Memento te Aurum

by Alice Greene

To those that crave being seen and accepted without conditions.
I see you, and you're always welcome here.

Trigger Warnings

Domestic Violence

Child Abuse (Physical and Verbal)

Self-harm

Mental Health Issues (Depression, Anxiety, Panic)

Arson

Drowning

Violence and Murder

Death

Graphic Sexual Situations & Kinks

Memento te Aurum deals with dark topics and includes a myriad of adult themes. Please be mindful of your limits and take care of yourself. Your well-being matters.

Playlist

The End of Everything - Noah Cyrus
Rhiannon - Fleetwood Mac
the 1 - Taylor Swift
Summertime Sadness - Lana Del Rey
It Will Come Back - Hozier
Angel of Small Death and the Codeine Scene - Hozier
Your Needs, My Needs - Noah Kahan
Kiss Me You Animal - Burn The Ballroom
Heartlines- Florence + The Machine
The Prophecy - Taylor Swift
Glitter & Gold - Barns Courtney
Clarity - Vance Joy

Act 1

Ayla

Spring, 1870

I t took us two weeks to get from Boston to Alder Bridge, New York. Two grueling weeks hopping train cars, crossing forests, and driving horses. Two grueling weeks with my parents relentlessly pestering me: 'Are we there yet?'

I've seen it in my dreams for months now, a farm out in rural New York, with rolling hills, ancient oaks, and an endless starry sky. A safe-haven for people like us.

My father, James, says we're blessed. My mother, Paloma, says we're chosen.

I always felt relatively indifferent on the matter. It gets me into trouble, and out of it.

My mother is a mind-reader, and a powerful one at that. With a single touch, she can see into your soul, the secrets you keep hidden even from yourself.

My father is attuned to the weather. He always knows when it will rain, or snow. He can bring down lightning and hail, make the streets flood and the pipes freeze. He can also make flowers bloom, but he never seems to have that inclination.

I can see into the future. Most often in dreams, sometimes in blinding flashes of knowledge that bring me to my knees. I have no control over it, I can't will them to come, I can't *look* into the future. It just lingers there, humming like a bothersome gnat. Always present, but out of my reach.Tools are the only way I can purposefully peek into the future, but those are muddy and vague at best.

This is why we're searching for Alder Bridge, for the Guild of witches that reside there.

In my dreams, it's safe, full of people with gifts like me that live peacefully and work together. A community of equals. A family.

I tried to go without my parents, to escape their cruelty, to escape their life of fleeing from town to town. No matter the circumstances, they could never be bothered to use their gifts for good.

My mother would mingle at parties, eavesdrop at the market, whatever she needed to do to figure out who was the wealthiest in town, and then a "natural disaster" would run them from their home. Maybe lightning set their roof on fire, or a strong wind blew a tree into their living room. Anything to make them evacuate, to clear the way so they could rob the family blind.

As a young girl, I would ask them why, and the answer was always the same. Because they could, they were entitled to it. Because they were blessed, and others were not.

I could never wrap my mind around it, and then the Universe showed me a way out. A safe-haven. So, I scrimped and saved, prepped and planned, and bid my time. But I didn't even make it out the front door before Paloma caught me and stole the truth from my own mind.

I saw an opportunity for salvation, they saw an opportunity for power.

My parents had always thought they were destined for greatness, blessed by the Universe with immeasurable gifts for some divine purpose. They believed it made them better, more worthy, than those without gifts, and had often expressed how weary they were of living among the "weaker" population.

I think they're absolutely insane. A lion is no more important than a fish simply because it has fangs. We all have our roles to play.

Early morning sunlight pours through the gaps in the trees, lighting the end of the trail leading to the Raith farm. We're greeted by an invisible field so strong it burns my eyes, like a repulsive stench.

"What the hell is that?" Paloma asks, wringing her headscarf in her hands.

"I was about to ask the same thing," a low voice comes from behind us.

We whirl around.

A teenage boy stands there. He's maybe a year or two older than myself, 17 at the most, with his arms crossed over his chest. A very large rifle is slung over his shoulder, along with two gray rabbits tied to his hip.

"We're looking for Absolon Raith," James says, moving to stand in front of my mother.

The boy looks us over, his eyes a warm bluish-green. His hair is a sandy brown color, fading to white blond where the tips reach towards the sun. A scratch of blonde stubble lines his jaw, and a deep tan gives his cheeks a ruddy, impish look.

"Why?" His gaze snags on me, his eyes traveling around my face, undoubtedly stuck on my nest of unwashed copper hair.

"That's none of your business, boy," James sneers, the breeze kicking up to a steady gust.

"Oh, no?" The boy smiles, foxlike. "My name is Algernon Raith, Absolon is my father. And this is our land you're trespassing on, sir."

Something in the back of my mind prickles at his name.

Paloma nudges my father aside and steps gingerly towards Algernon.

I've always known that my mother was a beauty, with shiny brunette waves and tan skin, eyes rich and as brown as a cup of espresso. There was nothing she couldn't flirt her way out of, or into.

"We're just looking for a little help, and we think your father might be the only one able to save us," she says, sashaying towards him.

To my surprise, and profound pleasure, Algernon appears to be unmoved by her charms.

"Save you?" His turquoise eyes flick back to mine, an eyebrow quirking up.

"We're like you," Paloma purrs, reaching out to touch the bare skin of his forearm.

Algernon catches her wrist in his gloved hand before she can touch him and lowers it back to her side.

After a moment of deliberation, he nods. "Follow me." He strides past us and through the barrier, the shimmering shield parting for him.

We hesitate, but fall in line behind him, with me bringing up the rear.

"It's a ward," he clarifies, picking through the woods until we reach a well-trodden path. "Keeps out anyone that isn't granted permission, and let's us know if anyone comes close to the property."

"Can you teach us how to do that?" My father asks, catching up to walk by Algernon's side.

He chuckles. "If my father welcomes you in, we can teach you anything you could possibly want to learn."

My father glances at me over his shoulder, a warning. None of that knowledge is for me.

Algernon leads us to an enormous log cabin, surrounded by a dozen or so smaller cottages and endless rows of crops and flowers. Animals graze openly across the property, both livestock and pets. We see a handful of people beginning what must be their morning chores. They pause to watch us curiously, all of them greeting Algernon warmly while glancing sideways at us.

When we reach the steps, the large front door swings open, revealing an older man with dark hair and the build of a grizzly bear. Beside him is a gorgeous blonde woman, who bears a striking resemblance to Algernon, and two other boys. One, with raven-black hair, looks to be around my age, 15, and the other looks to be in his twenties, the angles of his face severe.

"Al, you were supposed to be hunting rabbits," Absolon says good-naturedly, coming down the steps to embrace his boy.

Algernon mutters something in his ear and his almost comically thick eyebrows shoot up. He looks over at us, surprised, but unguarded.

"Welcome to Raith Farm. My name is Absolon, and this is my wife, Sophia." He gestures to the blonde woman. "You've met Algernon, and these are my other sons, Gideon, our eldest," The older boy nods stiffly in our direction. "And my youngest, Oberon." The dark haired one stares down at his feet.

"I'm James Abbott." My father shakes his hand firmly. "This is my wife, Paloma." She does a small courtesy. "And my daughter, Ayla."

Their eyes fall to me, and a wave of insecurity closes my throat. I've been wearing the same drab brown dress for days, and haven't brushed my hair in even longer. I probably look like a wild changeling, or a forest goblin.

"She's the reason we're here," James says, grabbing me by the arm and positioning me between this bear of a man and himself. He places his hands on my shoulders, a sham of tenderness. "She saw this place in a dream and knew it was safe."

"In a dream?" Sophia cuts in, walking down the stairs towards me.

"Yes." James shakes my shoulders. "She has prophetic dreams, and visions. A fortune-teller."

Sophia snorts, and tucks a stray strand of hair behind my ear, her touch cool and feather light. "Divination, darling?"

I nod, tilting my chin up. "Tarot is my specialty."

Gideon's eyes fix on my face, his eyes narrowing, but Algernon elbows him hard in the ribs and he looks away.

"And I can—" Paloma starts, but Absolon holds up a hand and silences her.

"Your abilities are irrelevant to me. I could sense the magic before you even crossed the border." His eyes land on me, then slide back to my parents. *Sense the magic?* "What matters to me, and this Guild, is the content of your character. We take care of our own here. We live off the land and nurture it, growing our relationship with Source."

"Source?" Paloma asks, visibly miffed that she was interrupted.

Absolon smiles. "You have much to learn, Abbott's. Gideon, come," he says, keeping his eyes trained on us as his oldest descends the stairs.

Gideon stops beside his father, gray eyes flitting back and forth between our faces.

"Gideon has a penchant for Psychomancy, manipulation of the mind," Absolon starts, placing a hand on Gideon's shoulder. "I'm going to ask a few questions, and do not bother lying. He'll know."

I notice my father's shoulders stiffen, but his expression remains neutral. My mother's fingers tangle with mine, her grip tight enough that her rings pinch my skin.

"Do they come with negative intentions?" Absolon asks, gaze narrowed at my father.

Why not ask me? I think, petulant. *Maybe I mean them harm.*

My mother digs her thumb nail into my palm, sending a flare of pain up my arm.

Gideon's eyes, now a burnished gold, flick towards me then down to our clasped hands, and my stomach hollows out. *Oh shit.*

"No," Gideon says after a beat. "They have no ill will towards us."

"Have they spoken truly?"

Gideon's gaze pauses at my mother, his brow furrowing slightly. "They embellish, but speak true."

"Are they decent folks?"

I almost laugh, but manage to bite my tongue. But of course, Gideon catches it.

My father's a dick, but we're not bad people. I think, hoping he can hear me. *We have nowhere to go.* Paloma's grip loosens, pleased that I vouched for them.

His brow lifts, but he concedes. "As decent as any of us, Father."

"Very good," Absolon smiles. "Relax, you've passed. All are welcome here, so long as you contribute to the Farm and cause no harm."

We all breathe a sigh of relief.

"Come, let me show you to one of our vacant cabins."

Algernon

Spring, 1870

"Are you going to waste the entire afternoon under this tree?" Gideon nudges my foot with his boot, drawing my attention away from the book in my hands. It's my grandmother's herbalism book, one of the few things my mother brought with her on the boat from Scotland. She'd have my hide if she knew I was reading it by the pond, but what she doesn't know won't hurt her.

"I'm working," I reply, shifting to a more comfortable position against the bark of the willow tree. "What else would you have me be doing?"

"Planting, maybe? Like everyone else?"

"How are we supposed to know *what* to plant if we don't learn about them?"

Gideon rolls his eyes. "If it's edible, we plant it. What else is there?" He plops down onto the blanket beside me, stealing a cookie out of my pack.

I flip through the book and show him the spread about dandelion. "We could make medicine! With the right ingredients, applied with scientific reasoning and a little Transfiguration, I could treat anything."

He mulls that over. "You know, I was half-hoping you were out here goofing off."

I chuckle. "You know me better than that." I grab my sandwich and unwrap the wax paper, the hard cheese and honey immediately assuaging the gnawing I'd been ignoring in my stomach. "It's not like I have much of choice."

Gideon drapes his arms over his knees, staring out at the sparkling water. A fish jumps by the shore, it's scales flashing gold.

"What do you think about the newcomers?" He asks, changing the subject.

Ayla's pouting face flashes through my mind, her eyes glacial despite their mossy hue, The thousand-yard stare, sallow cheeks, and bruised knees. She looked more like a wild animal than a girl.

"I'm not sure," I answer honestly. "Feels like they're hiding something."

"They are," he says flatly. "I just can't tell which one of them is the problem."

"So why didn't you say anything?" I polish off most of my sandwich and toss the crust to the spotted loons paddling along the surface.

"Because I couldn't imagine turning Oberon away."

I nod, a wave of affection toward my frigid older brother taking me by surprise. Often, I worry that Gideon is just a double of our father, but it's moments like these that remind me of his empathy, a critical factor our father lacks.

"What are you assholes doing?"

Speak of the devil.

Oberon jogs along the bend of the pond, half-dressed and elbow deep in dried mud. Despite his blase attitude, he did always like to garden. I'm about to tease him about his chipper mood when he drops onto the blanket beside us and heaves a long-suffering sigh.

"What's the matter with you?" I sit up and swallow the urge to fuss about his muddy boots on my woven blanket.

"I gave Leda flowers." He throws his forearm over his face, but I can see the blush crawling across his neck.

Gideon and I exchange a wide-eyed glance. Oberon's been in love with another Guild member, Leda, since they were children, but she's kept him at arm's length since puberty struck.

"And how'd that go?" Gideon prods.

"She scolded me for trimming mom's irises and called me a dimwit," he groans.

I can't help but snort a laugh, muffling it with my palm. "I'd say you're on the right track then," I chuckle.

"What do you mean?" Oberon drops his arm and props himself up, witless hope in his eyes.

"She cares more about you getting scolded than receiving flowers," I answer.

Gideon quirks a brow, as if surprised at my response.

"She cares about me?" Oberon sits up fully.

"Gods, you're thick," Gideon rolls his eyes and pushes to his feet. Out of the three of us, Gideon is the only one that retains a trace of our mother's Scottish accent and dialect. "She wouldn't let you follow her around like a puppy if she didn't, Ben," he continues, softening his tone slightly.

"C'mon," I say, getting to my feet and hauling Oberon up with me. "I'll help you make her something she can't say no to."

We gather up my stuff and trudge back towards the house. Gideon takes everything in and dismisses himself with a wave, so I lead Oberon to our parents library.

It's not a very large room, with a bay window taking up most of the space. On either side of it are bookcases as tall as I am, crammed full of books, maps, and assorted knickknacks. I've had to reinforce the shelves on more than one occasion to accommodate for their ever growing burden. Our mom even has a few plants growing in here, verdant, vine-y things that climb along the shelves towards the light spilling through the window. A nest of pillows and wool blankets pad the bench beneath the window, a half-drank cup of tea on the small stool beside it.

I drag my fingers along the spines. "What does she like to read?" I ask.

"Romance and fairytales," Oberon says, rolling his eyes.

I tug a book of the shelf and swat him with it before showing it to him. *Wuthering Heights.*

"What's it about?" He asks, flipping through the pages.

"Love, of course."

His lip curls with distaste.

"Read it, write some notes in it. Underline stuff that makes you think of her, doodle, whatever. Just put some thought into it. She'll love it," I say, leaning against the shelf. "And it wouldn't kill you to try something she loves. You might like it too."

"You're certain?" he asks.

"Cross my heart." I smile.

He sighs and claps me on the back before exiting the little library, nose already buried in the first page.

I glance out the window, about to take my leave as well, when I spot that feral little redhead picking her way along the treeline. She looks decidedly more like a regular girl today, her hair washed and hanging like a gleaming copper curtain over her shoulders. She's wearing a green dress and riding boots, not exactly fashionable, but I can't help but think she looks rather pretty, if a bit odd.

She seems entirely unbothered by the thorns snagging at her skirts, or the freshly tilled soil sticking to her shoes. I watch as she pauses beneath a thick pine, assessing it's branches, before she grabs hold of the lowest one and hauls herself up, up, up, until I can just barely see the toe of her boots and the flash of her hair through the needles.

Definitely odd.

She hasn't emerged once, to my knowledge, since they've arrived, and I wasn't going to be the person that discouraged her with unsolicited conversation. Why else would someone go up in a tree if not to be alone?

I resist the urge to go out there and introduce myself properly, and instead head towards my room to get my *actual* work done for the day.

Pushing thoughts of the odd girl from my mind, I sit down at my desk and heft the lead ingot my father left on my desk in my hand. I narrow my eyes at the flat gray surface, envisioning the web of molecules in my mind, and slowly, methodically, start converting those molecules to gold.

Gold acts as a heavy ward against most magic, and is my most favorite material on the planet. One I spend every day trying to master. Besides my ring, I always keep a sachet of gold leaf in pocket, just in case.

The transfiguration discipline is a common one, Oberon is quite adept at it as well, but I've always been too ambitious for my own good, and wanted to achieve the impossible. For science, of course. And, if I'm being honest, just to see if I *could*.

Turns out, I can do impossible things, like turn lead into gold and blood to bread. So, I've earned myself the title of Alchemist, one of only a handful in the world.

Gifts manifest differently for everyone, and usually fall within three categories: Transfiguration, Psychomancy, or Elemental Magic. As we grow and learn, it's common to more niche talents to develop, usually aligning with the witches personality, hobbies, and values.

On the rare occasion, something entirely new will manifest, for reasons we don't really understand. My father is the only person I've met like this. Most of his skills fall under Psychomancy, with a penchant for compulsion magic, like Gideon. But he can also manipulate magic, can sense it, dampen it, or strengthen it. Under his leadership, we are all stronger.

And more vulnerable.

Our father practically never used his magic, lest the circumstances called for drastic measures. It took a lot out of him, not that he'd admit it.

The three of us had become an extension of him, so he didn't need to actually *do* all that much besides point. My mother led the Rituals and offerings, and Gideon and I handled logistics, sustenance, and security. Oberon was only 15, but already the responsibilities were piling on. And if it wasn't for our meddling, Absolon probably would have put him to work sooner, like he did with me.

I remember taking inventory of the root cellar at 12 years old, counting how many days of food we had left in the dead of winter, and realizing we'd barely see through February if we didn't start rationing.

For Gideon, I imagine the burden started even earlier.

I shake the thoughts away, setting the heavy gold bar down on my desk and grabbing hold of that flicker of pride to wash away the melancholy.

This is how I could make sure we never starved again, that we can live comfortably, safely. My work is how I contribute, how I can provide for the people I love, and I'll work my fingers bloody, my eyes blind, if I must.

Ayla

Spring, 1870

The first few days are intensely awkward, and I spend most of them hiding in our new cottage. But, per usual, my parents have made themselves at home, and have charmed all twenty-five residents at Raith Farm.

I've only left the cottage for meals, and that was only because if I didn't, Sophia would leave a stocked picnic basket at the door for me. It was a kindness I couldn't stomach.

On the fifth day, well past noon, there's a knock on the front door. My parents have been gone for hours, and I assume they'd forgotten a key.

I pull open the door, only to be greeted by a dark haired girl in brown trousers, *trousers*, and a green linen tunic. There's dirt smudges on her cheek, and she smells vaguely of chocolate

I've seen her around at dinner, usually with the Raith brothers. Leda, I think.

"Hi! Were you sleeping?" she asks, staring pointedly at my rat's nest of hair.

"No." I cross my arms. "What do you want?"

"Absolon asked that you start joining us for our afternoon lessons," she says with a smile, unperturbed by my curt tone.

"I don't think so." My Father would have a damn conniption. I go to shut the door, but she sticks her foot in the way.

"We're sparring this afternoon." She wiggles her eyebrows. "You could take out some of that hostility."

"This isn't really a request, is it?" If Absolon ordered it, my father has let me learn, right?

"Nope!" She grabs my hand and drags me out into the warm afternoon and across the blooming field, to where a gaggle of teenagers and smaller children are gathered.

She plunks me down on a stump and starts grabbing at my hair, combing through it roughly with her fingers.

"Ow! What the hell?" I jerk away from her.

"You can't win a fight with all this," she laughs. "I fight dirty, and I'd hate to rip out a chunk of your pretty hair."

I can help but smile, finding her oddly charming, her honesty comforting.

"Ah, I see you brought the little fortune-teller out into the sunshine," Gideon says, swaggering towards us with Oberon trapped in a headlock under his arm.

Leda runs over and slaps at his bicep until he releases his younger brother, who shoves him before storming off, his cheeks flush with embarrassment.

"Don't be rude, Geo," Leda scolds, returning to my side and starting to braid my hair, which is no small feat, considering it's thick as molasses and reaches my low-back.

He puts a hand over his heart, though his eyes glimmer with mischief. "Rude? Leda, you wound me."

"Gideon!"

I look to my left and see Algernon approaching on horseback, with full saddlebags on either side of him. His hair gleams in the late afternoon sun, everything about him so much lighter, and warmer, than his brothers. He carries that same shine as his mother, that humbling kindness.

"Finally. Gods, Al, what took so long?" Gideon says, catching the reigns as Algernon brings his horse to a halt. It's the same piebald mare I always see him with, a spunky heifer he calls Selenium.

"*Al, what took so long,*" he mocks, imitating his brother's raspy voice and facial expressions with decidedly more drama.

He hauls the bags off of Sel, who seems annoyed that she had to carry them in the first place. He drops them onto the ground and pulls out a handful of handmade arrows. "I don't see you making 10 bows of various sizes and approximately 25 million arrows in a single afternoon."

Gideon rolls his eyes, but doesn't make any further comments.

Algernon glances over at me, a wide smile making his eyes crinkle at the corners. "Now, the real fun begins."

We line up in front of a row of oak trees wrapped in thick leather bands to protect the bark. Algernon goes down the line passing out bows and a handful of arrows to each person. I'm last in line, and he stops in front of me.

"Have you ever used a bow and arrow before?" he asks, craning his neck down to look at me. I barely reach his sternum.

I roll my eyes and take the weapon from him. I line up my shot and let the arrow fly. It whistles past him and beds itself solidly into the tree.

"Marvelous. Now I don't have to burden you with the pleasure of my company." He winks before heading back down the line to help the younger kids.

We toil the afternoon away with target practice, with Leda and I falling into frequent fits of laughter over any mishaps, of which there are *many*.

By the time we're finished, my arms are wobbly and sore, and my cheeks ache from smiling.

The sun begins to set, a vivid painting of purple and blood orange, and Sophia fetches us for dinner.

Everyone gallops down the hill together, whooping and laughing, but I fall behind and make a beeline for our cottage. I can't help but smile hearing their joy, the fizzy feeling of new friendship lingering as I climb the front steps and push open the door.

"Where the fuck have you been?" James booms, grabbing me by the collar.

"Absolon ordered me to join afternoon lessons," I snap back, the warmth in my chest freezing over.

"He's not your father," he says, dropping me and shoving me backwards. "You don't go anywhere without my permission." Thunder rumbles overhead as rain starts to patter down.

"I can't just disobey Absolon," I argue.

His sweaty palm strikes my cheek, throwing me to the floor with it's force. Searing pain explodes across my skin, and I rapidly blink to clear the blindness from that eye.

"You are not to attend another training session without my permission, understand? I will speak to Absolon."

I gather myself and make to run past him, but his hand wraps around the tail of my braid, jerking me backwards. But the ribbon Leda tied it with gives way, and I'm able to slide from his grip, my hair unwinding as I run to my room and slam the door.

I flop down on my bed, rubbing away the sting in my cheek and blinking back tears. I'll wake up early to *ask* if I can go to lessons tomorrow, before he heads out into the fields. Maybe then he'll be more amenable.

The rest of the evening is spent with my cards, an old tarot deck my mother had given to me on my 13th birthday, after my first cycle. It's

Italian, with faded colors and tattered edges, but the card stock is sturdy, and the messages come through clear as a bell, if a bit blunt.

Tonight, all it seems inclined to give me is Swords, the suit of mental turmoil. My signifier, the card my deck uses to identify me, la Luna, flies out first, then the Two of Swords, Eight of Swords, and Page of Swords, with the Magician lurking at the bottom of the deck.

I huff and reshuffle, only to get the Tower, the card of catastrophic change, and the 10 of Swords, the card signifying rock bottom.

The weeks tick by as we settle into routine on the Raith farm. Chores in the morning, lessons in the afternoon, not that I'm ever allowed to attend them, then supper and community bonding after sunset.

Leda and I have gotten quite close, and I spend most evenings at her house now, avoiding my parents like the plague. Thankfully, they seem to prefer my absence, while Leda and her mother welcome the company.

Algernon and Gideon have been teaching me to spar when they have free time, something my father refused to teach me himself. A bow was all he'd allow me so I could catch his dinner. The only person who could teach me about Divination is Sophia, and she'd never do something behind Absolon's back, loyal as bark to a tree.

It wasn't perfect, but it was more perfect than anything I'd known before. Despite my best intentions, I was easing into life here, getting more comfortable than I can ever recall being. It was peaceful.

Algernon swings his elbow at my head and I duck, throwing a punch at his ribs, an easy target considering he's built like a bean pole. He'd need four arms to effectively guard his torso.

"Lucky shot," he winces, dancing around me. Everything with him is more play than practice.

I snort and kick him in the shin.

He yelps in pain, dramatically falling to the ground. "That was uncalled for!"

"Maybe you shouldn't leave your limbs everywhere." I put my hands on my hips.

"Maybe you shouldn't be such a hellcat."

"Maybe *you* should stop breathing."

The summer air carries the sweet scents of blooming flowers and fresh grass. The field is alive with the vibrant colors of wildflowers in full bloom, attracting bees and butterflies, their iridescent wings glimmering in the sun.

He laughs in the annoying, good-natured way he does, and gets back to his feet. "You'd like that wouldn't you, hellcat?"

"Don't call me that."

"You don't like hellcat?" He raises a brow, eyes sparkling. "Hellkitten, then."

"Absolutely not!" I scoff, angry heat rising in my cheeks.

"Just kitten? Suit yourself." He grins. Before I can blink, he has my wrist twisted behind my back and his arm bracketed around my throat, his hold like iron. His body is solid, sun-warmed and strong.

I wriggle in his grip, but can barely move, the scrape of his ring across my jugular making my lungs freeze as a thread of panic winds around me.

He loosens his grip a fraction. "C'mon, you can get yourself out of this," he encourages. "Think, breathe. You can do it."

I take a sip of air, willing my heart rate to slow. *Think, think.* I tuck my chin into the crease of his arm to create some space, then use my free hand to grip his wrist and yank downwards, twisting as I go to immobilize that arm. I spin to free my other arm, effectively twisting him before I sweep his legs, dropping him onto his ass again.

All of this was done a half-speed, with Algernon letting me feel my way through it without resistance.

He smiles up at me, dimples showing through his tawny scruff. "Good! Now, do it faster."

We run through it a few more times, getting faster each time, until I see his jaw set, and he grabs me again, fast enough to give me whiplash, his arm around my throat actually cutting into my air. My arm protests at the painful angle he holds it at, a hairline away from popping.

Up until now, I realize with alarming clarity, he'd been using a fraction of his real strength. This time, he wouldn't go easy.

"I'm not going to hurt you, but you need to learn how to do it for real," he says, his voice gentle in my ear despite the painful hold.

I tuck my chin and try to force his arm down, but he doesn't budge. *Fuck.* I try again, dropping all of my weight into the motion, and this time his hold gives and I whirl around, my arms screaming at the effort. I make to sweep his legs, but he beats me to it, freeing himself and catching my ankle with his, spinning me around the throwing me off balance.

Halfway down, his body wraps around me, his hand at the back of my head, cushioning me as we land hard on the packed earth, the lush grass doing little to lessen the blow.

"Fuck, I'm sorry. Are you okay?" he asks, rolling off of me and onto his knees, his brow pinched with worry.

"Yes, you ass," I croak, sitting up and shoving him over.

He bursts out laughing, sprawled out in a patch of clover, the setting sun casting a golden glow across his skin. "Bested me again, kitten," he teases.

"Don't call me that!" I laugh, lunging towards him, but he's on his feet and galloping away from me and down the hill before I can throttle him. I may be able to land a few good punches, but that boy can run miles around a Clydesdale, his legs long and reedy.

I get to my feet, stretching my tired muscles. My stomach growls, but I take my time walking down the hill, suddenly feeling unsettled in my skin.

Of course, most of the food is gone by the time I get to the dining hall, save a few roasted potatoes and a hand-sized loaf of sourdough.

The dining hall is filled with people, laughing and care-free. It's stifling, hot and humid, their voices loud like a braying donkey. I see my parents sitting with Absolon and Sophia, deep in conversation. All the younger people sit a the table closest to the window, and Leda waves me over with a smile. Algernon glances up, and I notice a full plate of food in front of an empty chair between him and Leda.

I take a step towards them, heart warming, when the room tilts, whirling around me in a dizzying cyclone. The vision takes hold before I hit the ground, and there is nothing but the pictures flashing through my head.

Black cloaks and fire, bloody hands and blue lightning. Glass vials with glittering liquid, erased by black smoke. Algernon smiling, then screaming. Green flower buds and fresh lilac. A deer, alive, then dead, it's head laying a few feet away from its body.

"Ayla!" James' voice reaches me through the din, and I'm shaking, no, being shaken. "Ayla, baby, come back. We're right here."

"Oh, sweetheart, mama's here! I'm right here."

My eyes blink open and I'm immediately greeted by my parents contorted faces, their alcohol soaked breath wafting into my nose. On instinct, I try to crawl away but my father's hand is clamped around my ankle, the bones grinding together.

"What did you see?" He hisses, low enough that only my mother and I can hear.

"Just some flowers," I say through gritted teeth, my whole body aching. It feels like someone jabbed an ice pick into my forehead. Everything is too bright, too loud.

He releases me with a huff. "Go home and get some rest, honey," he says, louder this time, and yanks me to my feet hard enough to make my head spin.

The entire camp is gathered around them, staring at me with a combination of wonder and fear. My gaze snags on Algernon, who stands a head taller than everyone. His expression is too agonized, too pitying, for me to look at.

I push through the crowd and scurry towards our cottage, feeling tears start to burn behind my eyes. It's so embarrassing when they come on like that. It makes me feel so out-of-control, so helpless. Especially when there isn't anything useful to share, because then they're truly useless. I'm truly useless.

I sink onto the front stoop, dropping my head into my hands and trying to press away the burn. I will not cry.

I almost miss the crunch of footsteps approaching me in the dark. My hackles raise.

"Ayla?" Algernon steps into the meager lantern light above our front door.

Gods damn it. "You weren't in the vision either, asshole. Nobody was." I keep my eyes firmly fixed on the wood grain beneath my feet.

"I don't give a shit about your vision."

My head snaps up, shocked by his crude language. "What?"

"I just wanted to make sure you were okay. That seemed...painful," he says, crouching down to my eye-level.

"I'm fine." I roll my eyes and stand up. "Goodnight, Algernon."

"Hey, your nose—"

"I said goodnight!" I snap, wrenching open the door and slamming it shut behind me. I wipe at my nose with the back of my hand, leaving a dark smear of blood on my pallid skin.

Great.

I shove some tissues into my nostril and flop onto bed, not even bothering to take my shoes off. Tears rise again, but I force them down.

They never do me any good.

Algernon

Summer, 1876

I push Sel hard, flying through the dense forest around Silver Lake, careful to make sure her saddlebags don't catch on any trees. Gideon manages to keep up on his old draft horse, Apollo, but just barely.

We're riding back from a supply run to Albany, a miserable week-long ordeal. But our medicine stores had gotten dangerously low, along with essentials like salt and lantern oil.

The Guild can grow or make most things, but every now and then we have to venture out into society, more so now that our numbers have grown beyond 100 people.

I'm so close to a breakthrough on a medicine to treat infections, but haven't quite figured it out. I'm planning on cultivating mold later this afternoon to add to the recipe. It's the first stepping stone towards my ultimate goal, the Elixir of Life.

If I can treat infections, increase the bodies natural ability to heal, then what's to stop me from healing pneumonia, or even an external wound? By mastering the body's ability to heal, I could halt the natural aging process. We could live forever.

But, I have to get back to my lab to test my theory, *and* we have to get back in time for Ayla's 21st birthday.

"Will you slow the fuck down? You're going to put the horses into an early grave," Gideon hollers from behind me. I feel the prickle of his compulsion magic on the back of my neck and spin the gold ring on my thumb, pushing his magic back. Typically, he doesn't use it on us, but he will every now and then if we piss him off enough.

"Algernon!" He throws more force behind his words and I find myself pulling back on Sel's reigns.

Fucker.

He trots up beside me, and I feel a stab of guilt at how tired Apollo looks. "We'll get there in time, you nut. What are you so worried about?"

I use my shirt collar to wipe the sweat from my lip and push my hair off my forehead. "What makes you think I'm worried?"

"I have eyes. Look at you, you're an anxious wreck." He gestures to my feet, where I apparently put my boots on the wrong feet in my haste to leave this morning. "Are you going to court her?" His tone shifts from teasing to something more serious.

I roll my eyes and urge Sel forward. Heat creeps up my neck. "No, I'm not going to *court* her. We're just friends."

"Not according to her."

My head whips around hard enough I nearly fall off the saddle.

"What did she say to you?"

A grin stretches across his face. "Her exact words were 'Algernon is a ratbag motherfucker'."

"Oh, fuck off," I snap, turning my back to him and pushing Sel into a canter.

His laughter chases me through the trees, and I can't help but laugh at my own, pathetic expense.

Whatever she thinks of me, I wouldn't miss her birthday for the world.

We finally reach camp about an hour 'til noon. Sel practically bucks me off when we reach the stables, and Apollo gives me a dirty look. I make a mental note to bring them cake later.

I run up to the house, Gideon on my heels, and push open the door. I open my mouth to call for Oberon, but then I spot a tangle of black hair laying prone beside the chaise in the front room.

Fear propels us forward, but the empty jug of wine beside his head makes it abundantly clear what happened here.

Oberon is sprawled out on the floor, half blanketed in the table cloth from the dining room, the rest of which is neatly tucked around Leda, who is sound asleep on the chaise. I turn and spot Ayla curled up like a cat in my father's green velvet chair, red rivers of hair reaching all the way to the carpet.

"So, we have to haul ass to Albany while these dimwits get plastered on my wine and sleep all day," Gideon huffs, moving to wake Oberon before I catch his sleeve.

"Lighten up, it's her birthday. Go be a curmudgeon somewhere else."

He rolls his eyes and stalks off to the office he shares with my father.

I head to the kitchen, pulling a crinkled slip of paper out of my pocket. It's a recipe for a lemon rosemary cake I found in a cookbook at an old bookstore in town.

I flatten out the piece of paper on the counter and get to work collecting ingredients.

By the time I have everything collected and mixed, I hear stirring from the front room. I walk out there and immediately throw my hands up to shield my eyes.

Leda is on the ground with Oberon, straddling his hips and sharing a sloppy kiss, with entirely too much heavy petting.

"Fuck! Al!" Leda curses, jumping off of Oberon.

"I did not need to see that," I say, dropping my hands and chuckling at the mortified looks on their faces.

"What that hell have you been doing?" Oberon gapes.

I look down. I completely forgot that I threw on my mothers floral apron, which barely reaches past my hips, and I'm absolutely covered in flour and sticky batter.

Oberon gets up and ruffles my hair, sending up a cloud of flour and making us both laugh.

"My carpet!"

I whirl around and come face to face with my mother, who is trying very hard to look stern.

"I'm making a cake," I say, sheepishly.

"You can turn sand into diamonds but can't make a blasted cake." She smiles and shakes her head. "Come on, love. I'll help you."

I follow her back into the kitchen and hear Leda whisper, "Is he making Ayla a birthday cake?"

"He's a glutton for punishment," Oberon replies, chuckling. There's a soft smack followed by stifled laughter and I smile.

I stoke the coals at the bottom of the oven, somehow managing to burn my hand twice, while mom makes sure I haven't completely butchered the recipe. Deemed satisfactory, I transfer it to dutch oven and nestle it onto the rack above the coals.

"Is this for Ayla?" She asks, leaning against the counter.

"Everyone deserves a birthday cake." I shrug, starting to wipe down my mess.

"Be careful with your heart, my love." She says, crossing the room and pulling me down into a hug. I have to hinge at the hips to reach her. "That girl has walls higher than a Basilica."

"I don't know what you're talking about," I grumble.

"A mother always knows." She releases me and pats my cheek. "I expect the kitchen to be spotless before the cake is finished."

"Yes ma'am."

She leaves and I finish cleaning up the kitchen, then brew the largest pot of coffee I can using a pressing contraption I made a few years ago. I pour boiling water over the coffee grounds in a pitcher, let it steep for a while, then place the press over top of it. The mesh pushes down the loose grounds and traps them at the bottom of the pitcher, eliminating most of the grittiness.

Ayla was so excited about it the first time I showed it to her that she actually *smiled* at me.

Oberon pokes his head into the kitchen as I'm glazing the cake. "She's awake, and even more vicious than usual."

I raise an eyebrow, irritation lancing through me. "Watch it."

He holds up his hands and backs out the room, smirking.

I stick a beeswax candle into the cake and snap my fingers, creating a small flame. It's the only elemental magic I bothered to learn because it comes in handy with Bunsen burners. Air hardly seems relevant, water is fickle, and I don't particularly enjoy getting my hands dirty with earth.

I set the cake, the pot of coffee, a small mug with blue butterflies, and a present wrapped in brown paper onto a tray and carry it out to the living room.

The gift is a deck of tarot cards I found in the same bookstore as the cake recipe. The tiger on the front of the deck with flaming orange fur reminded me of her.

Ayla is sitting up in the chair, her legs curled to her chest. Her hair is a wild halo of copper, catching the afternoon sunlight to create a warm glow. She looks radiant and angry as a rattlesnake.

I set the tray in front of her, grinning at the scowl she gives me. "Happy birthday, hellcat."

She scrutinizes the arrangement in front of her and softens a bit. "You made me a cake?"

I nod, suddenly feeling bashful.

"You didn't have to do that," she says, picking up the mug of steaming coffee and sniffing it. "Thank you." Her eyes meet mine, and I see a flicker of emotion I've only caught once before, the very first moment I met her. She'd been covered in filth with dark circles under her vacant eyes. Exhaustion hung from her like a cloak. Then she saw me, and there was a flicker of...something. I won't say relief, or joy, but something. I've been chasing that look ever since.

"My pleasure," I say, a bit breathless, my heart thudding in my chest.

"This coffee is wretched, though," she mumbles, blowing out her candle and curling up into the chair with the warm mug pressed against her chest.

"I'm sure." I grin.

"Can I have some coffee?" Leda pipes up from the chaise.

"Ask the birthday girl. I'll be in the lab if you need me." I make a swift exit, that small victory planting like a seed inside my chest.

I head out the back door and across the field, to the greenhouse resting at the west corner of the property.

It took me nearly 2 years to take it from a moss and cobweb covered pile of glass to a functioning workspace with adequate ventilation, decent climate control, and ample storage. From the outside, it still looks mostly neglected, with tall thickets of blackberries and sprawling English ivy surrounding it. It was my dad's idea, to ensure outsiders don't start poking around.

Because inside, our Guild's most precious secrets are hidden, and I am their keeper.

I push through the brambles to my sandstone path, and approach the glass door. I take the heavy padlock in my hand and rub my thumb in a clockwise circle around the keyhole, unlocking the mechanism internally, and push open the door.

Immediately, humid air envelops me, along with the pungent smell of herbs, soil, and smoke. On the back wall are dozens and dozens of plants, all neatly arranged on a series of shelves or in their planter boxes. Mostly herbs, with a few exceptions for certain types of berries and peppers. The wall to my left houses my most treasured possessions, the dozens of notebooks I've filled with research over the years, and the hundreds of texts I've amassed in my travels.

Everything from herbal medicine, to blacksmithing, astronomy, organic chemistry, anatomy, and mythology can be found on these shelves. But the most extensive part of my collection, by far, is spellbooks. I've collected hundreds from all over the world, as well as the many that have been passed down or gifted to me for safe keeping.

I'm not sure how I managed to become the Guild librarian, but here we are.

On the right wall, protected by a black linen sheet, are my ingredient and experiment stores. The sheet protects light-fast ingredients from possible damage, as well as fends off wandering eyes with a Spell of Disregard. Not that any intruders would know what anything was anyways, I tend to be rather disorganized, and can't be bothered to write out labels for *everything*.

I push the fabric aside and grab what I'll need for today, my half-finished elixir to treat infections, a few glass jars and beakers, and a container of moldy blackberries.

I set everything on my large work table and unfold my gold wire glasses, slipping them over my nose. I pull my hair back into a bun to keep it out my eyes. My notes are still spread out from the day before, and I dive in where I left off.

As I work, the sun rises high into the sky, beating down into the greenhouse, but the irrigation system I connected to our well keeps it relatively cool by constantly circulating cold water around the walls and ceiling.

I think the mold may have been a breakthrough, the molecules for the elixir are vibrating at a different frequency than they were before, one that closely aligns with the natural frequency of the human body.

"Fuck yes!" I whoop, pumping my fist in the air as I seal the finished elixir.

"Sounds like things are going well in here," a deep, humor-filled voice says from the door.

I look up and see my father, holding a tray of sandwiches and a carafe of mead.

"I think I cracked the internal treatment for blood infections." I beam, setting the vial carefully on the table before wrapping it in cloth to protect it.

"Then lunch is well deserved," he says, setting the tray down on the table and sitting heavily on one of my rickety stools.

My father is as good-natured as they come, with a generous spirit and warm disposition, so long as you're on his good side, which I take great care to always be.

I grab a sandwich and take a bite before turning back to my notes. I'll be royally pissed if I forgot to jot something down when I go to replicate the recipe.

"Son," Absolon says.

I hardly register it, continuing to scribble on the sheet of parchment.

"*Algernon,*" he says again, more firmly.

"Hmm?"

"I need to talk to you about something."

I look up, a spike of anxiety rising in my chest. What could he want to talk to *me* about? Gideon was his right hand man.

"It's about the Abbott's."

My anxiety triples, kicking up my heart rate. I know he can sense it by the placating way he smiles at me.

"I see you watching Ayla."

I swallow thickly. "I don't *watch* her." I argue, taking a sip of mead in an attempt to settle my nerves.

"Uh-huh. Have you noticed anything..." He trails off, choosing his next words carefully. "...off? Between her and her parents?"

I bite my tongue. I'm not one to be hateful or violent by any stretch of the imagination, but when it comes to James Abbott...I see red. Ayla can hide the truth from everyone else, but I don't miss a thing when it comes to her. I see the way she cowers when he enters a room, the way that confident light drains from her eyes. I see the way that silver tongue falls silent when his eyes fall on her, and the rigidity of her spine when they touch her.

But my father always trusted him, enamored with his invaluable ability to control weather, so I kept my mouth shut, chalking it up to over-protectiveness.

"Why do you ask?"

"Oberon just told me that Ayla went home to rest before this evening, but returned not even a quarter-of-an-hour later with a cigar burn on her arm."

Without thinking, I lunge for the door, but my father catches me by the bicep with a steel grip.

"You will stay here. Your mother and I are looking into it."

I fight against his hold. "You expect me to just stand by after that bastard *burned* her?" I snarl, rage like I've never felt festering in my chest.

He tilts his head, watching me closely. "What has gotten into you?" His grip is crushing. "You will obey me, Algernon. I don't care what your feelings are for her." A spark of magic changes his green eyes to gold, a clear indicator of someone using compulsion magic, and I can't look away. "You will not interfere. You aren't strong enough to take on a witch like James."

The rage wheezes out of my chest and his compulsion takes hold.

"Tell me what you know," he orders.

"She's afraid of them. Something is wrong in that house, and James is at the center of it," I say, monotone, with no control over the words coming out of my mouth.

"That's everything?"

"Yes, father." I nod.

"Good." He blinks and releases the compulsion, and I stagger to the side, disoriented. "Anything you do to James will be done to you, do I make myself clear?"

"Yes, father," I say through gritted teeth.

"Good." He pats me on the shoulder and turns to leave, before pausing at the door. "She brings out something ugly in you, Algernon. You have *much* more important things to spend your energy on," he says, gesturing to the room. "Don't lose sight of that." He pulls open the door and shuts it quietly behind him before disappearing into the thicket.

I rest my elbows on the table and drop my head in my hands, my gold ring glinting up at me from the table. I always take it off when I'm conducting experiments, a bit of information my father definitely knew.

Rage simmers low in my stomach, followed by a sharp stab of shame.

Ayla needs someone, and now I'm powerless to help her, bound by my fathers magic.

I push aside the mead and sandwiches and dive back into my work, the one thing I *can* control. The one thing that's mine.

The sun has long ago set, the greenhouse lit by oil lanterns and a few stray candles. The hours slip by as I work, until a knock rouses me from my stupor.

"Al?" Gideon stands on the other side of the door, carrying a lantern that illuminates half his angular face. "She's looking for you, the party started over an hour ago," he says with a suggestive smirk.

Shit. I drop what I'm doing and wrench open the door, pushing past him and out into the night.

A bonfire lights up the horizon, with dozens of silhouettes dancing and spinning around it. The full moon hands heavy in the sky, casting Her benevolent glow over the festivities.

I stop at the edges of the party and Gideon nearly crashes into my back.

"Did dad tell you?" I ask, searching for her silhouette against the flames.

"Yes." Gideon nods. "He bound us all." His voice has a note of hostility. Despite being our father's most trusted confidant, their relationship tends to be strained.

"Why?" My chest is tight with anger and hurt.

"James is too valuable," he says simply.

Just then, I spot a copper trail of her hair as she spins around the fire, a bottle of wine clutched in her hand. She's wearing an emerald green dress with a fitted bodice and flowing skirt, making her fair skin and hazel eyes glow.

My breath catches in my chest, a confusing swirl of affection and possessive rage making my shoulders stiffen.

"He won't be so stupid to hurt her again, though," Gideon says, patting my shoulder. "Now that someone's noticed."

"No." I cross my arms over my chest, eyes locked on her. "He'll just get better at hiding it."

Gideon sighs and leaves me to stew, grabbing our mother and pulling her out to dance.

The night ticks on, everyone getting progressively drunker and louder, but I stay put, sober as the gallows.

Most of the adults have retired at this point, leaving the dozen or so 20 somethings to do what they do best. Leda and Oberon have snuck off to make-out behind a tree, leaving Ayla to dance with some less familiar people. A young man, probably close to her age, sidles up to her, a drunken grin on his face.

My simmering anger flares back to life.

He grabs her by the hips and yanks her into his front, grinding on her like a horny teenager. She whirls around and shoves him away, but he grabs her by the low neckline of her dress and tugs her forward, ripping the bodice a few inches.

Before I even realize that I'm moving, my hands are on the stranger's shoulders, small as a child under my grip, and I draw my fist back, punching him so hard that he staggers back several feet and collapses to the ground, blood running down his face.

He howls in pain and tries to throw some meager air magic at me, but I dodge it, a smile rising on my face.

"Touch her again and I'll turn your balls to lead," I sneer, something feral rising up inside me.

He blanches and scurries away, disappearing into the dark.

I laugh and start dancing to the music, taking Ayla's hand and spinning her in a circle.

"What is wrong with you?" She seethes, wrenching her hand away and shoving me as hard as she can before storming off between the houses.

I run after her, my long legs helping me catch up to her quickly. I grab her wrist to stop her, but she jerks away from my touch, sending a painful stab of guilt through my heart.

"I don't need you to defend my honor! I'm perfectly capable of doing that myself!" She shouts, face flush from anger and wine.

I cross my arms. "I'm not going to just stand there while someone disrespects you."

She scoffs and rolls her eyes. "Why do you even care? You disrespect me all the time."

"I tease you all the time, there's a difference."

"Explain it to me then, because it doesn't feel any different."

I grit my teeth, rage still simmering in my chest. "He just wants to *fuck* you, Ayla."

"Because that's all anyone wants with me, right? I'm just s-something to be used." Her words slur a bit and she scrubs her hands over her face, shaking slightly. "That must be what you want, considering you treat me the same way," she spits, indignation swallowing that brief flicker of sorrow.

I step towards her, chest to chest. "Do not accuse me of being the same as him," I growl. I know she's drunk, I know she doesn't mean it, but Gods, her words cut to the quick.

Her breath stutters in her chest, her pulse racing in the hollow of her throat. A flush creeps up her chest, brightening the green hues in her eyes.

Fuck, she's so beautiful.

"Then what do you want, Algernon?"

I can smell the wine on her tongue, the smoke clinging to her hair, the delicate, herby perfume oil she dabs behind her ears. I slide my hand up her neck and into her hair, tilting her chin up.

She's drunk, I can't do this. I won't do this.

I drop my hand and take a step back.

"Al—" she whispers.

"Oh my god, Ayla!" Leda runs into the alleyway, Oberon hot on her trail.

"Are you alright? I'm so sorry we left, what happened?" Leda babbles, fussing with the tear in her dress and rambling.

Ayla's eyes meet mine, the unanswered question weighing heavily in the air between us.

I duck into the shadow of the house and walk away.

Ayla

Winter, 1880

The first time I saw Algernon, heard his name, it struck a chord in me, plucking the harp string of a memory long-buried. Or so I thought.

I've seen Algernon's face, with varying degrees of clarity, in nearly every vision and dream that I've ever had about my future. He's always there, smiling at me with his stupid, lopsided grin, turquoise eyes full of an emotion I refuse to label.

As the years have passed, the dreams have only gotten more frequent. He's the sun, this constant presence of warmth, of happiness. He's been a guiding light in my life, long before I ever realized that he was what I was running towards.

But I've seen countless times how my story ends, I know what's waiting for me. And I refuse to torture myself with girlish hope. Because death walks alongside my visions of Algernon, a ceaseless shadow.

I've known from the moment I was born how I would die. My murderer held me moments after I breached my mothers womb, cut the cord connecting me to her, fed me and bathed me and rocked me. He guided my first steps, showed me my first snow, gave me my first bruise. He was a my first heartbreak, my first fight, my first punishment. He was there my first moments, and every other moment, and will be there for my last.

My father will kill me for a reason I don't understand.

My life will be brief, spent as a tool for others, something I accepted a long time ago. It's a life that's better walked alone. Minimal complications, minimal fallout.

I will blaze like a match, and be snuffed out just as quickly. It's what matches do, there's no need to mourn.

I thought Algernon and I could be friends, but the pull is too strong, too consuming, so I've started to avoid him, extricating him from my thoughts, my life, bit by bit. I keep waiting for the hurt to fade, to stop missing him, but every morning the longing steals my breath. So I let it serve as a reminder of what he'd inevitably suffer in the aftermath of my demise, and I push through.

I'd much rather shoulder that burden alone, than heave it onto him unwittingly.

I stare at the ceiling, lost in my thoughts, when there's a light knock on my door.

"Darling!" Paloma calls. "Could you help me with something?"

I groan and slam my book shut, getting up to open the door. "What?"

Her cheek is an angry red, almost as red as her swollen eyes. I feel a pang of guilt, but force it down.

She holds up her right hand. It's bruised and swollen, her fingers bent in the wrong places, a crude wrapping holding it all together.

"Oh, my god—"

She cuts me off. "I need you to do my hair. We're having dinner at the Raith's this evening with special guests."

"O-okay." I nod, too stunned to say no.

She turns her back to me and walks over to the dining room table, sitting down in one of the chairs.

I grab my hair brush and some ribbon and come up behind her. I start brushing through the tangles of her pretty brunette locks, jealous that there are barely any to work through.

She grabs her tarot deck from the center of the table and spreads the cards while I braid her hair into a crown. The Queen of Swords is the first card she pulls, her signifier. It's quickly followed by the 5 of Cups and Death. She turns the final card over, revealing the Devil.

"That's bleak," I mutter.

She laughs, a grating, shrill sound. "Isn't it? The Devil's been on my tail for weeks."

I secure the braided crown and sit down next to her. "I haven't seen anything."

In a strangely warm gesture, she pats the back of my hand. "I'm sure it's a devil that already walks among us. For some reason, it's choosing now to make itself known."

She holds up a spoon to look at her reflection, and grimaces. "You're terrible at this," she says, before reaching up and undoing everything I just did. "How did I birth a daughter that's so...uninspired?"

Tears burn behind my eyes, but I swallow them, baring my teeth instead. "The apple doesn't fall far from the tree, you crone."

I fully expect the ringing slap that comes next, but it still steals the air from my lungs.

Paloma pushes her chair back and stands, shaking out her wrist. She turns and leaves without another word.

I sit there for a long time, staring down at the Devil.

When the sun finally sets, I slink out of the house on a whisper of curiosity, clad in black trousers and one of Oberon's heavy black coats to disguise my shape. I keep my hair covered with a black scarf that I've wrapped to obscure my face as well.

Who's the 'special guest'?

I creep between the cottages until I reach the Raith home. Warm light spills from the windows, and I can see figures moving around inside. There's Absolon by the mantle, hulking but jolly as he laughs at something. I can see Oberon and Leda lingering by the edges of the kitchen, both of them looking apprehensively around. Gideon sits at the table beside a dark haired man I don't recognize.

He looks to be close to my age, handsome and angular. An onyx pendant glints around his throat, hanging into the deep v-neck of his green tunic.

My mother drapes her arms over him from behind, cooing something in his ear that makes his lips turn up into a wolfish grin. He waggles his fingers and blue glow dances between them before he brings them up to tap my mothers hand, which is somehow miraculously healed. Well, not somehow, I know it's because of Algernon potions.

She jumps back with an excited squeal, blushing fiercely.

Paloma Abbott *blushing*? I never thought I'd see the day.

"What are you doing?" a voice hisses from beside me and I whirl around, nearly crashing directly into a hard chest.

My heart stutters. Algernon.

"I, uh—"

"What happened to your face?" His eyes go from teasing to worried in an instant and he reaches out a hand to pull down my scarf.

I lurch away, smacking his hand before he can touch me. "Nothing, I was just going for a walk."

He stands to his full height, my head just reaching his sternum, and peers down at me. "A walk?"

"Yes, and if you'll excuse me." I shove past him and out into the field, racking my brain for a way out of this that doesn't include me walking into the snow-covered woods in pitch black darkness.

He falls into step beside me, having to dramatically reduce his gait to match my speed. "Where are you walking to?"

"None of your business," I reply through gritted teeth.

"I disagree." He doesn't miss a step as I veer to the left.

"I don't give a shit."

"You were spying." He grins.

I ignore him, heading straight for the food stores. Might as well get a snack.

As soon as we step into the lamplight of the food shed, his hand shoots out and fists my scarf, tugging it off my head.

"Hey!" I spin around and try to snatch it back, but he holds it well above my head. "Give that back!"

He catches my chin between his thumb and forefinger. "Who did this to you?" he says again, growing deathly serious.

I jerk my chin away. "No one. I fell."

"Liar." He tilts his head, serpentine. "Did he hit you?"

The air is knocked from my chest. *Does he know? How could he possibly know?*

"Nobody hit me, are you insane?" I bluster.

He clicks his tongue. "It'll be easier if you tell me, hellcat."

"Fuck off. We don't speak for months and suddenly you're going to act like you care about me?" I'm fuming, anger turning my voice into a snarl. "Save your breath." I turn my back to him and make to storm off.

"Ayla, wait." His hand wraps around my wrist and he pushes the scarf into my hand. "Just, tell me you're alright? Take some of this." He fishes in his pocket and pulls out an amber vial of what he calls 'Cure All', a serum that accelerates the bodies natural healing process. It took him nearly a decade to master, but the implications of it are enormous.

Too bad I can't partake without drawing my Father's attention.

I grit my teeth and keep walking, leaving his question hanging suspended in the air the same way he left mine. I stomp back to the house, having more questions that I left with. And zero snacks for my trouble.

Algernon's words swirl in my head. '*Did he hit you?*'

It's impossible that he knows what's happening in this house. I've been so careful, and they've barely laid a hand on me since my 21st birthday. And I earned the slap today, I know better than to talk back to my mother, especially after a fight with my father.

But it's the worry in his voice that lingers most in my mind, bringing a small smile to my lips. He's still on my side.

I hate how comforting that knowledge is. I crave his attention, despite knowing how dangerous it is, knowing that I can never truly have it, have him.

To have him is a guarantee to lose him.

The Devil still rests on the dining room table, taunting me.

Algernon

Winter, 1880

I watch Ayla storm away from me, the tails of her scarf lifting in the cold north wind. Her boots leave a trail in the snow, leaving a trace of her long after she slams the door behind her.

My legs ache with the impulse to chase after her, to find out what happened, to tell her she's safe, to apologize, to kiss her and never ever stop. I lift my foot and step beside one of her small footprints, leaving my own, much larger print beside it.

I drop my head back and sigh, the condensation of my breath billowing into the night air. Snowflakes catch on my glasses and fog the lenses. Resigned, I slip the vial back into my pocket and trudge back to the house.

The warmth of the foyer immediately starts to thaw the cold that has accumulated across my skin, welcoming me home. I can hear them all talking in the kitchen, my family, Leda, the Abbott's, and our guests, Amadeus Kennedy and his son, Keanu.

The Kennedy's have a reputation the precedes them in magic circles, one shrouded in mystery and a legacy as old as time. Rumors claim that there used to be dozens of them, sheltered in the thick mountains by the New

York-Canada border, a sunless pocket of ice and pine. But only two remain, and have come to my father for help, supposedly.

I step into the kitchen and force a wide smile.

"Algernon!" My father bellows, loping over to me and throwing an arm around my torso. "This is my middle son, Algernon, the smartest of the lot." He grins, patting me on the chest hard enough to sting.

"Algernon, it's a pleasure. Amadeus Kennedy." The man stands and extends a hand. He's dressed in a neatly tailored suit made of thick wool with tortoise shell buttons.

I shake his hand. "The pleasure's all mine."

"I must say, Al, I've heard your name a few times before," Amadeus smiles, confident even though I'm about a foot taller than him. Lesser men balk at my height, but Amadeus seems to barely register it.

"Good things, I wager?"

"Very," Keanu interrupts, standing up to shake my hand. "Word in Albany is that you're quite the inventor."

I see Oberon and Gideon bristle, but I offer what I hope is a placating nod.

"Yes, I've sold quite a few inventions at some trade shows in the city. And most of my patents were filed at the Albany Court House."

"Fascinating. Do you specialize in Transfiguration?" Keanu asks, tilting his head, dark eyes fixed on me. I've never felt small in my life, but something in his presence makes me want to curl inward.

"Enough gossip! Let's eat," My father interrupts, clapping Keanu on the shoulder.

For a split second, rage crosses those dead eyes, but he smiles a second later, all traces of malice vanishing as if they never existed.

We move out into the dining room, where my mother has set everyone's plates and piled food on the center of the table. Winter squash puddings, rosemary covered salt potatoes, garlic sauerkraut, steaming biscuits, and cured sausage with sage. A massive turkey rests at the center, glistening with fat and butter.

I take the carafe of cranberry wine from my mothers hands and pour everyone a glass. When I reach the Abbott's, I slow down, sifting through the molecules in my mind to separate out the alcohol, and triple it. The molecular structures appear like a puzzle in my mind's eye, and I can manipulate the pieces to create whatever image I want. It takes hardly a second, but it's enough to bring them just shy of alcohol poisoning.

I set the carafe at the center of the table and take my seat, some of my anger abated by that small taste of vengeance.

My father bows his head to begin the blessing. "I set a place at my table for the Gods, and ask them to join us here tonight. Our home is always open, and our hearts are open as well. This meal is the work of many hands, and I offer all a share. Sourceful ones, accept my gift, and upon the hearth, leave your blessings."

"Many thanks," we all murmur.

Everyone digs in, and my father and Amadeus dominate the conversation, talking about politics and the Anglo-Church.

I'm sitting between Leda and my mother, sheltered from *manly* conversation, although Keanu's gaze continually drifts back to me. My fingers close around the vial still in my pocket.

Amadeus and Keanu start sharing stories of their travels across the country and Canada, and soon, the entire table is absolutely taken with their charm and dry wit.

I try to follow the stories, but a niggling worry at the back of my mind keeps me suspended in uncomfortable reality.

What do they want from us?

Keanu's gaze seems to have shifted to the silent Oberon, and has turned into something else. Something curious, almost warm. They're close to the same age, and bear an uncanny resemblance, with their dark hair, fair skin, and sharp features.

My jaw flexes.

Oberon might be a man now at 25, built like a panther and twice as clever, but he's still my little brother, and I don't trust the Kennedy's as far as I can throw them.

I swallow the rest of my wine, and polish off my plate.

There's a lapse in conversation, and Paloma lets out a high-pitched hiccup and giggles. James' eyes are heavy, his jaw slightly slack.

I press my lips together to suppress a smile.

"Geo, Al, I think the Abbott's have had a bit too much to drink. Would you two escort them home?" Father says, stern.

We push our chairs out and haul them up by the armpits. James opens his mouth to protest, but Gideon mutters something in his ear that makes him clamp his mouth shut, eyes glazing over even further.

Paloma slurs drunken apologies as we guide them out into the night.

I suck in the cold air as the door shuts behind us and can't suppress the peel of laughter that bubbles up from my chest.

"I should have known you had something to do with this," Gideon grunts, dropping James into the snow. "I'm not saying they don't deserve it, but what's the crime?"

"One of them struck Ayla," I mutter, dropping Paloma beside her husband.

Gideon holds my gaze for a moment, then looks down at the Abbott's, who are too drunk to even shiver as the snow seeps into their clothes.

"Which one of you hit Ayla?" Gideon growls, crouching down to their eye level.

James snorts. "Which time? That little bitch."

My resolve snaps and I lunge, blinded by rage, but Gideon grabs me before I tackle James into the snow.

"The bind, Algernon," Gideon hisses, struggling to hold me back.

"I don't give a shit," I snarl and shove him off of me. I slug James in the jaw, pain sparking like flint in my cheek and snapping my head to the side. I hit him again, and another ghost punch cracks my temple. Dizziness fogs my vision and I stagger.

James is slumped over in the snow, unconscious and bleeding. Paloma has her hand over her mouth, suppressing her own scream.

Shit, I stretch my jaw. I can throw a godsdamn punch.

"Lets get them to their house, unless you want to let them freeze to death," Gideon says nonchalantly, prodding James with the toe of his boot.

"Not unless you want to die too," I mutter. I grab James by the shirt collar and start dragging him towards their house, Gideon erasing the trail of blood with his boot.

We drop them on the porch and Gideon bangs on the door.

After a beat, Ayla wrenches it open, and my breath falters.

"What the *fuck*!" she snarls, anger taking over her shock.

She's wearing her nightdress, a milk white lace thing that barely contains her breasts, which are flushed and heaving with anger. Her burnished hair is tied into a long braid, wispy pieces hanging by her ears and around her forehead, catching on her dark lashes. The cold air makes her nipples tighten, although she seems too pissed to notice.

I memorize her like a picture, half-drunk with desire, until Paloma stirs and weakly swats at my calf.

"Would you like to let them freeze on the porch?" Gideon asks Ayla, dutifully focused on her face.

She sighs. "I guess not." She steps aside to let us drag her parents to the fire.

We drop them onto the carpet and Gideon gives the fire a little boost.

"Do I want to know what happened?" she asks, pulling a heavy wool blanket over her shoulders to cover herself. Her eyes linger at my jaw, studying the bruise that's probably started to bloom beneath my beard. An exact mirror of the one on her father's face.

The corner of my mouth betrays me, curling up into a smile.

Gideon sighs. "Algernon has no self-preservation, and your parents have a drinking problem."

She rolls her eyes. "See yourselves out." She turns and stalks up the stairs, back to bed.

My eyes follow her all the way up the stairs until she's out of sight, my heart thudding. Again, my legs itch to run up there with her. I bet her sheets smell like rosemary and lavender, the scent of her skin. I could rest my head where she lays her cheek down every night, the sheets not nearly as soft as her.

"You really are a glutton for punishment," Gideon snickers, nudging my shoulder and dragging me back to reality.

I roll my eyes and shove him, trudging back out into the night.

Spring, 1881

The ground has just begun to thaw as we approach the spring equinox, and everyone in the community's effort has been directed towards planting for the coming season. Even Ayla seems to have thawed a little towards me, occasionally nodding in my direction to acknowledge my existence.

Dirt cakes the tips of my fingers and the knees of my pants, damp and fragrant. I scrape out another row in the soil and drop the sapling strawberry plants neatly down the line, covering their delicate roots with soil.

I sit up and run my fingers through my sweaty hair, when something hard and spiky beams me in the back of the head. A green pine cone lands to my right.

I pick it up and turn around, catching a flash of red hair before the culprit vanishes behind a tree. I rise to my feet and creep towards it, being careful to not make any noise. I get close enough to touch the bark, and Ayla jumps out, arm cocked and ready to throw another pine cone.

She shrieks when she sees me and throws the pine cone straight at my forehead.

I dodge it and jump to grab her, but she sidesteps and takes off through the rows of tilled soil and new growth.

I take up the chase, my long legs closing the gap between us in a heartbeat. I catch her around the waist and haul her up and backwards into my chest.

"You fucker!" she howls, kicking and thrashing like a rageful cat.

"You started it, wild thing," I chuckle in her ear, trying to ignore the wave of delight her herby scent sends through me. Her lithe body squirms against me, the heat of her skin radiating through our clothes and warming my blood.

I reach down and grab a handful of soil from a wheelbarrow beside us.

"Algernon, don't you fucking dare!"

I dump the pile of dirt on top of her head, cackling as she screeches. I drop her and run, covering a good bit of distance as she cusses me out and shakes the dirt from her hair.

Something catches my eye in the trees, a dark figure winding around the perimeter of the property and I freeze, alarm bells blaring in my head.

Ayla crashes into my back, leaping on me like a squirrel and clinging to my shoulders. She pauses there, loosening her grip slightly and angling herself to look at my face.

"What's wrong?" she asks, noting my frown and searching eyes.

"Someone's on the property," I mutter, reaching around to lift her off of my back, despite thoroughly enjoying the weight of her pressed against me.

I put my fingers to my lips and make a loud whistle, a signal my brothers and I have used to call each other from across the property since we were children.

A moment later, they both come running from different corners of the land, coming quickly to my side.

I'm about to tell them what I saw when Ayla suddenly sags to the ground, groaning low in her throat.

"Ayla?" Panic seizes my chest and I drop to my knees beside her.

Her eyes are squeezed shut, breath puffing from her nose in ragged pulses. A vision.

I go to pull her into my lap when her eyes snap open, their usual hazel replaced by chilly white.

"The Elixir," she murmurs, quiet enough that only I hear her.

My heart stalls. "What?"

She blinks and her eyes are back to normal, pupils dilating as she focuses on me. "He's after the Elixir," she pants.

"How do you know about—"

"There isn't time!" She shoves me backwards. "Go!"

Swallowing my questions, I tear my gaze from her and start running towards the greenhouse, my brothers hot on my heels. We push through the brambles and find the door wide open, the lock in broken pieces on the cobblestone.

My lab is torn apart, broken glass and torn pages littering every surface, A small, but rapidly growing fire is a breath away from the bookshelves.

Gideon immediately runs to put out the fire while Oberon stays outside to search for the intruder. I rush to my stock, finding the unfinished dose of the Elixir of Life exactly where I left it, in an indiscriminate vial by some drying moss.

I breathe a sigh of relief, then turn to my workstation. My current notebook lays open to notes I made when creating a new fertilizer to use this season. I flip through the entire thing, my eyes burning from the smoke, but no pages were torn out. Unless the intruder had the time to memorize the scattered notes I made about the Elixir *and* the intelligence to not only make sense of them, but finish the recipe, they didn't find what they were looking for.

Oberon runs back in, panting. "I think it was Keanu."

Gideon and I both look up. "What?" We say in unison.

Oberon lifts his arm, Keanu's onyx pendant hanging from his fist. The onyx is shattered, the chain broken.

"He sacrificed it to break the lock," Gideon says, approaching Oberon and inspecting the crystal.

"Did he...?" Oberon asks.

I shake my head. "I don't think so. The vial is safe and I highly doubt he'll be able to recreate it without an Alchemist." And as far as we know, I'm the only living one.

"Should we tell father?" Oberon asks, passing Gideon the onyx.

Gideon rolls it between his fingers, then pockets it. "I will this evening. But otherwise, this stays between us, clear?"

Oberon and I nod, relaxing a little.

I wrap my arms around their shoulders, pulling them into my sides and ruffling their dark hair. "You guys worry too much," I tease, tightening my arms so I have them both in a headlock.

Gideon punches me in the kidney and Oberon tries to hyper extend my arm, but I don't relent, dragging them both outside. They might both be more muscular than I am, but my height will always give me the upper hand.

Ayla and Leda stand at the end of the path, looking equal parts anxious and pissed off.

My brothers use that split second of distraction to slip free. Oberon jogs over to Leda and gathers her into his arms, whispering words of reassurance in her ear and kissing her deeply. My eyes lock with Ayla's and I give her a small nod.

Gideon seizes his opportunity and tackles me to the ground, pinning me with my arms behind my back. He takes a fistful of my hair and cranes my head up slightly, chuckling to himself.

I'm about to ask what he's doing, when Ayla crouches in front of me.

I can't help but smile, the mischievous glint in her eye making my stomach do somersaults, but then I see the fistful of dirt in her hand.

She gently removes my glasses and sets them aside at a safe distance.

I pinch my mouth shut and squeeze my eyes closed, preparing for the inevitable.

She shoves the dirt in my face, making sure to rub it thoroughly into my beard and hair.

"That's just rude," I sputter, blinking dirt out of my lashes when she pulls back.

Gideon drops my head into the grass, climbing off of me.

Ayla brushes my hair out of my face, my nerves electric under her soft touch. I lean into her fingers slightly, unable to resist the small amount of contact.

"You haven't seen anything yet, pup," she whispers in my ear, tugging at my hair before standing up and walking away.

"Ayla," I groan, shifting my hips to relieve some of the pressure on my stiffening groin.

My brother's and Leda stand there watching me, trying to suppress their laughter.

"Just leave me here to die," I grumble, arousal turning my brain to jello as I watch her walk away, the new pet name echoing in my mind.

Ayla

Spring, 1881

I rock against the pillow clamped firmly between my legs, biting my fist to suppress the breathy moans riding alongside the waves of pleasure rippling from my needy clit.

I imagine the scratch of his beard against the sensitive skin of my inner thighs, that silver tongue lapping at the honey dripping from me, rather than it soaking wastefully into my pillow. I imagine the hard press of his body against mine, remembering the way he curled around me when I tried to escape him, the way his long fingers dug into my hips, brushed against my tits.

My mind replays the breathless way he said my name, the heated look in his eyes when I called him pup. It took all of my control to walk away from him, and the closer I get to coming all over this pillow, the more I regret it.

Would he be with me now if I hadn't run away? His mouth or hips beneath me, undulating with me? Would his lips be on my neck, leaving bruises on my collarbone? Or on my tits, sucking a pink nipple between his teeth? Would he like the sounds I make? The way I taste?

My orgasm rushes towards me as I buck frantically on the pillow, his name on the tip of my tongue. But I don't dare say it, saying his name out loud while I touch myself would make it all too real. He'll stay in my head, where he's always been. Thoughts are just thoughts, nothing more. Nothing real.

The thought of him walking in on me flashes through my mind, the embarrassed but hopelessly aroused gaze I hope he'd wear. I can see the corner of his rose-colored lips turn up, the throb of his cock tucked into his trousers, that pet name falling from his lips. *Kitten.*

Sparks fly from deep in my belly, that sharp coil of pleasure snapping as my orgasm overtakes me. I fall forward onto the bed, smothering my cry in the thick quilt as I grind through the pleasure. I go limp as the last trickles of light flow through me, and my cheeks grow hot with shame.

What the fuck is wrong with me?

I roll onto my back, sighing at the ceiling, a gray rain cloud swirling in my chest and souring my mood. Why do I always want the things I can't have? I'm not naive, I know that I could have any other man in the community, or outside of it, but just when I think I might be attracted to someone else, Algernon flashes me that grin that makes his eyes light up, and I'm lost again.

But if I never have him, then it won't hurt as badly when I inevitably have to say goodbye.

I slide begrudgingly out of bed and change into a black dress, cinched at the waist, with a square neck lined with crude lace, and slip into my favorite heeled riding boots.

Dusk has just settled over the farm, casting a soft purple glow over the land. A bit of winter chill still lingers on the wind.

I meet Leda at her front porch and we link arms to walk over to the bonfire by the edge of the lake.

Sophia has arranged a new moon ritual this evening, and I desperately need some of that uplifting energy to cleanse me of my melancholy mood.

My father and a fire wielder named Marcus are feeding the flames, coaxing them high enough that the glowing flecks of ash seem to join the stars in the sky. Soft drums resonate with the heartbeat of the earth, stoking that primal spark of Source within us all, calling up the witch.

Leda drags us over to where the brothers stand to the side of the fire, and Oberon sweeps her into a sweet kiss. Gideon passes me a jug of cranberry wine, one of the last of the season, and I take a long drink, refusing to look at Algernon and his loose black tunic, lest I admire the way the firelight kisses the slope of his neck and creates shadows along the barely exposed muscles of his chest.

"Easy, kitten," that fox murmurs, and I nearly choke. "The night is young." He takes the jug from me, his long fingers brushing against the flesh of my palm, and he takes a deep pull.

My mouth waters, watching his throat bob as he drinks, imagining how the sweet wine tastes on his tongue. Heat swirls in my core, wetness pooling between my thighs.

"Everyone!" Sophia calls out, yanking me from my untoward thoughts. "Let us pray before we begin the festivities."

We all gather in a circle around the fire, joining hands, Leda on one side of me, insufferable Algernon on the other. I notice Amadeus and Keanu standing beside my parents. My mother looks like she might keel over from the white knuckle grip she has on the younger man's hand.

Keanu's wolfish eyes catch mine through the smoke, black as the charcoal at the bottom of the pit, and I shiver.

I considered going to Absolon myself, to tell him about my vision and corroborate the boys story, but I know that word would get back to my Father. And if he discovers that I kept a vision from him, the punishment will be swift and severe.

James is the only villain I have the capacity to worry about right now.

"You okay?" Algernon whispers, leaning towards me and squeezing my hand.

I nod, finding it difficult to tear my eyes away from Keanu. Fear coils along my spine, the air in my throat constricts, invisible hands squeezing.

Algernon follows my gaze and stiffens. Keanu's eyes flick away.

"What does he want?" I breathe, mostly to myself. But of course, Algernon overhears.

"An ass-kicking, apparently," he mutters, tugging me a little closer to him.

For once, I don't resist.

We aren't touching anywhere except our hands, but we're close enough that I can smell his sweet leaf scent, somehow fresh and spicy at the same time. The urge to curl under his arm and into his side is strong, the warmth of his body more acute than the fire, coaxing me closer.

Sophia's voice lifts as she begins the ritual, forcing me back to reality once again.

"Goddess, harbinger of fresh beginnings, a symbol of potential and growth, and we gather before thee, seeking thy gentle guidance. We ask for the fortitude to embrace the new opportunities that lay before us, even as thou emerge from the shadows of night to cast thy light upon the world.

We offer this collective prayer, our hearts brimming with gratitude and anticipation for the beauty and growth that you bring to our midst."

"Many thanks," we all murmur, watching the fire crackle happily and dance higher than before.

The circle breaks apart, but Algernon's hand lingers on mine for a heart stopping second before falling away.

I let Leda whisk me away into a dancing circle of women, and I try to lose myself in the spirit of the music, the power of our collective melody. But I can feel his eyes burning on my back, tracking my movements as if I truly was a lost kitten, and he a hungry fox.

I keep waiting to feel his hands slide around my waist, for his body to press up against mine, that spicy green scent to overwhelm me, but it never comes, and I can't decide if I'm relieved, or disappointed.

"You seem distracted, Ay," Leda says, pulling me in to slow dance with her arms around my neck.

"I don't trust him," I whisper, nodding my head to where Keanu reclines beside Gideon and Oberon, looking entirely too comfortable.

"Me neither," she whispers back, tipping her forehead against mine. "Want to get absolutely knackered?"

I grin, and we run off to steal a bottle of honey wine.

About an hour and two bottles of wine later, Leda and I are both blissfully drunk and skipping in wobbly circles around each other. Angry voices start to rise from the other side of the fire.

"That's madness, Amadeus! You can't seriously believe that?" Absolon shouts.

"You see the world we live in Sol! Famine, war, poverty, *that* is madness!" Amadeus fires back.

Oberon rushes over to us, wrapping a protective arm around Leda.

"What's going on?" I hiss.

"Amadeus—" Oberon starts, but is interrupted by a bright flash of golden light.

Absolon is *glowing*, his rage, and magic, spreading out into his aura. I've never seen anything like it before, his power too vast to be contained by his physical self. But Amadeus doesn't back down, the darkness at the edge of the fire racing towards him. *Shadow wielder.*

Everyone shrieks and rushes into the firelight, but it's impossible to hide from a shadow on the night of the New Moon.

The men keep screaming at each other, a jumble of words I don't understand, panic sparking like flint in my chest.

I see Gideon and Keanu run over to their fathers amid the chaos, Keanu pleading with Absolon with his arms open.

I start to wonder where Algernon is when I feel an arm slip around my waist and tug me backwards into something firm and fire-warmed.

"I'm here," Algernon murmurs, his hand splayed across my rib cage.

I let out a breath, some of my anxiety uncoiling. Algernon's right here, with me. He doesn't speak further, but I find myself nuzzling closer to him and he tightens his grip.

Suddenly, Absolon's voice booms loud enough for everyone to hear above the din. "*Get out!*"

"You'll regret this," Amadeus hisses. Then, the shadows swallow them up, a vacuum of endless black, and they're gone. It's rumored that Shadow Wielders could walk through their shadows, almost like portals, but the gift is so rare that there was never proof. But now, it's confirmed. And the Kennedy's are infinitely more dangerous than any of us realized.

I try to step away from Algernon, but stumble, and he hoists me fully into the air, cradling me in his arms. The world turns around me, blurred and wiggly. I snuggle closer to stability, which I realize belatedly is his chest.

"Mmm, fox," I murmur, grabbing at his tunic and bringing it up to my nose, savoring his scent mixed with campfire smoke.

He tilts his head, smiling softly. "Fox?"

"Kitten and fox," I slur, reaching up to touch his beard. It's thick and wiry, but softer than I expected, and a flush of heat throbs low in my stomach.

"I think you've had enough fun tonight, Ayla." He chuckles, holding me closer and starting to walk away from the fire, occasionally glancing over his shoulder at the chaos. But it seems so far now, the drunken haze and hum of arousal blotting everything else out.

I pout, attempting to cross my arms, but they don't seem to want to follow instructions.

"Why the pout?" he says, leaning down a bit closer, blocking my view of anything but him. Something explodes behind him. More shouting.

"Kitten," I grumble.

"Ah, I called you Ayla instead of kitten. Is that it?"

I nod, frown deepening. Some part of my brain is screaming to stop, that lines are being crossed and I'm veering into dangerous territory. But the wine, and my pussy, don't seem to care.

"My apologies, kitten," he hums, bumping his nose against mine as he jogs up the front steps of my house.

"Algernon!" Voices start shouting his name across the field, but they sound a million miles away.

He sighs, leaning his forehead against mine.

"Stay," I whisper, my walls falling to pieces around me, brittle as dried leaves under the heat of his sun. A single, small plea.

"*Algernon!*" The voices get closer, Absolon's rising above the rest.

He holds me tighter, brushes his lips against my forehead, takes a deep, shaking inhale.

"I can't," he whimpers, voice raw. "Stay inside." He sets me on my feet by the front door and wrenches himself down the steps and out into the dark night.

I stand swaying on the steps, tears burning behind my eyes. My stomach roils, rebelling against the wine and scalding embarrassment of rejection crawling along my skin.

I stumble inside and over to the kitchen sink, my body evacuating every drop of alcohol and bite of food I consumed, leaving me hollow and shivering. I slide to the floor as the tears finally come.

He rejected me. He didn't want me.

I was so sure, so sure that he felt the way I did, that we had some sort of connection.

But he doesn't, and I am so fucking stupid.

When will I learn? Being raised by the two people that are supposed to love you, but don't, should have been my first sign. Spending my formative years in a community that's close knit like a family, everyone standing together, strong against the outside world, while I sit off to the side, alone.

Watching my only friend in the world, who was raised with cinnamon tea when she cried and hand stitched blankets with her favorite flower, fall in love and find her way unimpeded.

Watching the world bloom around me, brilliant as mid-spring, while I wither to nothing. Because I am nothing, as significant to the world as a wrench.

The front door opens and I pick my head up, wiping my tears with the back of my hand. A tiny voice in the back of my mind whisperers '*Algernon?*'.

But it's my parents, with their heads leaned together, muttering to one another in hushed voices. They hurry down the hall and into their room. They don't even spare me a passing glance.

As horrible as they are to each other, at least they aren't alone.

I am on my own, I always have been. I have a singular purpose, and I know the cost of veering from the path Fate laid out before me.

I did this to myself. Over and over again, I break my own heart with hope, by wanting.

No more.

I stand and shake myself, smoothing my unruly hair down and wiping my nose.

Never again.

Algernon

Spring, 1881

Every step away from her is agony, but there's no turning back. If I turned my back on my family, I wouldn't be the kind of man she deserves. At least, that's what I tell myself, because it's easier than admitting I'm a coward.

I make it back into the ring of light around the fire, and my father is the first person to reach me. He crashes into me like a wave, his arms braced tightly around me.

"I thought they took you," he whispers, and I hug him back, my heart aching.

How did everything go so wrong?

My mother forces herself between us, squeezing my middle so tightly the air is forced from my lungs.

I hear voices rise a few feet from us, an argument, and we break apart. The Guild is scattered around the fire, in family clusters and small units, their faces fearful and words sharp. Clearly, the Kennedy's display got to them. Trepidation hangs heavier than the smoke in the air, and the hair on the back of my neck rises.

Gideon circles around the edge of the crowd, his head bowed, but I can still make out the gold shimmering at the edges of his eyes.

"What did Amadeus say to you?" I snap, turning towards my father.

"He wants to start a war," he answers, watching the crowd, his mouth flattened to a hard line.

"A war?" I backpedal. "Against who?"

"Humanity, Algernon." He looks back at me. "He talks of Source birthright, of magical superiority."

I suck in a breath. For as long as magic has existed, there's been those that believe we are higher beings, somehow more worthy of power. That our gifts are a sign from the Gods, or God, that *we* should be in charge. But it's been a long rejected belief, the antithesis of what Source and nature teaches us.

Naturally, after the War on Magic, this sentiment grew, but was ultimately snuffed out because, if anything, it proved that we are far more equal than magic purists would like to believe.

But apparently, in a desolate corner of the country at the hands of a once great family brought to ruin, the movement grew teeth. And now, those fangs have sunk into our own flesh and blood, and were tearing through.

A man charges up to our father, spewing insults, and Oberon steps out of the shadows to block him, but our father holds up a hand to stop him.

"You're a coward!" The man hollers, and I recognize him as one of the farriers.

"Because I don't give in to small-minded men?" Absolon bites back, the muscles in his neck bulging. My mother tries to step forward, but I snag her wrist and gently pull her back. Oberon comes up besides us, and I see Leda tiptoe over in my periphery. I have half a thought to ask her to go check on Ayla, but swallow it.

"You're the one that's small minded, Sol! We could be *great*, the most powerful Guild to walk the earth! But instead you'd rather us live in the fucking backwoods, hiding like vermin." His words spark like flint, and the surrounding crowd turns towards us, the rage in their eyes flickering eerily in the fire light.

I suppress the urge to step back. It feels like the ground is falling out from under my feet, and I'm hanging suspended at the mercy of folks I considered family. The turn was so swift, so staggering, I can hardly wrap my head around it.

But then other's come forward, their expressions softer, and they argue back, taking up from my father.

"Amadeus' promises are empty. As substantial as fairytales," Absolon says, raising his voice over the bedlam. "I gave you freedom. On this land, you live and breath Source, you don't have to hide to go to work, or to the store. You don't have to toil, squandering your gifts, to scrape up a few pennies to pay rent for an apartment the size of a stable. I gave you safety, family, purpose! But the second a stranger offers you power, you turn your backs?"

The crowd has fallen silent, the only sounds the roar of the flames and the drumming of my heart.

"If you want to join Amadeus, than go. I won't stop you. But do not leave under the delusion that it is for anything greater than personal gain." Absolon turns and storms back to our house, his energy like static around him, and my mother pulls from my grip, following in his wake.

Oberon and Leda follow them next, then Gideon, until I'm left alone by the remnants of the feast we'd just enjoyed. I watch as the crowd starts to thin, and wonder how many people will be here come sunrise.

I spot Ayla's parents on my left, talking with the farrier and a few others, their heads bowed. James' gaze flicks up to meet mine, and a sneer crosses his face before he turns back to the group. A few moments later, James and Paloma start back towards their house, wobbly from the wine and speaking in hushed whispers.

Making sure no one is watching, I move in silence a few yards behind them, dodging the lights from houses to stay shrouded in darkness. They stumble up the steps and into the house, slamming the door behind them.

I creep around the porch and peer into the kitchen window, praying Ayla's already gone to bed, but I spot her right below me, sitting on the ground in front of the sink. She has her knees pulled up to her chest, her head resting on her forearms, and her shoulders shake with sorrow.

The clawed hand of heartbreak punches through my chest and seizes my heart, tearing it clean from my body.

She's crying, and it's my fault.

I sag onto the ground, the damp grass soaking through my pants, and lean my forehead against the rough wood siding. Something in me rages to kick down the front door and bundle her into my arms, to tell her I'm right here and that I'll keep her safe. But my rationality keeps me locked in place, knowing that if I went in there now, she'd turn me away. She'd tell me that she *hates me*. I'd have a better chance of talking to a rabid animal.

She gave me a chance, let her walls down, and I blew it.

Besides, she was drunk, she may not have even meant it.

The thought is like salt rock rubbed into the gaping emotional wound in my chest, and a thick sob wells up in my throat, choking me. I wrench myself away from her house and stumble towards the greenhouse. I should probably go home, but the last thing I want right now is to be confronted by my family.

The doors open for me without a touch, and close gently behind me, the soupy warmth of the air almost suffocating. I collapse onto one of the armchairs, dropping my head in my hands, and mourn.

I wake up to brilliant sun shining down onto my face, and nearly fall over in my haste to stand. I fell asleep in the armchair, and now it was well after daybreak.

I need to talk to Ayla.

The spring breeze is sweet and fresh, the chirp of birds and hum of bees nurturing the sprig of hope in my chest.

I can save this.

But a few paces from her door, Gideon intercepts me.

"Where the fuck have you been?" he hisses, dragging me aside.

"I fell asleep in the greenhouse. Can this wait?" I look between him and her front door, shifting my weight back and forth.

"Fifteen people left," he says, and my sprout of hope withers slightly.

"Fifteen?" I echo, falling still.

"Father's holding an open house tonight, to try and curb anyone else leaving." He catches my gaze flicks back toward her door and narrows his eyes. "I'm not sure what's going on with you, but you need to get it together. We need to be a unified front."

"I know, I know." I place a hand on his shoulder and look him in the eye. "I'll be there."

He nods and walks past me towards the barn, probably to prepare for this evening. Our father only calls open houses when something is seriously wrong, and the thought makes anxiety coil in my gut. For a moment, I debate following Gideon to help, but I have to try and make this right before it's too late.

I know better than to knock on her front door, so I move around to the side of the house, which is thankfully obscured by the edge of the forest. Her bedroom window hangs twenty feet above my head, the glass pushed open to let in the warm air.

There's an oak tree a foot or so to the left of it, and I grab a lower branch, hanging on it to see if it can bear my weight. It groans slightly, the bark rough under my hands, but holds.

About halfway up, I realize this might be a terrible idea, but it's too late to turn back now. I stop right outside her window, obscured by the thick foliage, and see her sitting at her desk, her copper hair in a thick plait down her back, wearing a light blue shift, revealing her sun tanned skin and rounded shoulders.

Desire pumps through my blood, but I ignore it. Now is not the time for my cock to do the talking for me. I crawl closer, holding my breath as if that'll make the branch stronger, and place on foot on her window sill. I crouch down, and with a bracing exhale, I ease myself through and land on my feet inside her bedroom.

"Shit!" She shrieks, whirling around and brandishing a pen in my direction. "Algernon!"

I hold up my hands. "Don't freak out. It's not like I could waltz through the front door," I say, fighting the smile trying to curl my lips.

"So you break into my room!" she throws the pen down and yanks the quilt off her bed, covering herself up.

"I had to talk to you," I say, risking a step closer.

The anger in her face falters, her jaw ticking. "I don't want to talk," she bites, venomous.

"I should have stayed," I blurt, my long legs swallowing up the last few feet between us, but I refrain from reaching out.

She shakes her head, avoiding my eyes. "Don't," she whispers.

"Ayla," I try to tilt her chin up, but she jerks away from my touch. "You know how I feel about you—"

"It doesn't matter anymore," she says, and the words ring in my ears like a slap.

"It does, Ayla. We can do this—"

"I don't want you."

I take a step back, blood rushing from my head and making the room sway under my feet. "It doesn't have to be like this," I say, my voice breaking.

She doesn't reply, hugging the blanket tighter around her shoulders.

"Say it again, and I'll go. But it won't change anything."

She finally looks up, her gaze so hard it cracks through my sternum. "I don't want you."

I stare back at her, resolution twining through the cracks of my heart. "I won't push you, but know that I won't give up, either." I move towards the window, and with one last backwards glance, I climb out, telling myself that the tear rolling down her cheek was just my imagination.

Ayla

Spring, 1882

Six families have left the Guild, joining the Kennedy's burgeoning ranks at the Canadian border.

I have been left entirely out of the loop on what exactly is happening, and refuse to ask. All I've heard in passing whispers is that the group has begun calling themselves the Arcanum, and that they've begun gathering witches from across the Northern hemisphere. Their numbers grow by the day.

What they're planning is unclear. But it has Absolon terrified of another war against witchcraft, and our once safe corner of the world is vulnerable. The in-fighting is constant, causing our food stores to wither and our homes have begun falling into disrepair.

This community survived entirely on goodwill and camaraderie, two resources that have suddenly become scarce.

The Raith's have all but boarded themselves up in the house on Absolon's order, Leda and her mother along with them.

James and Paloma spend most of their time with their heads together, locked up in their room and ignoring me entirely. I should be sad, but frankly, its a reprieve.

I've considered running, nearly every day, but it's like James can smell it on me, appearing just when I work up the nerve to pull out my rucksack. He snaps my thread of hope with three words: '*You are mine.*'

Fall, 1883

The Arcanum has infiltrated Albany's government, and there are rumors that the Capital is next.

Things have reached an uncomfortable truce on the farm, with most of the families that would consider leaving having already done so. Only a handful remain, including mine, the Raith's, which Leda, as of today, will *officially* be a part of, and a few other's.

It's the Autumn Equinox, and Oberon and Leda are getting married tonight.

I slide into the delicate blue dress she selected for me, her only bridesmaid, and pull my hair up into a loose chignon. I pull out my rose petal rouge and start brushing it along my cheeks, hoping it'll mask the palid look of my skin.

"Ayla!" James' voice roars, my bedroom door slamming open with a gale force wind.

I barely lift my eyes and finish applying my makeup. "Yes?"

"Your mother's useless. I need you to read for me." The veins in his forehead are bulging. Bruises stain his knuckles like violent watercolor.

I sigh and pull out my deck, tapping on it three times, then starting to shuffle.

Immediately, the Fool flies out and I close my eyes, bracing.

"Are you mocking me, girl?" He roars, grabbing the deck from my hands. "Just like your mother, you fucking bitch!"

Wind whips around the space, a cyclone starting to form at the center of the room. Rain pelts me, soaking my dress and ruining my hair and makeup. I swallow the long-absent prickle of fear that crawls up my throat.

"I'll show you!" He whips my cards into the lit fireplace, all of them immediately going up in flame.

"No!" My heart shatters and I try to push through the wind, try to save some of them, but the force of it is too strong. I watch la Luna at the edge of the wood, it's edges curling and turning black, slowly burning away.

"How could you?!" I scream at him, voice cracking.

His eyes widen a fraction and the wind ticks down a notch, the rain letting up enough for me to breath.

"Vision. Now," he growls, stalking towards me. He grabs the crystal ball from my desk and thrusts it into my hands. "What do you see?"

I blink to clear the tears from my eyes, desperately trying to focus on the swirl of indigo colored energy within the crystal, to use it to channel a vision, but it slips from my grasp, refusing to connect with me.

"I can't," I say, forcing myself to meet his eyes. "You know it can't be forced."

"Like hell." He yanks the crystal ball out of my hands and throws it against the wall, shattering it into a million pieces. Then he freezes, the weather disappearing in an instant, leaving behind an eerie silence.

I hear someone downstairs calling my name. Oberon.

"This isn't over," he hisses, pointing a finger at me before hurrying down to greet the Groom.

Shaking, I attempt to fix my hair and my makeup, standing beside the newly fueled fire to dry my dress.

Satisfied with my appearance, I get on my hands and knees and reach under the bed, feeling around until my fingers land on a small package wrapped in brown paper. I pull it out and blow the thick layer dust from it before gently unwrapping it.

The tarot deck falls into my hand, a gilded orange tiger grinning at me from the front of the box. I open the top and pull out the deck, and small note falls to the floor. I pick it up and unfold it, trepidation swirling in my stomach.

Ayla,

This deck reminded me of you, hellcat. I know how much you love yours, but it can't hurt to have a back-up. Happy birthday.

Yours, A

My heart quickens, warmth flooding through my chest. I fold up the note and slide it back into the box with the cards.

Algernon and I haven't spoken in...Gods, I don't even know how long. He was persistent the first few weeks after that night, trying constantly to talk to me, to apologize, but seemed to give up when I refused to budge.

I slip the deck under my pillow and take a deep breath before heading downstairs.

Leda's wedding is all that matters tonight, and I won't let my own silly preoccupations detract from that.

The wedding ceremony is brief, and I somehow manage to get through it without a hitch, despite my emotions refusing to settle.

I linger at the back of the reception, nursing a warm mug of whiskey with pumpkin and a cinnamon stick. Leda and Oberon dance under the stars, blissful and bursting with love.

I'm happy for them, I truly am. The love they have is amazing, pure and sweet, uncomplicated. They deserve that and more.

"I wasn't sure if you'd come," a low voice says from beside me.

I steel my muscles, refusing to flinch. "I wouldn't miss her wedding."

"Hmm, I suppose not." Algernon steps into the light of the lantern hanging above my head. He's dressed in white shirt, crisp and new, with a tailored brown vest and trousers, accentuating his broad shoulders and narrow waist, his long legs and tan skin. "You look beautiful," he says softly, eyes wandering my face.

"I know."

"Are you enjoying the party?" He moves a little closer, tempting me with the earthy smell of his skin.

I don't trust myself to reply, taking a sip of whiskey instead. It's been so long since I've heard him speak, my body immediately is overwhelmed with the old desire to curl up into his chest, listen to the rumble of his words from the source.

"I'll take that as a no—" he leans against the light post "—it was a beautiful ceremony though."

I nod, refusing to look at him for fear of melting into a puddle under the heat of his gaze.

He sighs. "How long are you going to close me out?"

"I'm not sure I know what you mean," I scowl, taking a sip of whiskey.

The musicians tip into a willowy ballad, the notes light as air.

"Will you at least dance with me? Just one song?"

Everything in me screams to turn him down, to run and hide, but when he stretches his hand out towards me, I find myself reaching back. I slip my hand into his, the warmth of his touch seeping into my cold fingers.

As the music starts to build, he guides me towards the cleared circle by the riverbank where everyone is dancing, candles littering the ground around it, mingling with the moon to cast a soft glow over everything.

He pulls me close, his arm wrapping around my waist with a familiarity that sends shivers down my spine. The contrast of the cool evening and the heat of his body has my head spinning, every touch sending sparks along my skin. The world around us fades into the background, leaving only the two of us, lost in the embrace of the music and each other.

We move together in perfect harmony, our bodies swaying to the rhythm of the song. With each step, each gentle turn, I feel myself falling deeper under his spell despite my every intention. The years looming like mountains between us fall away to nothing.

It's as if time itself has stopped, freezing this moment in eternity.

I rest my head against his chest, listening to the steady beat of his heart, a reassuring rhythm midst the chaos of my thoughts. In his arms, I find solace, a fleeting escape from the constraints of my reality.

But even as I revel in the bliss of this stolen moment, a bittersweet ache tugs at my heart. I know that before long, I will be gone, lost in the sands of time. For him, nothing but a memory.

I push aside the inevitable, choosing instead to lose myself in the warmth of his embrace, in the promise of what could never be.

As the song draws to a close, he presses a soft kiss to my forehead, a silent confession. I hold onto him a moment longer, unwilling to let go, but reality beckons, pulling us apart once more.

"Ayla, I regret walking away from you every day," he murmurs, brushing a strand of hair off my cheek.

"You made the right choice," I whisper, turning away before I collapse into his arms, desperate for escape once again. But I can't escape Fate, can't escape my reality, and I can't destroy us both in the process.

"Let me choose you," he pleads, but I don't turn back.

We can never go back.

Algernon

Fall, 1885

I shelve another vial of the Elixir of Life, the final one. We have enough now for everyone in the Guild, along with a few extras just in case. My father wanted to offer them at the Full Moon ritual tomorrow night, the first one we've held in nearly 3 years. He's hoping it'll serve as a testament to our power.

With the Arcanum breathing down our necks and poaching our numbers, we've hardly felt inclined to celebrate.

My eyes drift back to my notebook, and the nagging fear that's lingered in the back of my mind for years. Did Keanu manage to crack the formula?

At first, I doubted it. But now that his power and ambition have made themselves blindingly clear, it's starting to seem possible. And would explain why he's been so desperate to have my brothers and I join their ranks, to aid in his fathers quest of political power.

Their mission was simple, those with Source, with magic, should control our world. It was basic Darwinism, survival of the fittest. To the Arcanum, we were the stronger species, so we should have all the governing power, that it was shameful for us to have to hide like rats when we could so easily crush humanity under our thumbs.

It was grotesque, and so misguided. So misaligned with the natural world and all it's teachings. It was a greedy power grab masked as a righteous revolution, and hundreds of witches were falling for it.

I clean up my work station and ruminate on it all, as I so often do, but, like always, thoughts of Ayla creep in.

I've watched her hollow herself out, turn to icy recluse over the last few years, and I hate myself everyday for it. I broke her heart that night, and I knew it in the moment, but I was too much of a coward, too afraid of standing against my father, and it cost me everything.

I waited nearly a decade for my shot with her, for her to let me in. And the moment she did, I stomped all over her because I was afraid of getting crushed myself. It was selfish and cruel, and I spend every second wishing I could redo that night. Wishing that I held her tighter, kissed her lips, told her I was hopelessly in love with her, and ran the fuck away from all of this with her safe in my arms.

I could have saved her, saved us. But I didn't, and now we're both suffering with a distance between us that I have no clue how to bridge. I thought that after the dance at Oberon's wedding, I'd maybe cracked through her defenses, but as soon as the music ended, she blocked me out again.

Locking up, I step out into the chilly night. It has to be close to midnight, the nearly full moon hanging heavy directly overhead.

"*Leda!*" A harrowing scream tears through the night air, making the hair on the back of my neck stand up. *Oberon.*

I run towards the sound, dropping everything and bolting across the field to Oberon and Leda's home. My heart slams in my chest, cold terror seizing me as he screams and screams.

I find Oberon in the yard, doubled over with agony, screaming his throat raw. His bare torso is covered in blood, and he looks strangely pale, almost ghostly. Something in me recoils at the sight of him, an instinctual revulsion kicking up in my stomach, but I push forward and try to pull him into my arms.

"She's gone," he wails, shoving me away. "I can't feel her." He tugs at his hair and punches the ground.

I feel others come running up, but they linger at the edge of the yard. My father's voice cuts through the din.

"Algernon, get away from him."

I whirl around. "Are you insane?"

His face is cold and emotionless. Everyone around him looks equal parts horrified and devastated, except Gideon. He wears the same emotionless expression as our father and my heart sinks. Then I notice Absolon's hand on his shoulder, knuckles white, gold glimmering between his fingers. Gideon's face isn't expressionless, he's hiding the agony of being crushed under our father's will.

"Do as he says, baby. Please," my mother calls out, tears streaming down her cheeks.

Oberon screams again, clawing at his chest, covering his ears.

"I don't understand," I say, torn between loyalty to my mother and father, and loyalty to my little brother.

"Kill me!" Oberon suddenly lunges at me, grabbing me by the shoulders. "I'm supposed to be dead," he wails, eyes black as coal, his veins darkening at an alarming rate. He leaves a dusting of black powder on my tunic.

My stomach does another flip of primal revulsion, and then understanding dawns.

He *is* supposed to be dead. He was killed, but came back.

"Necromancer," I breathe, terror coiling in my legs, urging me to flee. Necromancy is the darkest magic of all, forbidden in every circle of magic since the dawn of Source. It goes against the very laws of nature, it's the kind of power that belongs in the hands of the Gods. The kind of power that will turn the soul of the kindest man black and cruel.

"Algernon, please," Oberon cries, clutching my chest, sobbing. "I didn't mean to. I tried to save her, I tried—" anguished sobs swallow the rest of his words, and he collapses to the ground.

"Leave him, Algernon." My father orders, gold flashing in his eyes, but the compulsion doesn't take hold, too much of his power directed at keeping Gideon rooted to the spot.

"He's a Necromancer," I call out, looking down at my brother, shattered into a million pieces, his whole world stolen from him.

"He's dangerous," Gideon answers this time, but his voice sounds odd, stilted and mechanical. My father working the muscles of his jaw and vocal chords, playing him like an instrument. My stomach roils.

"We have to go inside, now," my mothers says, tearful. "The killer might still be out there."

Oberon looks up at me, terrified. "Please, stay."

I place a hand on his shoulder. "I will not abandon my brother." My cowardice cost me Ayla, it will not cost me my brother and closest friend. Not when he needs me.

"But you'll abandon us?" My mother clings to Gideon's arm, and I watch her heart break.

"No, *you* are abandoning your son," I snarl, looking at their faces, looking at everyone I grew up around, that helped raise us, turning their back on him over a mistake made in a moment of desperation so complete I can't even begin to fathom it.

If I was in his position, if it was Ayla that needed me, I would have done the same thing. I would have given up everything to try and save her.

I haul up Oberon, wrapping my arm around him and pulling him into my side. "I'm here," I whisper to him. "I'm not afraid of you."

Ayla pushes to the front of the crowd and those hazel eyes catch mine, watery and wide. Her father has his hand clamped on her wrist, white knuckled so she can't come any closer.

I hold her gaze. "I stand with my brother."

The smallest flicker of pride lights up her eyes, and I know I've made the right decision.

"Everyone, back to your homes and lock your doors. Be on high-alert. Gideon, James, and I will search for the culprit," Absolon barks.

With that, the crowd slowly dissipates. Ayla is dragged away by her parents, and my family follows them.

Oberon and I are left alone, with the bloody remnants of Leda's murder and the stench of dark magic.

We search for Leda for weeks to no avail. It's like she completely vanished, lost to the wilderness.

I watch Oberon grapple with his new found power. I watch him bring their dog who was killed during the attack back to life, and force food and water down his throat when he's bed ridden for days afterwards. He teeters on the verge of madness, consumed either by the debilitating weight of his new power, his bottomless grief, or copious amounts of alcohol.

It's everything I can do to keep him alive and relatively sane.

We know that the Arcanum was responsible, that Leda was murdered to send us a message. Submit, or we'd be crushed like ants.

To protect my brother, to protect Ayla, there's something I have to do.

In the cover of night, I sneak into the greenhouse, trying to be a stealthy as I can at my height. I unlock the door and slip inside, closing it silently.

I turn and nearly jump out of my skin.

Ayla is sitting on my workbench, swirling a vial of Elixir in her hand. She's wearing a long green tunic and black stockings, her hair a tumbled mess of copper around her shoulders. Her lashes cast long shadows on her skin, the tip of her nose a delicate pink from the cold.

"Hey," she says, not meeting my eyes.

"How did you get in here?" I take a few steps towards her.

She shrugs and sets the vial down. "It's not hard to pick a lock."

"It's a warded lock!"

"Set better wards."

I sigh. No point in arguing, it hardly seems important anymore. I come up beside her, sitting on the stool to the right of her crossed legs.

"Have you told anyone?" she asks, tilting her chin towards the vial.

"Just my family. And you saw it in that vision."

"Good," she murmurs. "Does it work? Make you live forever, I mean?"

I nod. "I think so."

She looks more closely at the vial, then back at me. "Can I ask you something selfish?"

"Of course." I resist the urge to run my fingers across her ankle, up her delicate shin bone.

"Don't give any to my parents."

I meet her eyes. "Never."

We sit in silence, listening to the roar of crickets and toads, the rustle of falling leaves skittering across the ground.

"You taught me the greatest lesson of my life," I say quietly, giving in to the urge to rest my hand on her ankle. Her skin is cold under my touch, bright and burning, even with the thin fabric barrier. She doesn't flinch away.

"What's that?" she asks.

"To do what's right, rather than what I'm told."

She chuckles, mirthless. "That's a good lesson."

"I meant what I said at the their wedding. I would give anything to go back and choose to stay with you that night. But I was a coward." I stand up and face her, looking her in the eye. "I'm so sorry, Ayla."

Her eyes search mine, unreadable. Then she sighs and looks away. "I'm not angry with you, Algernon. You made the right choice."

"I disagree," I say, placing my hands on the slope of her rib cage and lean closer, drawn in by the familiar scent of her skin.

She places a hand on my chest, stopping me. "It's what's best. Trust me."

The words sting, but I relent, lowering my hands to my sides. If there ever was or will be a time for us, it isn't now. Not with the world falling apart around us.

"Did you come here to take it?" I ask, changing the subject.

"I came here to destroy it," she admits, picking up the vial again.

I nod in understanding. She didn't want her parents to get a hold of it.

"Well, I came here to take it."

She looks up at me, surprised. "You haven't yet?"

I shake my head. "I wasn't sure if I wanted to, but now..." I trail off. "He'll need me."

Her touch surprises me as she pushes the vial into my hand. "Go on then."

I take the vial and pop the cork with my thumb.

"It might kill me," I smirk, wafting it's medicinal scent into my nose.

"Doubtful." She smiles. "You're too good for that."

My heart warms, and I tip the contents of the vial into my mouth, swallowing it slowly. It tastes like nothing, but the warmth spreads from my throat through my chest, almost pleasurable. I fail to suppress a giggle that bubbles up, giddiness overwhelming me.

"Your eyes," she murmurs, reaching up to touch my face before stopping herself. "Did it work?"

I look down at myself. I don't look any different, but I *feel* like I could run circles around the world. Like I'm finally brave enough to lay her out on this table and ravish her the way I've dreamed about.

I grin. "Yes, I think so."

"Well, then congratulations. You're immortal." She slides off the table and starts to walk towards the door.

I snatch her wrist, harder than I intend, and spin her back around. "Take it," I say firmly, using my other hand to grab another vial from the shelf.

She tugs her wrist away. "I don't want to."

"I don't care." Confidence soars through me, giving me a steadiness I've never felt before. Something in the back of my head is alarmed, but I'm far too gone to acknowledge it.

"Algernon." She starts to back away, but I match her step for step.

"I won't watch you die," I snap, suddenly angry. I feel out of control, feral.

She opens her mouth, then closes it again. "Algernon, it's pointless."

"Take it." I thrust the vial towards her.

A flicker of consideration passes through her eyes, before it's replaced by trepidation. I can see the curiosity in her eyes, the want lingering in the back of her mind. And that's all I need.

I grab her by the throat and pull her into me, stealing the air from her lungs. My hand slides into her hair and for a second I consider kissing her, letting her taste the Elixir on my tongue. But I resist, this is more important.

I can feel her heart racing, the small pants of breath falling from her lips, her pupils blown wide.

"Al," she breathes.

"Open," I growl in her ear.

Her lips part slightly, whether in acceptance or to protest, I don't know, but I seize my opportunity and pour the Elixir down her throat.

She takes every drop, licking her lips after. Then she smiles slightly. "I hope it's not wasted on me," she says, eyes wandering my face.

"Never." I lean down, aching to taste her, to feel her lips against mine, exhilaration slamming through my veins.

But she steps back and looks away.

"Thank you, Al," she whispers, touching her chest gently, where I know the same pleasure must be swirling beneath her skin. "I have to go now."

I grit my teeth, my heart splintering a little bit more. I nod, not knowing what else to do besides fall to my knees and beg.

She turns and dashes out the door, leaving me standing there brokenhearted. And I can't even be angry, because she shattered me as gently as she could. More gently than I did.

I sink onto the ground, head in my hands. I try to remember back before any of this happened, when my days were stacked with laughter, with sunshine. When my biggest concerns were whether or not Ayla wanted me, and if my mold was cultivating properly.

I can barely remember it now, those golden days. Now, my days are soaked in shadow, and I'm staring down the barrel of forever, no light in sight.

A knock jars me from my stupor and I lift my head. Gideon stands on the other side of the glass, looking sallow and slightly haunted, his under eyes dark.

I haven't seen him since the night Leda disappeared, besides catching a glimpse of him on horseback leaving the property in the middle of the night, when Absolon is sleeping.

Is he here for the Elixir? I wonder. I push to my feet and meet him at the door, but don't unlock it.

"What?" I ask, crossing my arms over my chest. I know he couldn't do anything that night, but instead of coming to see us while Absolon slept, he was probably getting piss drunk and fucking his feelings away. A luxury Oberon and I no longer have.

"Don't look at me like that," he says.

"Where have you been going?"

His eyes flicker with surprise, but it quickly dissolves back into disinterest. "Into town," he says after a beat.

I snort, turning away from him and shaking my head. "You know that he's been asking for you?" I snap. "When he's drunk, or sleeping, or so consumed with hurt that he can't think straight? He asks for her, and for *you*." Sorrow blooms in my chest, a feeling I haven't allowed myself to indulge in, too busy holding Oberon's pieces together. And still, he asks for someone else.

Gideon looks like he's been struck. "Al, I didn't—"

"He needed you, and you disappeared." *I needed you.*

"I'm trying to fix this, I'm trying to find—"

"There's no *fixing*!" I roar, slamming my fist against the glass, splintering it and making him jump. "You can't fix this," I repeat, the rage wheezing out of me as quickly as it appeared.

"I know," he breathes, leaning his forehead against the cracked glass.

"Why are you here?" I ask finally.

"I was in the stables when I saw Ayla walking home." He looks up at me, frowning slightly. "She was crying."

"What happens between Ayla and I is none of your business," I growl, getting defensive.

"Fuck, Algernon. I'm not trying to get in the middle of whatever pining thing you guys have going on. I just wanted to make sure *you* were alright."

Me?

"Can you let me in? It's fucking freezing."

I flex my hand over the door handle, debating, then pull it open. Hesitantly, he steps inside, taking a deep lungful of the warm, petrichor tinged air. He collapses into one of the arm chairs by the bookcase, pinching the bridge of his nose like he has a headache.

I watch him closely, my big brother, one of my favorite people in the world. The man that taught me to ride a horse, that would make a fool of himself so I'd smile when I was sick, that saved my ass more times than I can count. The boy that placed himself like barricade between us and our father, that took every blow with a smile so we wouldn't be afraid. But even still, I feel like I barely know him, even though he's as familiar as my favorite sweater.

Someday, I'd like to know him, the *real* him.

I move to the cabinet of finished serums, grab a bottle of the Elixir, and set it on the small table beside his chair before sinking into the other one. "For your headache," I explain, well, lie.

He uncaps the vial and swallows it without question, and I see the furrow in his brow immediately ease, the color come back into his cheeks. He shifts a little in his seat, presses him hand against his sternum. A laugh bubbles up, but he fights it down with a frown.

"What the hell was that?" He asks, a bark of laughter bursting out. He claps a hand over his mouth, his eyes wide.

"The Elixir," I smirk, corking the vial and tossing it into the trash.

For a moment, I wonder if he'll be angry, but then he chuckles, still rubbing his chest where I know that buzzy warmth is spreading.

"You little shit," he laughs.

I produce a bottle of crystal clear moonshine from an icebox in the corner and pour us each a shot.

"To eternity," Gideon says, raising his glass.

"To eternity." I clink my glass against his and swallow the vile brew, grimacing.

The next morning, Oberon shakes me awake.

"Al, wake up!" He smacks my face.

"What?" I grumble, trying to swat his hands away.

"The Abbott's are gone."

My heart freezes, panic squeezing the air from my lungs. "What?!" I jump up, already running out the door.

He chases after me. "They packed up and left. The last families went with them."

I stop at the bottom of the steps leading up to their front porch, Oberon bumping into my back.

"She's gone?" All the strength is sapped from my limbs, and I feel like I might collapse.

Oberon puts a hand on my shoulder, a strange display of strength from him. "I'm sorry, Al."

We head inside, and sure enough, all of their belongings are gone, save a few pieces of furniture and scraps of things. I walk to her room, holding onto a thread of hope that she'll be sitting there when I open the door.

But I push it open and find it empty, besides a bare bed and dusty desk. I walk around the perimeter of the room, searching for something I can't name, taking deep breaths as if that will brand her scent on my lungs, keep her with me for a little longer.

When I reach her desk, I spot a folded slip of paper and snatch it up.

It's the note I left her in that tarot deck all those years ago, worn and faded with time. I bring it to my nose, the smell of her hair soaked into the parchment.

I turn it over, half-sick with hope, and let out an audible gasp when I see her familiar scrawl.

Fox,

None of this was my choice. I'm sorry.

Yours, A

Act 2

Ayla

Spring, 1924

Finger-bone branches whip my skin as I run through the forest, the scant glow of the first quarter moon lighting my way into town, to the train station. The humid air lay thick on my lungs, coating me an uncomfortable sheen of sweat.

I don't think anyone is following, but I can't be too sure. The Arcanum is vast and cunning, and I'm completely alone. To them, I was no one. Another body in the army, a grunt. Not a person, but a tool. So, really, it wasn't much different than my life before, how my life had always been.

I just have to make it to the train station.

The meager station comes into view just as the sky begins to blush, and I allow myself a single moment to catch my breath, mainly so I don't look like a mad-woman. I try to smooth my cropped hair into somewhat presentable waves, and pinch my cheeks to add some life to my exhausted face.

Blessedly, the station is almost entirely empty at this hour, save for a gentleman or two, the conductor, and the ticketmaster. The train rests regally on the tracks, heaving thick breaths of steam, it's red paint gleaming.

"Traveling alone, doll?" The elderly ticketmaster asks, his dense white brows masking his expression.

"Visiting family in the city, actually." I flash my brightest smile.

"That'll be \$32.00, miss. Train leaves in a few minutes." He holds out his hand, a ticket pinched between his pointer and middle finger.

Internally, I cringe at the price. I knew it would be expensive, but that was nearly every penny I've saved over the last year. Keanu hadn't allowed anyone but his inner circle to work, so I had to hock nearly everything I owned over several months to scrounge up the cash I'd need to escape.

I count out the bills and slide them across the kiosk.

He doesn't count the money, just hands me the ticket and smiles. "Enjoy your trip, doll."

I scurry away, clutching the slip of paper close to my heart.

Freedom.

I board the train and settle into a cramped, but comfortable seat with a small table, decorated with a white cloth and jar candle. I settle my small suitcase under the seat, hooking the handle with my heel so it doesn't slide.

Twenty minutes later, at 7 a.m. on the dot, the train begins to move, and I can finally breathe.

It would be hours before someone noticed my absence at Folke, I'd slipped out when last night's Sacrifice tipped from ritualistic to raging, and it was likely that most people had only just climbed into bed.

By the time anyone would notice, I'd be lost in the web of the city, forgotten and free. I had only one friend in the entire organization, and I had to trust that he'd understand what I was doing, and keep his mouth shut.

My eyes are heavy, my blinks getting slower, and I rest.

I all but run out of Grand Central, the crush of bodies overwhelming in the late-afternoon rush. I throw myself into the nearest phone booth, double then triple checking the locks before I dig a scrap of paper out of my pocket. My desperate lifeline.

Albany's favorite inventor takes the Big Apple by storm! Raith's new digs are fit for a king, and rumor has it, he's made some high-rolling friends down in the concrete jungle. Ready to take on Addison and Teslo, Al?

A blurry photo of a sizable estate rests next to the brief article, my only clue as to where he is. I take a few deep breaths, try to settle my nerves, then exit the photo booth and start walking.

The gentle warmth of a spring afternoon envelops me as I traverse the lively streets. The sun bathes the city in a soft, golden glow, casting a warm hue upon the brick facades and blooming trees that line the sidewalks. Delicate blossoms flutter in the breeze, painting the air with the sweet fragrance of renewal.

As I walk, the rhythmic tapping of my shoes on the pavement harmonizes with the melodic tunes of street musicians, creating a symphony of urban life. Storefronts boast displays of pastel-colored dresses and wide-brimmed hats. Street vendors peddle vibrant bouquets of tulips, and the cheerful calls of children playing echo through the air.

As I turn corners, I discover pockets of greenery tucked away in unexpected places, providing a peaceful retreat amidst the urban hustle. The air is filled not only with the scents of blossoms but with anticipation, a future filled with endless possibilities. Promise lingers at every sunlit bend.

But the hours drag on, and I walk until my feet are bleeding. The sun has long ago set with no luck, and what was promises around every corner has turned to threats. I stop under a streetlight, half prepared to accept defeat and sleep in the alley when I look up, spotting a taxi lingering by the curb.

I swallow my nerves and run over, sliding into the backseat.

The cabby barely looks up. "Where to, miss?"

I tear off the picture and pass it to him. It's a long shot, like finding a needle in a sewing kit the size of an elephant, but I have to start somewhere.

He takes it and looks at it over the rim of his spectacles, then chuckles. "Raith's? Coulda just said that, love. That's a hot spot tonight."

"I—what?"

The cabby passes the picture back to me and closes the privacy window before I can ask an questions, pulling out into traffic.

Not even 20 minutes later, we're pulling around the curved driveway in front of the estate, a sprawling white Colonial beast blanketed with ivy and glowing with warm light.

He gets out and opens my door, grinning mischievously. "Make good choices, doll."

"What do I owe you?" I ask, chewing my lip.

"Nothing, hon. Mr. Raith covers the fees of his guests. Generous, that one."

I open my mouth, then close it, and step out of the cab, clutching my bag to my chest.

My shoulders creep up to my ears, the thud of my heart suddenly getting louder, my throat dry. For a moment, I consider getting back into the cab, but he's already pulling away.

What did he mean, that it's a "hot spot"? I can't see a soul in any of the windows. I squint, and can just make out the glimmer of a protective glamour. Clever.

I steel myself and approach the massive front door, grasp the golden lion knocker, and knock three times.

After a few agonizing moments, the door opens with a flourish, and I'm greeted by a comely woman wearing a white apron. Thunderous jazz explodes into the silent night air, and I can see at least a dozen people crowded in the foyer, laughing and dancing.

"Uh, hello, ma'am," I say awkwardly. "I was wondering if Mr. Raith was in tonight?"

She snorts. "A'course. He's always in. Is he expecting you, dear?"

I blanch. "No, but, ah, I'm an old friend."

Her eyes skate over me, pausing at my hair. "Ayla?" she asks.

My heart stalls. "Yes ma'am."

She tuts, then ushers me in. "Mister's going to platz," she mutters to herself, practically dragging me through the house and up the massive staircase.

The house is luxurious, if a bit overstuffed, near to bursting with people and music. Folks of all color and creed litter his halls, drinking, laughing, and dancing the night away. Many are laid out on couches and tables, some even laying in piles on the floor, languid and grinning obscenely.

The deeper into the house we go, the wilder things get.

One room is full of folks sprawled out on luxurious pillows, all angled towards a beautiful woman performing an aerial act with shimmering silks. Another full of half-dressed bodies, in varying states of kissing and heavy petting, gentle moans floating through the air, sensual and lush.

"What is this place?" I ask, a bit anxious, but sinfully curious at the same time. I was raised so sheltered, and any fun at the Arcanum was violent and calculated. I couldn't help but drink in a little debauchery.

"It's a safe haven, dear," she answers, smiling knowingly at me.

We approach another room, this one filled with completely naked bodies, the erotic slaps of fucking, shrill moans, and breathless pants creating a symphony of pleasure.

As we walk each room gets darker and darker, with one resembling what I can only call a torture chamber, full of leather and chains, stone and steel. A woman is suspended from the ceiling, not doing artful aerial tricks, but bound and gagged with thick black rope, a man in a gimp suit beating her raw with a wooden paddle.

I've never seen anything like it, and I'm not one to judge, but the thought of Algernon partaking in all the festivities going on under his roof makes me feel a bit queasy.

"Here we are, dear," the woman says, stopping in front of a rich brown door.

Panic fully seizes me.

He's right there, on the other side of this door.

It's been almost 40 years since I've laid eyes on him, when he poured that delicious Elixir down my throat with his hand tangled in my hair, a heartbeat away. The night I disappeared.

And here I was, showing up out of the blue, without a penny to my name to ask for his help.

Before I can brace myself, the maid is knocking on the door and pushing it open.

"Mr. Raith, pardon the interruption."

My breath freezes in my lungs.

There's Algernon, sandy hair and long limbs, gold framed glasses and full beard. He's wearing a white button-down, half-way unbuttoned to expose curls of chest hair between corded muscle. Leather suspenders attach to his tan trousers, rolled at the ankles, revealing mismatched argyle socks. He has the plunger of a glass syringe between his teeth and is tightening a tourniquet on a flushed woman's arm.

Years had passed, but it felt like mere moments. Sand through the hourglass.

A few other people crowd the room, but they blur into the background. I can't look anywhere but him, my heart thundering in my chest.

He looks up then, and our eyes lock together.

His eyes are cold, gray instead of glimmering turquoise, devoid of all the joy and mischief that used to live there. The light of his soul, extinguished.

"Ayla?" He takes the syringe from his mouth, wide-eyed, but doesn't stand.

I wave, offering a crooked smile that I hope appears nonchalant. "Hi, Algernon."

Quickly, he inserts the needle into the woman's arm and depresses the plunger. Her yelp of pain immediately melts into a moan of ecstasy, her eyes going glassy.

"Atta girl," he murmurs, patting her arm and undoing the tourniquet. "Back to the party with you. All of you," he says, a bit firm on the last three words.

The dozen or so guests scurry out, leaving me, Al, and the maid.

"Thank you, Magda, I'll take her from here." He winks at her and she swats his arm, blushing. "Have a glass of champagne, aye? You earned it."

Magda laughs at that, a shrill, buoyant thing, and hurries out the door, shutting it with a click behind her.

He moves back across the room to what I now recognize as a doctor's chair and a small steel tray, holding a variety of needles and things.

"I'm sorry to intrude," I start, hating the nervous quiver in my voice.

He shakes his head. "You could never intrude," he says, but doesn't look at me.

I see a small vial of whatever he injected into the woman on the small table by the door and pick it up. "What is this?" I hold the vial up to the light, swirling the thick, honey colored liquid.

He finishes cleaning up the station and perches on the arm of the doctors chair. "Opium, basically. Minus the addictive qualities. Much safer, you'd fall asleep before you can take enough to overdose," he says, and I find myself desperate to make him smile.

"So, you're a drug dealer," I tease, leaning into the much more comfortable dynamic we had as teens.

"That sounds so undignified." He picks up a mostly empty glass of red wine from the tray and swallows the last of it. "But yeah, basically. I offer the Synth, they bring the party."

"Synth?"

"Synthorium, that's what I named it."

"Do you—"

"Partake? No, I just administer and host. I'm actually usually in bed by now," he chuckles, his shoulders lowering an inch.

A flicker of relief floats through my chest, uncoiling some of my anxiety. There's a tiny glimmer of that old sparkle behind his eyes, carving through the layers of ice around him. All the swagger, none of the depth. He's walled that part of him off, the soft part that made him so...Algernon.

I shake my head, knocking the thought away. He grew up finally, it's a good thing. We both did what we needed to survive. It was better this way, with his walls up. Safer.

"So, tell me what happened after you joined the Arcanum." He crosses his arms over his chest.

I bristle, my hopes that we could avoid this conversation all together dashed. "It's not important. I escaped, end of story." The way he's looking at me...it's like there's a window to my soul only he can see. The vulnerability makes my skin crawl.

His brows furrow, but he doesn't pry. "Are my brothers—"

"Brainwashed pricks? Yeah." The words land as harsh even on my own ears, but his questions struck a nerve, panic clawing up my chest.

He sighs. "I was going to say alive, but that more or less answers the question."

"Look, I'm not interested in rekindling a friendship," I snap, anxiety sharpening my tongue. "I just need a bed until I can scrounge up some cash tomorrow."

He smirks, finally meeting my gaze. "You haven't changed at all, kitten."

I narrow my eyes at him, the old pet name landing on my ears like a blow. "I'll see what I can find on the street. Good night." I turn to storm off, but he moves faster, the damned giant, his long fingers wrapping around my wrist. The touch is scalding, sharp and jarring as a bee sting.

"Ayla, wait. I'm sorry. Please stay tonight." The ice in his gaze dissolves even further despite my attitude, the corners softening like melting snow. "I'll leave you be if that's what you want."

"Are you sure there's space?" I quirk an eyebrow, referring to what must be several hundred people in his house.

"For you, always. I'll get you sorted myself, I'm sure Magda's already well acquainted with a bottle of Chardonnay."

"Thanks." I offer a small smile, relieved he didn't throw me out onto the street like I half-expected. Like I deserved.

He nods and opens the door, striding down the hall.

I jog after him, dodging the flock of people that try to swarm him like he's some kind of celebrity. Which, I guess to them, maybe he is. Men and women fall all over him, rubbing against him like cats in heat, begging him to join them.

He politely declines each offer, pushing through them at a steady pace. At some point, he reaches back and takes my hand, ensuring I don't get lost in the shuffle. I should take my hand away, should bury any familiarity between us, but his touch is a salve on my raw nerves.

"I can find my way if you want to join them," I say, mostly to gauge his response.

He glares at me over his shoulder. "I have no interest in joining *them*," he says with inflection, although it doesn't read as judgmental.

I bite my tongue to stop myself from asking *whom* exactly he wants to be with instead.

As we move further into the house, the crowd dissipates, allowing me to get a better look at the mansion he calls home. Although, it hardly looks like a home in this portion of the house. In fact, it hardly looks lived in at all, with scant furniture and no decorations.

I open my mouth to ask, but he cuts me off.

"It's a lot of house for one man. I figured you'd be more comfortable away from the party."

"Where is your room?" The question slips out before I can stop it, and my cheeks heat.

"The crows nest," he says, smirking. "The stairs are that way." He gestures to the left, down a dimly lit hall. "I prefer to stay away from the party myself."

"Then why have it all?" We come to a stop in front a a pretty oak door carved with laurels.

"Like I said, it's a big house for one man." He pulls out a key and unlocks the door.

A sharp pang spears my heart. I hadn't considered how lonely he must have been the last few decades. Everyone he cared about was gone, left him behind, including me.

The guilt eats at me, but I can't think about his heartbreak right now. I have more than enough of my own.

I step around him and into the bedroom. It clearly intended to be the bedroom for the lady of the house, delicate and ornate, with sage green floral wallpaper, plush carpet, and endless rows of books. I nearly drool at the sight of the overstuffed bed and claw foot tub. It's immaculately clean and looks freshly fluffed, diligently maintained.

I ignore the strange flair of emotion in my chest, push away the thought that maybe he had kept the room prepared for my sake, just in case.

"I hope you find it comfortable," he says, watching me as I explore the space.

I scoff, swallowing the lump in my throat. "I slept in a dorm room with six other women. This may as well be the Taj Mahal."

"What?" He narrows his eyes, and my stomach flips.

"This is very kind, Algernon. Thank you." I gently take my suitcase from his hands, hoping to steer him away from my flippant slip.

He slips the key off the ring and sets it on the small table by the door. "Stay as long as you like. Feel free to find me or Magda if you need anything." There goes those walls again, tall and glacial. Formal and chilly where he was once warm and jovial.

"Goodnight, Al."

"Goodnight, Ayla." He turns on his heel and walks out, closing the door gently behind him.

I flop onto the bed and stare at the ceiling, my racing thoughts competing with exhaustion as I try to hatch a semblance of a plan for the rest of my life.

Algernon

Spring, 1924

I lean against her door and try to catch my breath.

She's here.

After all these years, I'd given up on any hopes of seeing her or my brothers again. I burned my bridge with the Arcanum a long time ago, refusing to exchange freedom for safety, and it seemed more likely that I'd die before anyone escaped Keanu.

But, she's here. She escaped, somehow. Not only from the clutches of Keanu, but her parents, who were still alive thanks to a bastardization of my life's greatest work.

Keanu had stolen my recipe after all. How he managed to actually create it is unclear, not that it matters much now. The inner circle of the Arcanum is alive and well, including my brothers, Paloma and James, and several other past members of my father's Guild.

Keanu stood firmly at the helm now, thanks to a pinch of patricide at the turn of the century. My own parents are gone as well, having disappeared before I could administer the Elixir, heartbroken and hollowed out by guilt. Opting to run away rather than confront their short-sightedness. They passed awhile ago, their bodies returned to Alder Bridge in wooden boxes.

Their burial was the last time I saw Gideon, at least 15 years ago. Oberon had disappeared as well at that point, drunk on his misery.

My heart thumps with anguish, a strange spiral of guilt and anger. I loved them, but what they did to Oberon was despicable. Even though, as loathe as I am to admit it, they may have been onto something.

My little brother took to the Arcanum like a drunkard to the barrel, fooled by their righteous intentions.

They've created a school in Alder Bridge, Folke University, and the underground School of the Old Arts, in an attempt to rally young witches to their cause. The Hail Mary of good intentions: offering an education to those without.

Gideon fell for it, then Oberon, and now they're both lost to greed and false promises.

I had hoped Ayla's story was different, that she would *see*. And, evidently, I may not have been far off.

I push off the door and head down the hall, ascending to my Crow's Nest. I strip down and run the bath. I skim my fingers along the surface of the water to speed up the molecules vibration. Steam rises into the cool air, and I sink into the bath, relishing the deep sting of it's intense heat.

My glasses fog, and I let them, my head leaning back to rest of the lip of the ceramic basin. Drowsiness settles in, the room a foggy blur, and I doze.

A sharp pinch in my arm jars me awake.

I jerk my arm back and the needle snags my skin, tearing a gash down my bicep.

"Gah, what the fuck!" I cradle my arm to my chest, blood dripping into the now tepid bathwater. I look up at my assailant, and am not at all surprised to see Ayla blinking at me from the dark. "Are you trying to drug me?"

She sidesteps towards the door. "No…"

"You were trying to drug me!" I gape at her, trying to hide the laugh simmering in my chest.

"Only a little." She reaches for the doorknob.

I flick my wrist and slam the door shut before she can scurry out, locking it and welding the metal together for good measure.

"You can't dose me with my own creation, hellcat," I chuckle, standing up a split second before I remember I'm naked.

She doesn't bat an eye, gaze fixed firmly on my bleeding arm. "Worth a shot." She shrugs.

I step out of the tub and try to walk casually to the towel, wrapping it around my waist. I do my best to clean up the blood with another towel, and then concentrate hard on the gash, trying to zero in on the cells of my skin to knit them back together.

Working with living tissue is a relatively new experiment of mine, and I've found meager success with it. At most, I can make my beard grow a centimeter or two.

Every time I get a grip on the material, it slips away when Ayla inevitably distracts me. It's impossible to concentrate with her in the same room. I huff and admit defeat, winding some gauze around my bicep.

"Why exactly were you trying to drug me?"

She shrugs, avoiding my eyes.

"To snoop around?"

"I wanted to visit one of the kink rooms without running the risk of bumping into you." The corner of her lip turns up and she tucks a copper strand of hair behind her ear. It's odd to see her with sheared hair, but she looks as beautiful as ever, enchanting in the candlelight.

"I'd be happy to accompany you." I smirk, crossing the room and opening the door.

She rolls her eyes. "Fine, I wanted to snoop."

I smile. "Thought so. Snoop away." I gesture to the room and grab my robe from the door, tying it around my hips. "Although, I doubt you'll find anything interesting."

"Oh?" She quirks up an eye as she migrates towards my desk, flipping open my notebook.

"Mm, there's not much of note up here, besides, well, me." I lean against the bedroom door, custom designed so I don't hit my head.

She continues flipping through the notebook, her eyes skimming the page, but clearly not absorbing any information.

"How about a conversation rather than an investigation, aye?" I ask, scratching the back of my neck. "It's been nearly forty years since I last saw you."

She pauses, running her fingers over my inked handwriting. "No funny business?"

I place a hand over my heart. "I promise to behave."

Ayla snorts and brushes past me, wafting her rosemary perfume into my nose, tinged with smoke and pine, fresh as forest air.

It's going to be harder to keep that promise than I thought.

I trail behind her and into the small sitting room at the top of the staircase. The loft is littered with couches and floor cushions, nestled atop a plush faux fur rug. Moonlight bathes the space in a blue glow, pushing back the orange light from the lit sconces around the walls.

Ayla sits gingerly on my favorite leather armchair.

I pour two glasses of Cabernet, hoping pathetically that she might leave behind a trace of herself in my home. I hand her a glass and sit across from her, stretching out like a cat on the velvet chaise.

"Shall I go first?" I ask, swirling the wine in the glass, admiring the way the deep red compliments her skin.

"Fire away." She takes a sip.

"Did you know you were leaving that night?"

She nearly chokes, coughing into her hand. "Right to it, huh?"

I blink at her, waiting, my stomach in a knot. It's the question I've been asking myself from the moment I knew she was gone.

Had she come to my lab to say goodbye? Or just for the Elixir? Or was it mere happenstance?

She sighs. "Yes, I knew."

"Did you—"

"Ah, ah." She wags her finger. "My turn."

I huff and lean back.

"Did you ever find Leda?"

The question takes me aback. "No, of course not. If I had found her, I would have brought her home."

Her shoulders creep down a fraction.

"Do you know who killed her?" I ask.

"Keanu claims it was a hit ordered by Amadeus, someone on the outside."

"Lies," I say, teeth grinding together.

"Of course. Are you parents still alive?"

"No."

"You didn't give them the Elix—"

"My turn," I interrupt. "Are my brother's hurting people?"

She takes a long pull of her drink. "We all are."

"That's not an answer." I lean forward, resting my elbows on my knees, wine glass dangling between my fingers.

"Yes, it is." She kicks off her heels and tucks her legs underneath her. "Have you been alone this entire time?"

I avoid her eyes. "More or less."

"That's not an answer," she counters.

"Yes, it is." I swallow the rest of my wine and get up to grab the bottle. I refill mine, then walk over to her, holding it up in offering.

She nods and holds out her glass, watching my face closely.

I refill her glass, meeting her eyes. "Did you miss me?"

"No." The skin of her neck flushes, and her eyebrows furrow slightly, barely at all. But she's never been able to lie to me.

I smile and turn away. *I missed you too.*

"Do you regret making the Elixir?" She asks as I sit back down on the chaise.

Another question that plagues me every day, despite knowing the answer.

"No, not at all."

She raises an eyebrow. "But if you hadn't—"

"You wouldn't be here," I answer, holding her gaze.

She lapses into silence, seeming lost for words.

"Would that be so terrible?" She asks after a minute, looking down into her wine glass.

"It would be the most terrible thing imaginable," I say, the thought alone stealing the air from my lungs.

"Algernon—"

"You can lie to me, Ayla. But I refuse to lie to you. Tell me about Keanu, the Arcanum. How did he replicate the serum?"

She swallows the almost full glass of wine and sets it down on the coffee table between us. "There's a skilled Transfigurationalist on staff, but he's no Alchemist. He cracked the serum on sheer luck. And who knows if it's even the same as yours, it could be anything."

I nod, rubbing my beard. That serum could be very, *very* dangerous.

"He killed his father some time ago and has full control. He has Guilds all over the world. He's created this..." her voice wavers. "This web of power, winding it tighter until he's ready."

"Ready for what?" I ask, anxiety raising the hairs on the back of my neck.

"To take over," she says simply. "I'm not sure he even cares about Birthright, or anything for that matter. He's doing it just because he *can*." Anger rises in her voice, her jaw flexing, shoulders creeping up to her ears.

"Ayla—"

"I think it's time for me to go to bed." She stands, smoothing out her skirt.

I watch as she picks up her shoes and pads across the carpet, her small toes sinking into the black fur, and down the stairs. The entire time, I wrack my brain for something make her stay, but no words come.

I'm such a fucking coward.

Ayla

Fall, 1925

I slipped out as early as I could that morning after finding Algernon, an envelope stuffed with cash buried at the bottom of my suitcase. He'd left it on my pillow while I slept, marked only with an 'A'.

Inspired by his savvy in turning his gift into wealth, I built a career on the back of the spiritualism movement as a psychic, the dark haired Madame Allegra Veil.

Was it real? Not particularly. Was it ethical? Probably not. But it paid the bills on my Upper East Side studio and secured invites to the biggest parties in the city.

Tonight was perhaps the biggest event of my career, a gala at the Biltmore Hotel. I'd been hired by some Senator's wife, with whom I'd made acquaintance at a seance last month.

I add the final touches to my makeup, a bit of pale powder to my nose and a sweep of burgundy lipstick, and ensure my wig is seamless. I loathe the wiry thing, dyed so dark it's nearly black and sheared into a blunt bob that barely reaches my chin, with heavy bangs that make my face look too round.

But, anonymity is essential. I can't risk the Arcanum tracking me down, or worse, my parents.

I grab my black tasseled clutch and ensure everything I need is inside: lipstick, powder, my tarot deck, a hag stone, a selenite wand, and my Colt .25.

A car is already waiting by the time I make it downstairs, and I'm barely in the seat before we hurtle into the night, speeding towards the illustrious hotel.

When we pull up, dozens of beautifully dressed party goers crowd the street in front of the hotel, and I have to push my way through them to reach the crimson clad doorman.

"Madame Allegra Veil, I'm expected in the ballroom?" I say, tuning out the hushed whispers at the mention of my name. My reputation often proceeds me these days.

"Of course, right this way." He smiles, gesturing me inside with a sweeping arm.

In a few short moments, we cross from the formal lobby into the infamous ballroom.

I'm immediately swept up by the atmosphere of sheer elegance and extravagance. The buzz of excitement fills the air, mingling with the smooth jazz melodies pouring from a corner stage. As I cross the threshold, the sight before me is nothing short of breathtaking.

The ballroom is a vision of opulence, with its intricate decorations, cascading chandeliers, and glittering crystals casting a warm, inviting glow. Luxurious fabrics drape the walls, and the ceiling seems to stretch into infinity.

I try not to ogle the guests who fill the room, each one dressed impeccably. The women's flapper dresses sway gracefully as they dance, and their hair, cropped into chic bobs, is adorned with stylish headbands. The men are equally stylish in their well-tailored suits, their hair slicked-back with dark grease.

On the polished dance floor, couples glide and twirl to the rhythm of the music, their dance moves energetic and jumpy. Laughter and animated chatter fill the air.

On the arm of the doorman, we cut through the crowd and I'm deposited at a velveteen booth at the back of the room. There's a glass of champagne and silk altar cloth already set up for me to receive guests. A small note rests against the champagne flute, I assume a note for my employer for the evening.

Give 'em a show.

A

I pull out my deck and begin to shuffle, the same deck I've enjoyed for decades. I've acquired many in my travels, but this funny little deck gifted from Algernon has always been my most reached for.

We understand each other.

I let the deep blue of my third eye spread through me, tapping into my gift. As soon as I lay out the first card, a group swarms, holding out dollar bills or simply firing off questions.

I sigh, slap on my most seductive smile, and take the first bill.

The hours melt together as I read card after card, with barely enough time to breathe in between. Blessedly, the crowd lulls around midnight, and I'm able to rest.

I reach for my champagne, the same glass from earlier, but it's flat and tepid.

"Care for a fresh glass?" A glittering, gold rimmed flute of champagne is set in front of me, a man sliding into the booth beside me.

"This isn't in lieu of payment, is it?" I ask, resisting the urge to swallow down the chilled wine and instead look over at the intruder. My heart stutters to a halt as my eyes meet his turquoise ones, crinkled by his fox-like grin.

"Of course not." Algernon slides a neat stack of bills over to me. "How much time will this buy me?"

I pick up the glass and take a long sip, parched from hours of repeating myself and chanting nonsense. "You've got me for the rest of the evening." I smile, a bit disconcerted by the well of emotion rising in my chest at the unexpected sight of him, the familiarity of his presence.

"So, what's my future?"

I start shuffling the cards, feeling them vibrate in my hands. "It's not so simple," I chastise, putting on my Madame voice. "We must understand our past to make sense of the future."

Three cards jump out, landing on the altar cloth. The Empress, the Fool, and the Seven of Swords. I flip the deck over, revealing the Ace of Swords.

I snicker to myself, but of course he catches me.

"Something funny?" He raises an eyebrow, smirking.

"No. You just always were a mama's boy."

"That is not what the cards say," he huffs, trying to slide the cloth over to himself.

I snatch it back. "I'm the psychic here!"

He rolls his eyes. "Sure, *Madame.*"

I look over the cards again, assembling the message in my mind. "Most of your life was guided by strong women. They impacted you more than anything else, more than your father or your brothers."

He hums in acknowledgment but remains silent.

"You approached everything with an air of optimism, and naivete. Always seeing the best in others. But much of this optimism was a front, a way to protect yourself so others don't look deeper. A way to ensure no one could take what little you had. You kept much close to your chest, despite appearing to others as an open book."

His eyes study my face, taking in my words. Most shy away when I cracked open their chests like this, peered at the ticking of their heart, but Algernon didn't flinch.

"You had ambition, a clear path, although few knew it. It's guided you from the beginning, and continues to this day." I meet his eyes. "You will do whatever it takes to stay on the path you've decided for yourself."

He nods, tracing the border of the Ace of Swords with his long finger, golden ring glinting in the candlelight. "You always could read me like a book," he says softly, looking back up at me.

"It helps when the subject is connected to the cards as well." I gather them up and start shuffling, mentally asking the deck to reveal something about this path he's on. I can't help but be a little nosy.

The Nine of Wands slips out.

I roll my eyes, setting the deck off to the side. "You have overcome much, and have further to go."

He rubs his beard, looking thoughtful. "But it'll be worth it? The waiting?"

I turn over the deck, revealing the Seven of Pentacles. I reach out to touch his hand, the contact sending a current of sparks up my arm, magnetic. "Yes. It will all be worth it, Algernon."

He squeezes my hand in return, nodding slowly. "Good to know."

I take another sip of wine as we sit in silence. I find myself looking him over, looking for any signs of misfortune or hardship. But he's dressed to the nines, in a sharp plaid suit with a dark gray vest and silk tie. His sandy, sun kissed hair is swept back, but isn't greased, a single, wispy piece falling over his eyebrow. His beard is sharp and clean, if a little long for the current trends.

Gods, he is so handsome. Statuesque and gentle, with the hands of a scientist and the mind of a scholar.

"You know better than to look at me like that," he says, voice low.

I avert my eyes, heat flaring in my cheeks and my lower belly. Gone is the gawky teen I grew up with, here is the man he's become, confident and self-assured in ways I can't wrap my head around. A man that knows what he wants, and I have a suspicion that should he choose to pursue it, pursue *me*, I'd be powerless to stop him.

"Can I show you something?" He asks, slicing through the heady tension.

"I suppose." I shrug, sliding out of the booth.

He stands and offers me his hand.

I hesitate, but place my hand in his, twining our fingers together, and he guides us out of the room, carefully dodging party goers and overloaded drink trays.

We weave through the halls until we reach a set of double doors, which he pushes open with a flourish, revealing a moonlit courtyard with marble statues, crisp topiaries, and wrought iron benches. In the middle rests a gorgeous white fountain, the Queen of Cups at the center, pouring water from a vase.

I gasp, moving closer to the fountain. "She's gorgeous," I whisper, leaning over my hands to get a closer look at the smooth folds of her dress.

"Yes, she is," he hums, sitting on the ledge beside me. "Red or white?"

"Huh?" I glance over at him, confused.

"Red or white, hellcat."

"Ah, red?" I answer.

He smiles and dips his fingers into the water, sending delicate ripples across the pool. Burgundy bleeds out from his fingers, slowly overtaking the clear water and transforming it to wine.

I gape at him, awestruck by his strength. It was an incredible feat to transform so many gallons of water into something else entirely. And despite a slight furrow of his brow, he hardly seemed to exert himself at all.

When he's finished, he produces two wine glasses from inside his jacket, dunks them both into the pool, and hands one to me.

"Here's to inevitability." He smiles, tilting his glass towards mine.

I clink them together, and take a long drink.

Inevitable victories for some, inevitable loss for others.

If only one of us could win, I'm glad that it's him.

We drink and talk about nothing for hours, eventually getting absolutely, mind-numbingly drunk. We laugh and joke and poke fun, forgetting for awhile how different our lives have become since the first day we met, how our paths have divulged countless times. Yet somehow, by some trick of fate, our journey's continue to cross.

Like we're set on a collision course, and no matter how many times we pivot, we end up crashing together.

I wake up in a hotel room, sunlight slanting through the drawn curtains, still in my dress, my wig tossed onto the bedside table.

There's a glass of water and note beside it.

You know where to find me. Be safe.

Your Fool, A

Algernon

Spring, 1927

It's pouring down sheets in New York tonight, sending a chill deep into my bones. It's April's like these that make me hate this city. Dingy and dark, lonely in a city of thousands.

I walk the ten blocks to the Oyster, an underground dive off of 11th Street.

When I received the invitation, I almost declined, but something itched at the back of my mind, urging me to accept. It's been a few months since I played with Carone and his goons, may as well lighten their pockets.

The door is opening before I raise my hand to knock, and a giant with a bowler hat ushers me inside. The hall is dimly and dingy, the aches and groans of old city infrastructure echoing around me. Plenty creepy to deter anyone without the thick card stock invitation.

I reach another door at the end of the hall, manned by a behemoth in a pinstripe suit, a M1911 in his grip.

"Mr. Raith." He nods in greeting, then unlocks the heavy door.

I step inside and am immediately swallowed up by loud chatter and saccharine sweet jazz, all the bustle and grit of rich New York, of mobsters.

I'm guided to Carone's preferred Poker room by a shot girl, dressed in nothing but strings of pearls.

Before I can enter though, she presses me up against the wall, her five foot height barely reaching my sternum.

"You're the inventa', right?" she says, brushing invisible lint off my tweed blazer.

"That's right." I smile, amused by her boldness.

"Lookin' for a new assistant? I can be *real* helpful." She bats her painted lashes at me, her breasts pressed uncomfortably against my diaphragm.

"Not currently, doll. Apologies. But keep the whiskey coming, alright?" I give her a wink and slip a twenty into her hand.

Her eyes bug out and she nods vigorously before scurrying away.

I straighten my bow tie and take a deep breath before pushing open the door.

Carone sits at the head of the velvet green table, facing the door. There's a lacky in each corner, and six other players seated at the table.

I skim their faces, finally landing on the only woman in the room. I nearly trip, my heart lurching in my chest.

Ayla sits casually beside the dealer, stacking her chips into neat little piles. I immediately recognize her, even though she's dressed as her alter ego, Madame Veil.

She glances up at me, but doesn't flinch, just turns back to her chips and takes a sip of what appears to be a whiskey neat, with a dissolving sugar cube and orange peal garnish.

"Ah, my scientist!" Carone booms, pushing his chair back and rising to his feet. "How are you, Al?" He offers his hand, which I shake firmly with a smile.

"Just fine, Al, just fine." I grin. "Looking forward to bleeding you dry."

He roars with laughter and claps me on the back. "Arrogant son-of-a-bitch! We'll see." He graciously shows me to my seat, right beside

Ayla, and returns to his own chair on the other end. "You remember Webber, Santori, and Herschel." He gestures to a few of the familiar men seated at the table, who all acknowledge me a with the same sullen nod.

I took them for every penny they had last game, and clearly they hadn't forgotten.

"Pleasure, gentleman." I tilt my hat to each of them.

"And that's Martino, DiMizzio, and our guest of honor, Madame Allegra Veil." Carone leans forward, conspiratorially. "She's a psychic," He divulges, waggling his brows.

"Hardly seems like a fair Poker opponent," I jest, smirking at her. She rolls her eyes, taking a sip of her drink.

"It's getting too easy," Carone laughs. "And she promised to be a good girl." His beady eyes sweep across her, and I bristle.

Thankfully, my shot girl tiptoes in and places a whiskey beside me so I can wash the bitter jealousy out of my mouth.

"Dealer!" Carone shouts, and everyone falls into silence as the cards are dealt.

I check my hand, holding back a grimace and take a long swallow of whiskey, savoring the burn in my chest.

"You have a terrible poker face," Ayla whispers, breasting her cards.

"And you are a dirty hustler," I retort, looking back at my cards and trying hard to hide a smile. "You shouldn't even be allowed to play poker."

"Shh," she mouths, winking.

I can't seem to focus on the game, my eyes tracking her every movement: the flutter of her fingers, the rise and fall of her exposed decolletage, the slight purse of her lips as she thinks. When she licks a bit of sugar off the rim of her glass, I nearly fall out of my chair. Every time I see her, she's more breathtaking, more confident and alluring.

I remember those few moments of closeness we shared in our youth, her chest pressed against mine, her breath in my ear, her hands on my skin. I've regretted every moment I let her move away. Every moment I didn't grab her and swallow her whole.

We play a few rounds in friendly quiet, with the gangsters mostly chatting amongst themselves. Neither Ayla or I make any moves the first few rounds, and Carone absolutely delights in beating a "Science-man" and a psychic.

"If I didn't know better, I'd say you were a phony, dollface," he jeers, ogling her openly.

"Would you like to play with my cards instead?" She teases back, batting her thick lashes and pursing her glossy red lips.

My cock stirs in my trousers, wanting to bite into those lips like the pulp of an overripe strawberry. I feel almost mad with it, the longing to touch her, to taste her. I could throw her on the table right here, claim what is rightfully mine in front of these greasy pricks.

"Doll. Why don't you come sit right here on papa's lap?" Carone drools at Ayla, spreading his stubby legs wide and patting his knee.

Before I can think better of it, I'm up in a flash, stepping up easily onto the tabletop, walking across it, and depositing my 6'7 self into the pint-sized gangster's lap.

"I thought you'd never ask, *papa*," I flirt and lift off Carone's flat cap, tossing it onto the table.

"Get off me, you fucking dandy!" Carone tries to shove me off, but I move faster, slipping Carone's gun from it's holster and holding it under his chin.

"Speak to her that way again and I will blow your tongue out of your mouth, clear?"

Carone holds his hands out to his goons, freezing them in place. He nods, eyes bulging.

"Excellent," I rear back and clock Carone in the temple with the handle of his own gun, knocking him out instantly. I jump up, dodging fists and reach for Ayla's hand. "Shall we?"

"You're insane," she rolls her eyes, but takes my hand.

"Now's not the time for dirty talk, kitten," I wink, then sprint out the door, dragging her behind me in a flurry of gunshots.

We barrel outside and down the alley, ducking and weaving between buildings until we're a considerable distance from the Oyster, the sound of shouting long since faded.

In the dark of a strange alleyway, I turn and grab her by the throat. Before I catch my breath, chest heaving, I collide my mouth with hers, devouring and hungry, incendiary. She will not run from me this time. I refuse to continue breathing for another second without knowing what she tastes like, what she feels like, what pretty little sounds I can coax out of her.

She moans against me, low and sinful, and kisses back, letting my tongue slip past her teeth and taste her. Sweetened whiskey and blackberries, campfire and moonlight. She's intoxicating.

I'm delirious with desire, driven mad with hunger.

I scoop her up and fasten her legs around my waist, pushing her up against the wall, creating delicious friction between our bodies.

Her tongue slides between my lips and swirls with my own, drawing a groan from my throat as we melt into one another. She sucks lightly on my tongue, dragging her fingers along my scalp.

Holy fucking hell.

We break apart to breathe and I trail kisses along her cheek and jawline, tilting her head back so I can nibble at her throat, inhaling her sweet scent.

"This means nothing," she pants, voice breathy and high.

Yeah, right.

"Whatever you say, hellcat," I smirk, sucking a bruise onto the junction of her shoulder in a tiny act of rebellion. She'll remember this, one way or another.

She yanks my hair back and devours my mouth, our teeth scraping together, sharing moans like air.

The soft sounds she makes go straight to my cock, spurring me on. *More, I need more.*

I want every sound that falls from those pretty lips to be just for me, only me. I want to hear her gasp, moan, whimper, scream. I want everything. Every smile, every tear, every laugh, every sarcastic comment, every jab. I want her joy and her sadness and her rage and her sex and her love. I will have it all.

Her body goes rigid, the breath catching in her lungs. "Stop, stop!" she cries and I immediately drop her, wrenching myself to the other side of the alley as reality rushes back in, heart thudding in my chest.

She sinks to the ground, clutching her head in her hands, knuckles white.

Another scream tears from her chest and I run back over. I try to pull her into my arms, but she shoves me away, curling up into a ball, muttering incoherently. Her hazel eyes are white as freshly fallen snow, crimson blood drips from her nose.

I pull her into my lap anyways, holding her and rocking her gently, guilt clawing at the inside of my ribs.

My heart hurts watching her suffer, knowing there's nothing I can do to ease her pain. All I can do it be there, something I've failed miserably at for most of our lives.

"I'm here, Ayla. I'm right here," I whisper into her hair, holding her even tighter as she begins to tremble. "Say the word and I'll never leave your side." I nuzzle into the back of her neck, kissing along the top of her spine.

She shakes her head, fists my jacket, and pulls me closer. "This can't happen again, Algernon. I can't—" a sob chokes of the rest of her sentence.

"Don't worry about that now," I say, smoothing her wig, and wiping away the blood from her nose and lip. "Right now, you're safe. I'm safe. Focus on the here and now."

She takes a few hiccuping lungfuls of air and relaxes slightly.

"I wish things could be different," she whispers, lifting her head up to meet my eyes.

"You wish right now was different? Or the future?" I tuck an escaped strand of her real hair behind her ear.

"The future," she sighs, leaning her forehead against mine. "Right now is good."

"Can I kiss you again?" I ask, sounding so pathetic I almost cringe.

Her fingers come up and brush against my lips, and I kiss the pads of her fingers, light as a feather.

"This is the last time," she breathes. She leans in and molds her lips against mine, soft and slow.

My heart feels like it could burst, aching so intensely I fear I may perish on the spot. But, would that be so bad?

I kiss her back, trying to communicate decades worth of feelings without words, with only a shared breath, a single kiss. A kiss that could go on forever, and still wouldn't be long enough. I cup her jaw, desperate to keep her close, to stay in this moment forever, but she whimpers, and on a reflex I let her go.

She staggers out of my lap, wiping her cheeks with the back of her hand. "Goodbye, Algernon," she whispers, eyes dim.

"Until next time." I correct, tears clogging my throat.

Our time will come, even if I have to take on fate itself.

Ayla

Fall, 1929

I duck behind Addison, swallowing my disgust as the men leer down at the wretch in the stripped jumpsuit, who is being secured to an electric chair in orderly fashion.

There have been countless moments where I've regretted my contract with Tom Addison, the famed inventor and lightbulb enthusiast, but none have resonated quite like this one, a person's life teetering on the edge, about to be, quite literally, struck down like a tree in a lightning storm.

I've never seen Addison so worked up, practically frothing with anticipation, as he is now. Armpit stains spread through his gray sport coat, his neck and cheeks flushed pink with delight.

I feel like I could hurl.

The guards beyond the glass begin the countdown.

"Three."

Addison presses his forehead against the window, creating moist rings on the glass as he exhales.

"Two."

The other men scooch in, jostling for the best view.

"One."

The lever is flipped. I can hear the chair rattling against the floor, banging like a screen door in a thunderstorm, but the victim makes no sound, and then he's dead. Fried from the inside out.

Addison, and then his peers, begin to clap.

"Good show! Well done, everyone." Addison laughs, taking off his flat cap and bowing as the others return his praise tenfold.

"How many must die by your invention until you're satisfied, Tom?" I ask, squaring my shoulders.

He barely glances at me. "Science, and electricity, have no limits, dear. I am but a vessel, a conductor," he says, voice heavy with grandeur. "Couldn't expect a soft-hearted woman such as yourself to understand." His gaze finally fixes on me, cold. A warning. "If your morality is deeper than your pockets, I'm sure Teslo would love to have you on staff." Nick Teslo, Addison's greatest competitor and perpetual thorn in his side.

I stiffen, then sigh.

Being on Addison's payroll was the only thing keeping me off the streets, and out of the Arcanum's reach.

A little over a year ago, I received a telegram from a Mr. Keanu Kennedy, demanding my return to the Arcanum and Folke. He claimed that he'd "allowed" enough gallivanting and it was time that I returned home.

Client by client, he stripped away my livelihood and destroyed my reputation, going so far as to have my home and car repossessed, and draining every account I had.

I was naive to think that Keanu had just let me go, that'd I'd been able to escape with repercussions. He was just withholding his hand, which means that somethings happened that forced him to use it.

What exactly that is remains a mystery.

Addison's wife had been a client of mine, one of the few that Keanu didn't know about due to the discrete nature of her needs. It was her faith in me that convinced Addison to hire me on as a consultant and advisor, and my perfect track record of sniffing out sound investments that kept me around months later, despite my inability to keep my mouth shut.

But it was only a matter of time before Keanu found me again, and the second time, he won't stoop to petty harassment and bribery.

I trail the group out of the prison and into a row of black Model-T's, sliding in beside Addison and his assistant, Terry.

I stare out the window, mostly ignoring their conversation, something about the dinner at the mayor's house this evening.

Addison nudges me. "Allegra! For God sakes girl," he laughs.

"Sir?" I try to look apologetic, and not at all like the kind of girl that would punch him square in the nose.

"The dinner tonight, any insights?"

I roll my shoulders and withdraw my pendulum from my waistcoat pocket, ever the performer. I concentrate on the swaying point, and start asking the questions I know Addison cares about.

"Will they grant us funding for the project?"

Yes.

"Will we have to share it with others?"

Yes.

"Teslo?"

Yes.

"Under the mayor's oversight?"

No.

We all glance at each other.

"Is it a for a federal initiative?"

No.

"Agh," Addison huffs. "It's broken. That's enough."

Before I slip the pendulum back into my pocket, I can't help but ask the question that plagues me everywhere I go.

"Will Algernon be there?" I think.

Yes.

I swallow thickly, my throat suddenly going dry, remembering the last time I saw him. The comforting warmth of his body, the scalding burn of his touch. The way he smelled and tasted, decadent and honey-sweet. Lithe and delicate, but solid and self-assured. Exactly how I imagined he'd be and more.

Some part of me had desperately hoped he'd be a terrible kisser, but I'd been so so wrong.

I'd never been grateful for a vision before, but had one not struck in that moment, I probably would begged let him fuck me in that alley. Hell, I would have followed him to the courthouse like a lovesick puppy.

But those could only be fantasies, little dreams I only allow in the dead of night, in the deepest parts of myself, where not even the Gods can see me.

I shake myself out of my reverie and put the pendulum away.

Addison hums in thought, rubbing his doughy chin.

"Would it be alright if I accompanied you?" I ask, as sheepish as I can manage.

"Of course not. A business dinner is no place for a woman," he grunts, turning back towards the window and lapsing into silence.

Terry shrugs apologetically, then turns to his small notepad, where he always seems to be cataloging...something.

The remainder of the drive to the office is quiet, and I escape from the car as soon as it comes to a complete stop.

I trudge up the six flights of stairs to my office-slash-temporary studio apartment and start digging through my few boxes of clothes, searching for something I could pawn off as a maids uniform. The need to see him is too strong, overpowering any sense of self-preservation. Just the idea of him lays my self-control to waste.

I pull out a mid length black dress, with long sleeves and a high neck. Perfect. With an apron lifted from the servant quarters, my natural hair in a french twist, and a bit of glamour magic, I should be able to blend right in.

At least, to everyone but the one person that matters.

Night comes quickly and I slip out the back door of the office building, navigating the few blocks to the Gracie Mansion concealed in shadow.

I creep along the brick wall, searching for the rusted gate used as the Servant's entrance, and am lead directly to it by an older woman in a nearly identical dress to mine.

I slip in behind her, thankful that I opted for a spell that not only obscured my appearance, but presence, from anyone that wasn't searching for me directly.

It was a costly spell, one that left me feeling a bit sluggish, but it was well-worth it.

In another moment, I'm inside the kitchens, easily securing a white apron and bonnet, and hoisting a silver tray of champagne flutes onto my shoulder.

I follow another servant up to the party.

The men linger around the parlor room in a small group, sipping freshly distilled moonshine and smoking cigars. I spot Addison by the bar cart, Terry beside him looking a bit green, and a few other unfamiliar men.

Nick Teslo loiters by the piano, looking sullen and uncomfortable as usual.

I dare a glance at the bookcase, and find that Algernon is already looking at me, his head at an impish tilt, with a lopsided smile on his face.

I gingerly set down the tray, snagging a glass for myself, and walk towards him.

"If you needed work as a maid, you could have called." He smirks, eyes sparkling as he takes in my disguise.

"I'm not a maid. I work for Addison," I reply, leaning against bookshelf beside him.

"You work for *Addison*?" His eyebrows shoot up.

"Mhm," I hum, rolling my eyes as Addison tells a terrible joke, then waits patiently for uproarious laughter.

"Why on earth would you subject yourself to that?"

"Not all of as are millionaire inventors, Raith." I scoff.

"If you want to be on my payroll, just say that," he teases, nudging me lightly. I ignore the flair of heat his touch sends skittering through my blood.

"I'm doing just fine, thank you."

"Never thought I'd see you work for someone, not after the Arcanum," he says thoughtfully, maybe even a touch concerned.

"Well, the Arcanum didn't give me much of a choice. I'd rather be on Addison's payroll than Keanu's," I mutter, taking another swallow of my drink.

"They found you?" Algernon stands up a little straighter, now much more than a bit concerned.

"Sure did. And burned my little kingdom down."

He sighs and sags against the bookshelf. "They offered me a position at the School of Old Arts."

"What?" Now I jerk upright. "When?"

"Nearly every week for the last year or so. They've gotten quite pushy, to tell you the truth." He takes a sip of whiskey, and suddenly all I can think about is the way it tasted on his tongue.

I take another sip of champagne to clear my head. "You haven't seen anything yet."

"No, I expect not. From what I hear, things have escalated quite a bit. Keanu fancies himself Alexander the Great, with Oberon as his Hephaestion."

"In more ways than you know," I snort, and he shoots me a bemused look.

"He's in danger. Gideon and him both are," he says into his whiskey glass, forlorn.

I soften a bit. "I know, but Keanu has them wrapped around his finger. The Arcanum is like a snare trap, the harder you try to escape, the deeper you're tangled. They couldn't leave if they wanted to."

He's quiet for a moment, chewing absently at his lip. "Have you ever thought about fighting back?"

A laugh forces it's way out of my throat, jarred loose by surprise. "*Fight back*? With what, a crystal ball and potions?"

He chuckles, a smile breaking through the fog of worry. "Something like that."

"Not a chance. I'm riding the Addison train to Michigan next month, then on to California."

His jaw ticks. "Coward," he mumbles.

"What?!" I whisper-shout, shoving his side, his muscles hard under my fingers.

He doesn't budge an inch. "What?" He grins, but it doesn't meet his eyes.

"I am not a coward." I cross my arms.

"Whatever you say, kitten," he murmurs, taking a sip of whiskey.

I open my mouth to retort, but the double doors open and the Mayor strides in, sucking all the air out of the room with him. An all-too familiar dark haired man hovers to his left, a gleaming collar of bone around his neck, looking rather pleased with himself.

Keanu.

My stomach plummets and Algernon grips my hand, dragging me quickly into the Aviary branching off of the Parlor.

He presses his hand flat against a massive pane of glass and in a blink, it vanishes, the humid September air gusting in. He shoves me through it, wasting no time.

"Run, now," he orders, glancing quickly over his shoulder.

"Al—"

He turns back and cups my cheek, fear making his eyes bright. "He knows I'm here, but not you. *Go.*"

I swallow the tiny protest that rises up, my instincts rebelling against leaving him here, abandoning him again. But I nod anyways, and turn, running through the garden and out the rusty gate.

I round the corner, looking over my shoulder, and crash straight into someone. I look up from the ground and see my mother, haloed in a yellow streetlight, and my heart stops.

"Oh, darling!" she cries, trying to scoop me up and hug me close.

I shove her away, try to run, but a frigid blast of wind shocks me still, and his hands land on my shoulders.

"Ayla, honey, We've been looking for you," my father growls in my ear, vodka wafting with his hot breath into my face. Small sparks of lightning course along my neck and down my arms, singeing me and leaving smoking tendrils in the fabric of my dress. Excruciating, web-like burns climb up my throat and over my jaw, spreading across my face, so hot they feel like ice.

I grit my teeth through the agony and throw my elbow back, managing to catch him by surprise, and slip out of his grip. I draw my gun from the garter of my tights and aim it at his head.

"Leave. *Now.*" I snarl, gesturing down the street with the barrel.

"Honey, please—" Paloma starts, eyes wide.

"I will give you ten seconds."

"Drop that. Now." James barks.

"Ten."

He sends another blast of icy air my way, but I hold firm. There isn't a trick in his book he hasn't used on me, that I haven't learned to withstand.

"Alright then. Five." I click the hammer. Adrenaline hammers through my blood, making my vision pulse red.

"James—"

"Three."

"This can't go on forever," James sneers, then walks towards Paloma, seizes her by the upper arm, and drags her down the street and out of sight.

I count to ten, willing the adrenaline to keep flowing, to keep the agony of the burns at bay, before I turn and start running, gun still clenched in my fist.

I'm not sure where I'm running to until I stumble up the front porch of Algernon's house. "Magda!" I scream, throat raw with a metallic grit.

I see the door swing open, and Magda's polished Mary Janes before the adrenaline wears off, and blackness overtakes me.

"*What did you do?*" Someone shouts and I feel warm hands cradle my face, tilting my head gently on its axis.

"She was in so much pain, I—" Magda starts.

"How much did you give her?" Algernon cuts her off, voice tinny with worry.

"Just half a syringe, less than what you usually administer," she answers.

He exhales slowly. "Alright, alright. I'm sorry, Mags. Thank you for taking care of her," he says softly, dabbing a cloth to my forehead.

"'Course, sir. Holler if you need anything."

I hear the door click shut behind her.

As I emerge from sleep, I can feel the drug pumping through me, warm and tingly. Liquid sunshine. The burning inside my skin ebbs, my headache floats away.

"Ayla, love, are you alright? Can you hear me?" Algernon murmurs, wiping more sweat from my brow and the hollow of my throat.

My eyes flutter open, the room tinged a yellow gold. Daffodils and butter, summer lemons.

"I can hear you," I mumble, my tongue velvet soft and heavy.

"How do you feel?" His brows are knitted together in concern. "Your pupils are enormous."

"I feel good," I hum, reaching up to touch his face, to stroke the golden glow around him.

"I bet." He cracks a soft smile.

My fingers drift from his cheeks, down the arched bridge of his nose, to his lips. "You're very handsome," I slur, a distinct, flickering burn kicking up in my lower belly.

"Thank you?" He sits back a little, but I follow him, holding onto his neck.

"Handsomest ever. Prettiest boy," I lean forward, try to kiss him, but he evades me, the drug making me slow. Gods, all I want to do is kiss him.

"Hellcat, you need rest. You don't know what you're saying." He tries to take my hands off of him, but I cling tighter and start trying to tug his tie over his head.

In a distant part of my brain, I know I'm acting insane. But that part is quiet and far away, and he is right here, beautiful and kind. My Algernon.

"I need you," I breathe, shifting to straddle him. My hands wander over his torso, popping the buttons to expose the muscled plains of his chest. I lean in and start kissing his neck, tasting the salt of his skin, bathing in the familiar scent of his cologne.

His hands fall to my hips, gripping me tightly.

I can feel his pulse rise, a flush creeps up his neck. His cock stirs in his trousers, nudging against my core.

"Fuck, kitten," he huffs, holding my hips still. I hadn't even realized I was grinding down on him, a feral beast in heat.

"Please," I moan into his ear, nibbling along the hard line of his jaw.

"Have mercy," he pants, sliding a hand into my hair and yanking my head back, exposing the collar of burns around my throat. He sucks in a hard breath, and pushes me off and onto the other side of the couch.

"Not like this, baby," he says, voice low, holding a hand out to me to stay. "When I fuck you, it will not be like this." He stands and storms out of the room, slamming the door shut behind him.

I sag back into the cushion, shame overwhelming me.

The rest of the night passes in a hazy blur, my mind a soupy mixture of Synth, adrenaline, and guilt. I wait for him to return, hoping that I didn't ruin this, whatever this was. But he doesn't.

At the first sliver of morning light, I gather my strength and slip out the front door, limping pitifully to my apartment, feeling the sting of long healed scars reopening.

Algernon

Fall, 1929

The smoke infiltrates my dream, casting a thick, gray haze over the lights of the city, over Ayla's face, eclipsing the moonlight.

I jerk awake, and already my nostrils are burning, my eyes gritty and raw. Sweat beads along my forehead and drips down my spine, my shirt already soaked through with it.

Flames lick underneath my bedroom door, dance outside the windows. The smoke is so thick I can barely see my own hand in front of my face. The house is ablaze, and has already reached the Crow's Nest.

"Ayla!" Her name tears its way out of my throat, sharp as razor blades before any full thoughts form, and then I'm up, hurtling down the smoldering steps.

Most of the hall has already caved in, nothing but curled wallpaper, blackened carpet, and flaming bonfires of antique furniture. I can't get to the room I had left her to rest in, it's barricaded by a wall of blue flame, so hot I can smell the tips of my hair singeing.

I try to grab hold of the oxygen to suffocate the flames, but their too hot, too volatile. Enchanted, I realize.

Blood thunders through my veins, thick and stupid from the flames gobbling up any spare oxygen. I half-fall down the stairs, and the smell that greets me makes my hair stand on end.

Dozens of charred bodies litter the hall, burned beyond recognition. Just black husks, melted to the carpet fibers.

I can't look at them, can't process them, because one of them might be her, and that's an impossibility. That simply cannot happen.

I push through the smoke and flames, and out into the morning sun. White burns my eyes, sending bolts of searing pain straight to my frontal lobe. Someone throws their arms around me, squeezing me tight, reeking of smoke.

"Mister! Thank *God!*" Magda cries, blubbering into my sternum. "I was so worried!"

"Did anyone else make it out?" I rasp, grasping her gently by the shoulders and crouching to her eye level.

"Some, but I haven't seen Ayla," she says, reading my mind.

My stomach lurches, a sick twist of terror. *Gods, please tell me she snuck out and went home.*

The fire department roars up the driveway, the siren ear splitting. My head is an echo chamber, every sound rattling around against nothing, just building onto itself.

"I'll be back." I lie. "There's a fire proof safe in the lab. The code is 81355. All the money is yours, burn everything else. Promise me?" I stare down at her, my only friend and caretaker for the last decade. The person that force fed me when I spent too many hours in the lab, that put blankets over me when I fell asleep at my desk, that kept me from teetering off the edge into darkness more times than I care to admit.

"I promise," she says, tears welling up.

"Thank you for everything." I bend down to kiss her sooty cheek then take off up the driveway, dodging the sputtering crimson trucks. I must look like a madman, half-dressed, black with smoke, barefoot and burned.

I run the few blocks to Addison's New York office, ignoring the raw blisters at the bottom of my feet screeching at me to stop moving.

With a wave of my hand, the back door opens, the lock melted to a puddle of steel. I bound up the steps, and start pounding on her door, too frightened to consider that my intel on her address might be inaccurate.

But the lock clicks, the door opens, and there she is, looking lovely and sleep-tousled and annoyed and *alive*.

Relief floods through me, giddy and bright, more potent than even the Elixir of Life, and I nearly tackle her with the force of my embrace.

Stunned still, she allows it. "What the hell happened to you?"

"The house," I pant, burying my nose in her hair, her rosemary scent a balm to my burned nostrils.

She gasps. "The house burned down?"

I nod, cuddling her closer, wanting to tuck her inside my ribs where nothing can ever reach her. Where she'll be safe with me.

"Al, you're choking me." She pushes lightly against my stomach.

I take another lungful of her scent, then let her go, closing the door behind me and locking it. "We have to go. Now." I push past her into her apartment and start throwing her stuff into the first bag I find.

"What? We?" She crosses her arms, but doesn't try to stop me.

"They must have seen you go to my house, Ayla." I stop and face her. "It was an attempt on both of us."

She sucks in a breath, understanding dawning. "What about your lab?"

There's a hollow pang in my heart. I hadn't thought about my lab. Thankfully, I have backups for all my notebooks stored in the Greenhouse, a precaution I took back during the Great War, but that doesn't spare the score of machines I had built, the countless cases of antibiotics and medicine, the dozens of crates of Synth. My entire livelihood. A lifetime's worth of work.

I sag onto the couch, dropping my head into my hands, winded from the realization.

Gently, she takes the duffle bag from my hands and continues packing. I watch her in silence, numbness overtaking me, dulling my frayed nerves, snuffing out the pain thrumming all over my body.

When she finishes packing, she sets a fresh set of clothes in my lap. "Shower and change. I know somewhere we can stay."

I nod and rise stiffly, shuffling to the bathroom in a haze of grief.

I shower quickly, watching the chalky gray ash wash down the drain, but the smoke smell clings to my skin, my hair. I dress, refusing to wonder why she has an old set of my clothes, and emerge back into the living room.

She's sitting on the floor, a spread of cards in front of her. The Three of Pentacles catches my eye.

"Our paths have realigned," she mutters, mostly to herself. "We have to work together." Her eyes flick up to me, her gaze softening a bit as she takes me in.

I probably look like a kicked puppy. I slick my hair back and roll my shoulders, sliding my mask back into place.

"A travesty," I say, winking at her.

She rolls her eyes and collects the cards, tucking them neatly into their box and then nestling them into a green velvet pouch.

"So, where are we going?"

"Away," she says, hauling the duffle bag over her shoulder and heading out the door.

I jog after her and snatch the bag from her, but let her lead us out of the building.

She guides us out the parking lot and over to a black Model A. From her hair, she pulls two steel pins, and starts working them into the small lock on the door handle.

I could unlock it in a blink, but the little furrow between her eyes is far too sweet to pass up. I watch with fascination as she pops the lock and the door springs free.

"Where did you learn how to do that?"

She smiles, a little sheepish. "Leda taught me when we were kids."

My jaw drops. But before I can beg her to elaborate, she's climbing into the front seat and starting the car.

"How did you do *that?*"

"You ask a lot of questions. Get in the damn car."

I scurry around the vehicle and cram myself into the passenger seat. I spot the keys in the ignition and raise an eyebrow at her.

"Terry locked his keys in it this morning," she grins, and speeds off down the street.

We drive all day, barely speaking and stopping only when absolutely necessary, and make it nearly to Lake Ontario. We trade on an off, until eventually neither of us can keep our eyes open.

She parks the car in an alley and points out a brick inn bathed in red streetlight.

"*Tsk, tsk,*" I click my tongue at her, smirking.

"What? They're discreet. And I know the owner." She hops out of the car and starts walking across the street.

I grab the bag and catch up to her right as she pushes open the front door.

"Ayla, *darling!*" An elaborately dressed, very buxom woman rushes to greet Ayla, swallowing her up in a bone-crushing hug.

"Hello, Auntie Tilda," Ayla says, smiling in spite of herself. "Got some rooms to spare?"

"You're in luck, Chickadee. We've got one left!"

Ayla's smile drops to a scowl, and I beam at her.

"We'll take it," I say, sliding a hundred dollar bill into Tilda's palm and flashing her a wink.

Tilda's cheeks flush, and she fans herself a little. "Good catch, Chickadee," she whispers to Ayla, whose scowl deepens. She slips the last key off the hook behind the desk and hands it to me, her fingers heavy with diamond rings.

"Now, get some rest, you two," Tilda giggles, shooing us up the stairs.

We traverse the halls, pointedly ignoring the chorus of moans and slaps bleeding through the walls. I find the room number marked on the key quickly, 22, and unlock the door. It's a simple room, just a fireplace, a love seat, and a small table with two chairs. And one, queen-sized bed.

I waggle my eyebrows at her.

"Can't you turn that couch into another bed?" She crosses her arms, annoyed.

I kick off my shoes and flop onto the bed, yawning and stretching my arms. "Can't do it. Too tired. The wood...isn't right."

"Algernon!"

I close my eyes and put on my most obnoxious fake snore.

"Fucker," she grumbles. After a few minutes of silence, the other side of the bed dips as she slides in. She flicks her hair over her shoulder, smacking me in the face with it, sending a waft of rosemary and mint.

I run my fingers down the waves gently enough that she doesn't notice, feeling her silken strands of hair. I rub the ends between my thumb and forefinger, resisting the urge to bring it to my nose.

She sighs, adjusting to get a little more comfortable, and scooting a little bit closer.

My hand rests in the empty space between us, itching to slide around the dip of her waist and pull her into me. Her breaths deepen as she drifts to sleep, but I already know that there's nothing but wakefulness in store for me tonight despite the exhaustion in my bones.

Slowly, so slowly, I inch closer to her, letting my fingers brush against her satin slip. *Fuck, she took off her clothes.* I shiver at the contact, chastising myself for crossing this line.

She makes a soft noise and shifts a little, moving closer to me, forcing my hand against her hip.

"Mm," she mumbles. It's impossible to say if she's asleep or awake.

I move closer, letting my arm fall over her waist and rest on the bed in front of her. Her back is a wisp away from my chest, as thin as her slip.

I let my head fall forward on the pillow, resting my cheek on her hair, breathing in her herbal scent. I take a deep breath, my chest expanding enough to barely touch her. Her warmth seers my skin and I nearly gasp aloud. It takes every ounce of strength to not crush her to me.

It's moments like these where I know I would die without her. That she is the beginning and end of me. That without her, I couldn't go on. There'd be nothing left for me.

Everything I am is devoted to her.

I am completely in love with her, and have been for as long as I've known her, longer even. My soul is hers. My life is hers.

But I will not have her begrudgingly, with hesitation and fear. I will have her completely, body and soul, or not at all. I wouldn't survive anything less.

She shifts again, pressing her back flush to my front, branding my skin with hers. Molding me into the shape of her. I try to ignore the way her ass is cradling my hardening cock, wanting to focus on her softness, her openness that's rarer and more beautiful than a precious jewel.

I'm not sure if she's asleep, but with her body so close, I can't seem to care. I bury my nose into her neck, breathing her in, drowning in her. The need to taste her is overwhelming, like I'll die if I don't feel her skin under my tongue.

She is a drug, I'm an addict even though I've barely gotten a taste of her.

I can't stop myself, and I place a delicate kiss along the curve of her neck, letting the tip of my tongue dab against her skin.

She shivers against me, letting out a tiny breath.

That one taste is enough to drive me mad but, for her, I tamp down my impulse and lower my forehead to her shoulder, closing my eyes and praying for sleep to come and end this suffering, or else have her turn over and devour me whole.

Soft mewling sounds reach me through the din of sleep, infinitely more pleasurable then the rude awakening from the day before.

My senses rush back to me, the heat of skin, the smell of her hair, the slip of her nightdress, the gentle swirl of her hips—wait, *what*?

I notice it now, the smallest undulation of her hips, a wave traveling down her spine, rolling against my chest and painfully hard groin. Breath-less sounds fall from her lips, soft as goose down and sinful as the scalding desire darkening my vision.

I grasp her hip hard, stopping the lazy rock of her ass against my cock. "Ayla," I warn, my heart in my throat. But she doesn't reply, just continues to murmur and squirm. Fast asleep.

Something feral inside me rears up, showing it's teeth, demanding I wake her up with cock inside her tight little cunt. I grip her tighter, now encouraging her rocking hips, grinding against her sumptuous ass, feeling the heat pulsing from between her legs.

A fuller moan slips past her lips, a sound rich like honey and even sweeter, that sounds almost like my name.

My hands scramble to grab a hold of the bottom of her dress, sliding my fingers along the soft skin of her thigh, dipping down to the fiery center of her.

Her breath hitches, and I lose my nerve, scrambling away from her and onto my feet, running into the bathroom and kicking the door closed with my foot.

The scrape of my trousers against my throbbing dick is agony. I fist my cock, withdrawing it from my pants, and start pumping it furiously, so desperate it's nearly painful, and come hard enough to make my knees shake. I bite my fist to stifle the moan that bubbles up, milking every last drop of release from my balls into the porcelain sink.

When the orgasm finally dissipates, I realize it's done basically nothing to sate my lust, this rageful, feral thing she's woken up inside of me. I sag against the wall, tucking my cock away and try to take a few steadying breaths.

I glance over at her, a spike of anxiety shooting through me when I realize the door is ajar, but she hasn't stirred, apparently able to sleep through just about anything.

What the fuck is she doing to me? Maybe my father was right, she does bring out something ugly in me. Something wild.

I splash some cold water on my face and clean up the mess I made before venturing out of the room to find a bracing cup of coffee, and hopefully my sanity.

Ayla

Fall, 1929

Algernon grinds against me, his cock like granite. His grip on my waist is bruising, decadent in it's harshness.

It takes everything in me to keep mostly quiet, to feign sleep. My clit throbs with arousal, swollen and sliding between my clenched thighs, racing towards an orgasm. I can't hold back the needy moan that escapes my mouth when I crest that peak of pleasure, my orgasm crashing over me like a wave of fire.

His hand is sliding down my side, gathering up the bottom of my dress, caressing the slope of my thighs, so close to where I need him.

Oh, Gods, I could come again, a second orgasm barreling towards me. I draw in a sharp inhale.

Algernon lurches away from me and across the room. The bathroom door bangs against the wall.

I hold still, listening to him fumble with his pants, and a low groan hiss through his teeth as I hear the unmistakable slap of a cock being stroked. I risk a peak over my shoulder, and see Algernon through a gap in the door leaning over the sink, his hand braced against the wall, furiously pumping his cock.

The veins in his forearms are bulging with effort, his knuckles white and teeth barred, something animalistic in his eye. I've never seen him like this, ferocious and uninhibited. He's so deliriously beautiful, and my heart thuds like a galloping horse, sending another dizzying gush of pleasure through me.

His hand comes off the wall to bite his fist as the first pearly rope of release flies. A gritty moan blooms from his chest, barely muffled by his fist as he paints the sink in his seed.

I lick my lips. What a sin to waste such a delicious gift.

His orgasm tapers off and he sighs, dismayed.

I flip back over, praying he didn't see me watching him.

A few moments later, I hear him exit the bathroom and pull on his boots, before stepping out into the hall and shutting the door behind him. The edges of it glow gold for a moment, then return to normal, a ward settling into place.

I flop onto my back, the smell of his hair wafting up around me. Gods, he's been gone a few moments and I already miss him.

I snuggle into his pillow, taking deep inhales of his warm, spicy scent, still tinged on the edges with smoke. Maybe it was tolerable because it was a constant, an ache you learn to live with. I'd missed him for 40 years. But now he's here, is *staying* here by my side. There's no other option. To separate is to fall into the Arcanum's web. Together is our only chance of freedom, and, a small, naive part of myself hopes, a chance of survival.

But, I'm being selfish. Too concerned with my own freedom to worry about sparing Algernon's heart. I have to keep him at arms length, it's the only way to protect him. What happened this morning, and after the Mayor's dinner, and after the poker game, and the millions of little moments before, cannot happen.

It'll only destroy us both.

But how many times have I said that? Have I told myself to not touch him, to not let him touch me, and failed miserably? How many times have my walls crumbled around me at a single glance from him? A single touch?

I can't deny it anymore. The truth is a rotten tooth, agonizing, but demanding to be prodded. Demanding to be acknowledged. I care for him, maybe even love him. I want him so desperately it consumes me, snuffs out any and all rational thought.

But I can't condemn him to a life of heartbreak. I can't allow him to hope for something we can never have.

I hug his pillow tighter, tears brimming. How much easier would it be to be selfish, though? To take him, make him mine, to love him completely, then cease to exist having known what it's like to be loved. Having felt true, unconditional, uninhibited love.

And leave him alone, heartbroken, having experienced the same rush, only to have it ripped away from him.

How could I let him love me, knowing that he'll lose me?

No, I couldn't. It's much kinder to hurt him gently, small rejections and digs, than to smash his heart to pieces. To gut him the way Leda's death gutted Oberon.

I'm a lot of things, cruel is not one of them.

I crawl out of bed and change into a fresh pleated, knee-length skirt and white collared shirt. Settling onto the couch, I start brushing through my tangled hair, which has nearly gotten as long as when I was a teenager. It spent so much time up in a wig or pulled back that I didn't bother to cut it to suit current tastes.

Footsteps approach from the hall and the door is pushed open. Algernon squeezes through carrying a loaded tray. With an exaggerated sigh, he sets the tray on the table in front of me. "My lady." He bows.

On the tray is a large coffee pot, two mugs, a small carafe of cream, and a plate overflowing with breakfast food. Butter yellow eggs scrambled to fluffy perfection. Golden toast smeared with a pink, rose-scented jam and bright lemon curd, a few juicy sausage links, and a *very* generous portion of roasted potatoes. All of my favorite things.

I meet his eyes, lost for words, and he smiles softly, almost apologetically. Like he's sorry for making me happy, but just can't help himself.

I know that he'd choose to have loved and lost than to have never loved at all. But it isn't his choice to make. I won't allow it.

He pours the coffee and flops onto the couch beside me, nibbling on a triangle of toast.

"So, what's the plan, hellcat?"

"I suppose running is pointless," I grumble, taking a sip of the bitter beverage, savoring the warmth in my chest.

"I suppose you're right."

"But what are we even trying to do? Kill Keanu? That's insanity." I spear some eggs and potatoes with my fork, suddenly ravenous.

"Let's start with learning what they're up to, then maybe we convince Gideon and Oberon that Keanu can't be trusted. Maybe I can even throttle your dad along the way," he chuckles to himself.

I raise a bemused brow at him, feeling the phantom throb of the burns my father left on my skin. Thankfully, Algernon's Cure All had healed them completely, but the nerves remember.

"Not if I get to him first," I counter, shoveling more potatoes into my mouth.

"Together, then." He grins. "We can't take down the Arcanum without them. We just aren't strong enough. And we can't free them without exposing the truth of who Keanu is, what he's doing."

"I'm not sure Oberon will survive it," I say quietly, looking down at my cup.

"How do you mean?" Al sits up a little straighter.

"After Leda, he had nothing. Keanu became his something, his every-thing—"

"He had *me*," Algernon snaps, setting down his mug hard enough to crack it, which he quickly mends before it can spill onto the table. "I was right there," his voice catches, and spears my heart.

Hesitantly, I set a hand on his shoulder. "He wasn't in his right mind. You couldn't understand what he was going through," I say, voice stilted. Comforting people is not my strong suit.

"Oh, I understood." His eyes lift to mine, stormy and sad. "I'm probably the only one that did."

"It doesn't matter," I reply, pulling away from that look in his eye. "It's done now. The only way to free them is to show him the hurt that the Arcanum is causing. That Keanu's mission is inherently flawed and selfish. We have to knock off the rose-colored lenses."

Algernon nods, wringing his hands together.

I'm tempted to reach out and hold them, to comfort him in the only way I know how, but I resist.

"Okay, so what next?"

"Alder Bridge."

I bark out a laugh, gaping at him in disbelief. "You can't be serious."

He looks up at me again, expression stony. "I'm very serious. I need my Greenhouse."

"It's been decades. Your Greenhouse is probably rubble by now!"

"I can assure you, it is not," he says cryptically. "The farm is exactly how I left it."

"How *you* left it?" I ask, confused.

"Who do you think owns it? Gideon and Oberon forfeited everything when they joined the Arcanum."

Understanding dawns. "So you're—?"

"The sole heir of the Raith estate, yes."

A thought prickles at the back of my mind, one so profoundly heartbreaking I almost don't want to ask.

"How long were you there alone?"

He sighs. "I was alone longer than I wasn't," he says quietly.

"Algernon, I—"

"We should get going," he cuts me off. "Long drive."

I nod, swallowing the guilty tears clawing up my throat at the image of him completely alone on the giant Farm. No one to talk to but livestock and the Moon.

Silently, we gather our things and head to the car.

Algernon drives for hours, not saying a word. Dark circles make his face look sallow, his hands shake on the steering wheel. Eventually, after he nearly runs us off the road, I demand to take the wheel, and exhaustion finally overtakes him.

He slumps in the seat, snoring softly. He looks so uncomfortable, curled into himself so he doesn't hit his head on the ceiling, his knees nearly touching his chest.

Gently, I guide his torso sideways until his head is resting in my lap, his legs able to stretch out a bit more with the added room. I run my fingers through his sandy hair, noting the few frazzled ends from the fire, the smell of smoke still clinging to his skin.

Tears threaten again as I look down at him, looking so vulnerable, angelic almost. My poor, hunted fox.

I press a kiss into my finger tips and brush it against his cheek, his eyes, his nose.

He sleeps for a long time, long enough that the roads start to look familiar, the trees creating a distinct silhouette against the setting sun.

The driveway is longer than I remember, and overgrown enough that I can barely discern where the woods end and the road begins.

The car pushes through a final thicket of blackberries, and the headlights land on the looming cabin, looking just as menacing as it did the first time I laid eyes on it, age having done nothing to soften it's edges.

I nudge Algernon gently, and he sits up, rubbing his eyes blearily.

We're home.

Act 3

Algernon

Spring, 1930

I focus on the electric current rolling down the wire across the table, rapidly gaining momentum. It barrels towards a wafer thin glass beaker, and a collision would mean certain destruction.

Normally, I'd focus on the wire, bend it away to protect the beaker. But for the last six months, I've been working smaller, trying to master not only the molecules and compounds within matter, but the atoms themselves, electrons, protons, and neutrons. The fabric of creation.

I zero in on the air directly in front of the beaker, the tapestry of atoms filling my minds eye. Millions and millions of stars, jostling around in the open space. I focus on the hydrogen and oxygen atoms, and slowly start knitting them together. Well, it feels slow, here at this little loom in my mind, but in reality I have about four seconds before there's a mess to clean up.

I bring the hydrogen and oxygen together, two hydrogen to each oxygen, and water molecules start to fill the empty space, an infinitesimal flood. The friction in the air begins to increase, higher and higher, even though visually, nothing changes.

The wire ends, a spark of lightning leaping off the end and directly into the wall of friction. Every other attempt at this, all 75, had failed. 75 broken beakers, 75 fruitless attempts at stopping kinetic energy. But this time, the lighting breaks apart, fizzling to nothing but static, the beaker completely intact.

I pick up the beaker, staring dumbly at it. I created friction. I stopped the kinetic energy. So maybe, with practice, I can deflect Keanu's energetic blows. Maybe, we have a fighting chance.

In a rush, I scribble down some notes, then run out to find Ayla.

We've been co-habitating on the farm for a few months now, having weathered a harsh winter together and now bringing the long dead garden back to life. She lives in her old house, and I in mine.

Our relationship has stayed purely platonic, if a bit clinical. She's made sure of that. We've fallen into a stilted routine, me spending 20 hours a day in the Greenhouse, her bringing the property back to life. Any time spent together is riddled with words unspoken, but she's here, safe and whole, and that's enough.

When it comes to her, I have a million and one selfish desires, but the singular, selfless one stands stronger. As long as she's safe and comfortable, I'm satisfied. It's more than anyone else has given her, and the bare minimum as far as I'm concerned. But she's made it abundantly clear that it's all she's ever wanted, and I won't risk the small amount of trust I've earned.

I find her in the orchard, clearing away a blanket of dead leaves so the roots of the trees can breathe, now that the risk of frost has passed. Gold dust dances in the air around her, glowing in the early afternoon sunlight.

She's wearing too-large trousers and one of my old sweaters, her hair pulled back with a black ribbon. There's a dirt smudge on her nose, and tiny drops of perspiration cling to her temples.

"Ayla!" I call, making sure I don't startle her while she's concentrating.

She glances up and wipes her brow on her sleeve. "Unless you have water, don't bother me."

"How about a little—" I waggle my eyebrows "—friction?"

Her eyes go wide. "You did it?"

I nod, grinning.

"Algernon!" She squeals, bounding over to me and pulling me in for a hug, forgetting herself in the excitement. "This is it," she murmurs in my neck.

I can feel her heart racing against my chest, the herbal scent of her hair mixing beautifully with freshly dug soil and spring rain. My resolve starts to crack, wanting nothing more than to draw her closer.

But she pulls back, sliding her mask back into place.

"So, when should we...?"

"The humidity will be high tomorrow, more moisture, more friction." I force a smile, despite melancholy settling over my excitement like smog. It's a near constant companion now, having her so close, but so far. Knowing that if one thing had been different, everything would be different today.

"Is it that simple?"

I smirk. "Simple, no. But enough to give us an advantage? Absolutely."

That's what we're after, what I've been devoting nearly every waking minute to: figuring out how to weaken Keanu's power so we stand a fighting chance. The only thing that can stop or dispel kinetic energy is friction. If I can increase the friction of the air around us, hypothetically Keanu's magic couldn't reach us, it would be broken apart by friction. Even if it bought us a few moments, it could be the difference between life and death.

Ayla inhales sharply, jarring me from my musings. She staggers back a few feet, eyes wide as saucers.

"Hey, are you—"

An ear splitting scream rips from her throat as she falls to her knees, clutching her head in her hands. I drop down beside her and try to gather her up like I normally do when a vision hits, but she slaps me away.

"It *hurts!*" she screams, shaking violently enough to chatter her teeth.

"I'm right here, love. I'm right here. Tell me what hurts." I try to keep my voice steady, but my heart is ricocheting against my ribs. A vision has never *hurt* before.

Blood starts to drip from her nose and ears, her eyes rolling back in her skull, bloodshot and vacant as she convulses.

I do my best to pick her up without jostling her too much, cradle her to my chest, and run back to the main house.

I make her a palette on the floor, afraid that if I put her on the couch or bed that she'll fall and hurt herself. The vision goes on and on and on. It must last at least an hour, her body never relaxing once. It's far and away the longest she's ever been captive inside her head. I don't leave her side for a second, my hand clutched tightly in hers.

I've never been this afraid in my life, the thought of losing her a noose around my neck.

Suddenly, she goes still, the tension leaving her body all at once. Her hand goes limp in mine.

"Ayla?" I lean over her, brushing my fingers across her cheek, but she doesn't react. Her chest rises and falls sporadically, like it's forgotten the rhythm of breathing. "*Ayla.*"

Blinding terror grips me, panic making me grab her roughly and pull her to my chest.

"Gods, Ayla, please. I can't lose you," I sob, burying my face her neck. Her pulse thrums weakly. "Please. I never told you that I love you. You can't go before I tell you. You can't." My heart feels like it's splintering, shards of glass carving up my inside, mutilating me with every breath.

Not yet, please.

Through my sobs, I almost miss her lashes flutter. She takes in a big lungful of air, then lurches sideways out of my arms, vomiting something horrible and blue all over the carpet. It vanishes almost as soon as it vacates her body in a puff of cerulean smoke. She coughs and sputters, panting. Alive.

"Al," she whispers weakly, reaching out to me, her hand trembling in the air between us.

I crush her back into my chest, dizzy with relief. "Oh, thank Gods," I mumble tearfully into her hair, not caring how pathetic I probably look.

"You love me?" she croaks, voice raw, pulling back to meet my eyes.

"I always have," I almost laugh, tucking a strand of sweaty hair behind her ear. "You know that."

"You never told me." She reaches up to touch my face, and I lean into her chilled skin.

"I love you, Ayla," I whisper. "And I'm so tired of acting like I don't."

Her eyes are glossy, heavy-lidded with fatigue and emotion. "Nothing's changed. I don't know what that was, but I can't, Al—"

"Can you tell me why?" I cut her off, anger flaring as my adrenaline rises. "You've kept me at arms length our entire lives. I know you feel something, so why deny it?"

She sighs, rubbing her face. "I don't want to hurt you."

"You won't—"

"I *will*."

I cup her face, forcing her to look at me. "I just want to love you, to be yours. It's all I've ever wanted. However much you think you'll hurt me, it can't be worse than living for eternity without loving you the way you deserve."

Tears stream from her eyes, her cheeks flushed and glowing.

"And what if you lose me?" she whimpers.

"It changes nothing. It's foolish to waste your life worrying about an inevitability like loss. I almost lost you tonight, but I don't regret a single moment of loving you. My only regret was that I didn't tell you, that you didn't know how I felt. If I lost you, I'd be lost too, whether you love me back or not. My fate is sealed."

She exhales sharply, like I've punched her in the chest, then she's on me, devouring my mouth with hers, kissing me as if I were life itself.

I flip her underneath me, not letting our mouths part for a second, drowning in the sweetness of her surrender, her love. My heart thumps with giddy elation, so overwhelmed I can barely breathe. All I can do is kiss her and hang on for dear life, finally swept away in her current.

But, I can feel her shivering, and her hands are cold as ice sliding under my shirt and up my chest. Something is wrong.

I break the kiss and lean my forehead against hers. She's burning up.

With more will power than I've displayed in my life, I gently remove her hands from my skin and sit up. "I'd love nothing more than to show you *exactly* how much I love you, but you need rest, kitten. You're on fire," I say gently, placing the back of my hand her cheek.

She nods, looking a bit bleary eyed. "Something wasn't right about that vision."

I scoop her up. "I know, but we'll figure it out. You'll be alright, love," I soothe, kissing her hair as I take her upstairs to my old room.

I almost chuckle to myself, how many times did I dream of carrying Ayla to my bed when I was a teenager? Countless.

Her shivering has intensified, so I put her into some clean clothes and bundle her up in bed, piled high with quilts. She falls asleep almost immediately, and once I rally the courage to step away, I rush back out to the Greenhouse.

I rummage through my stock cabinet, apparently having hidden it so well from her that I nearly hid it from myself. Finally, I pull out the small velvet box and open it, revealing a delicate golden locket.

It's oval shaped, with a sweeping 'A' on the front, surrounded by rosemary and lavender springs. On the back, there's a small engraving of a fox jumping over the full moon.

I click open the locket. It's empty, but maybe one day it'll house a picture of us.

I hadn't planned on giving it to her yet, the jury was still out on whether or not it would work at all, but I needed to do something to protect her. And a golden necklace may be just the thing to not only keep her safe, but add credence to my theory that gold can not only ward against external magic, but suppress internal magic as well.

Now, I just need to activate it.

I grab the locket, my notebooks, a few tomes, and a giant bottle of my Cure-all Elixir. I've never tried it on a magic-induced sickness, usually just head colds and stomach bugs, but maybe it would help ease some of the discomfort.

As soon as that's done, I run back to the house and set up shop at the small desk in the bedroom.

I tiptoe over to her and place a few drops of the Cure-All on her lips. Almost immediately, her color improves and her breathing levels out. I heave a sigh of relief, hopefully she'll feel much better in the morning.

Now, the locket.

With tiny shears, I collect a thin strand of her copper hair from underneath and snip an inch or so off. I hold my breath, but she doesn't stir.

I click open the locket again and set the strands of hair inside, then close it. I cup in in my right palm and close my fist around it, searching for the amino acids of her hair. They leap right up to greet my energy, like they're eager to be transformed. I concentrate on them, and one by one, start converting the molecules to gold.

It takes only a few minutes, and when I click open the locket, the hair is solid gold, fused to the inside of the locket. The pitch of it's vibration has changed, resembling Ayla's own unique signature.

I grin, that's a very good sign.

Carefully, I slip the chain around her neck and clasp it under her hair, letting the locket lay gently on her chest. It suits her perfectly, the yellow gold bringing out the same tones in her hair. I can only imagine how it'll compliment her hazel eyes, how it'll shine against her tanned skin in the summer.

I sit and watch her sleep for awhile, stroking her hair and holding her hand. I wonder how much of tonight was fever-induced hysteria, if she'll even remember it all. Either way, I've made my decision, I meant what I said.

She's mine. And I'm going to love the shit out of her whether she likes it or not.

Rising with fresh determination, I get to work figuring out what the hell happened to her, who the hell did it, and how I can make their death as painful as possible.

Ayla

I wake up sweating, stifled under the weight of what must be a hundred blankets. I kick them off and sit up, rubbing my eyes to make sure I'm not seeing things.

I'm in Algernon's room, wearing his clothes and a ...locket? I pick it up to inspect it. It's solid gold, with an A on the front an stunning botanicals framing it. I turn it over, revealing a delicately etched fox leaping over a full moon. I click it open and find some strange ridges, but no photo.

The night before returns to me in a fuzzy rush. I remember the spring breeze, hugging Al, and then agony, like someone had shot me in the head. I can hardly remember the vision, even though it went on for what felt like an eternity. I just remember blood, and piles of bodies, the rank stench of dark magic, my hands covered in the sooty remnants of it. It was horrific.

And then I heard his voice, distant and fearful. I clung to that, to him, and he brought me back from the abyss.

He had said he loved me.

Warmth floods my chest at the memory, hearing those words for the first time in my life, and finally letting go. Finally letting him love me. And letting myself love him.

I know I kissed him, but then things get fuzzy again. I must have slept, but I don't recall having any dreams, which has never happened once in my entire life. In fact, I actually feel rested, my mind strangely quiet. The constant hum of my power is gone, leaving me feeling weightless, unburdened.

I look at the necklace again. Could this be why?

"Morning, love." Algernon pushes open the door and steps into the yellow beam of sunlight streaming in from the large windows. He's shirtless, wearing only a pair of brown trousers, and carrying a pitcher of water.

He looks good enough to eat.

"Good morning," I say, hoping he doesn't notice the heat climbing up my cheeks.

He sets the water on the bedside table and reaches towards me, placing his hand against my cheek. A soft smile lights up his face. "No fever, you must just be happy to see me." He winks, stroking a thumb across my cheekbone before walking over to his desk on the other side of the room.

"Fox," I call out, suddenly hating the space between us that used to bring me comfort. This *thing* left unresolved.

"Hmm?" He glances over at me.

"Tell me about last night." I pull off the heavy sweater he must have dressed me, feeling overheated and claustrophobic, realizing a half-second too late that I'm not wearing anything underneath it. I roll my shoulders, too late to backtrack, might as well act like it was on purpose.

"I realized something, kitten," he hums, turning on his heels and stalking towards me, his voice smooth as honey.

I curl my knees up to my chest, but don't pull up the covers. I don't tell him, no, to stop, because my skin is electric with need, every nerve-ending begging for him. Years of denial crash down around me, kicking up a wave of arousal that makes my head spin. My heart hammers in my chest, entranced as I watch him kneel on the bed and start crawling toward me.

He places his hands on either side of my head, leaning against the headboard, dwarfing me under his size, his presence.

"I am so fucking tired of waiting." His head dips into the curve of my neck, his scalding tongue tracing my jugular, sucking on my pulse and making me see stars. Something about him swearing makes my insides shiver. "I won't risk losing you without having tasted you first, without loving you the way I was born to."

"You said you love me," I pant, sliding my hands down the solid planes of his chest.

"I do love you," he murmurs against my skin, licking and biting the peaks and valleys of my collarbones, his beard tickling the delicate skin. "I've loved you from the moment I laid eyes on you."

I suck in a breath, arousal sinking deep into my bones, electric warmth fizzing through my blood. I take a fistful of his hair and yank his head up, crashing my lips against his and sliding my tongue into his mouth.

He growls with approval, his tongue immediately twirling with mine, as natural as breathing. The kiss is indulgent, slow and savoring, blooming with promise. I scrape my teeth along his lower lip, earning a soft groan as his hands fall to my breasts, rubbing the rough pad of his thumbs over my pebbled nipples. I bow into him, melting under his confident touch.

"That feel good?" he whispers, dragging his tongue along my jaw.

I nod, arching closer to him, practically purring.

He chuckles and shifts downwards, bringing his head between my breasts. He hefts them in his hands, admiring them with heavy-lidded eyes. "So fucking pretty," he says, before laving a long, wet stroke across each nipple with his tongue.

I cry out, my legs falling open to make room for him to lay flush against me. My hips rock upwards, but because of his height, my clit grinds against his hard stomach, sending a delicious wave of pleasure through me.

"That's it, kitten. Keep doing that," he encourages, before sucking my left nipple into his mouth and swirling around it with the tip of his tongue.

I obey, rocking my hips against his body like I used to ride my pillow, dreaming that it was him instead. I've never been touched like this before, never been plucked like a fiddle under attentive fingers.

"I can feel how wet you are, baby. Are you going to come already?" He looks up at me through long lashes, the sun slanting across his face.

I can only whimper, my core muscles burning from desperately grinding against him. Close, so close.

"Has no one ever touched you like this?" He licks a long stripe between the valley of my breasts while his long fingers tweak my nipples.

I shake my head, panting like a cat in heat, too horny to be embarrassed.

His eyes darken, shifting to that same feral look he had back at the brothel. "You were waiting for me, hm?" He bites down on the skin above my heart, sucking hard enough to bruise.

"Yes, fox!" I cry out as my orgasm begins to crest, close enough to taste, my toes curling painfully.

"So was I," he whispers, capturing my lips again.

I don't have time to process that before I come, the force of it knocking the wind out of me. But I still manage to scream, shaking like a leaf as pleasure consumes me.

"That's one." He grins, sliding his hand between our bodies and cupping my still spasming sex. He gently swipes two fingers through me, collecting the wetness pooling at my entrance. "I will make you come once for every year I've known you. Two for the years you left me," he promises, kissing my neck sweetly.

My eyes bug out. "That's like 100!"

"I didn't say it would be all in one day," he chuckles. "But I'm happy to get a jump start." His fingers dip inside me, curling deliciously. "Fuck, kitten. So tight," he groans.

Gods, his fingers feel fucking amazing, stretching me while gently massaging my walls, coaxing them to relax so I can take him. Soon, I'm a moaning mess again, rocking against his hand.

"You swear you've never done this before?" I pant, brushing the hair from his face so I can see him better.

"Never," he says, turquoise eyes fixed on mine. "You're the only one I've ever wanted."

My heart catches and tears burn behind my eyes. He waited all those years for me.

"Although, I would occasionally sit in on the shows at my house back in the day," he chuckles, his expression somewhere between guilty and mischievous.

"Oh?" The sound comes out more like a moan than a question.

"Mhm. Wanted to make sure that when I finally had you beneath me, I knew exactly what to do." He smirks and curls his fingers slightly upward, hitting a spot that makes white explode behind my eyes.

I cry out, a second orgasm slamming into me. It's stronger than the first, but dissipates quicker, leaving me ravenous rather than sated.

"Good girl," he praises, slowly fucking me through it. "That's two." He grins, kissing my forehead. "Getting tired yet?"

I grab him by the shoulders and flip on top of him, catching him by surprise. I straddle his hips and lean over, a breath away from his mouth. "Quiet, pup."

He's not the only one that's picked up a few tricks along the way.

His cock immediately jumps to attention, prodding at my soaked pussy through his pants.

Exhilaration rushes through me, having him beneath me, *all mine*. I shift down, kissing and nipping along his bearded jaw, his throat, and down his chest, making sure to pause and mark him in the same place he marked me.

Restrained whimpers fall from his mouth as I work, egging me on. I want to make him scream.

I finally get down to his hips and hold the zipper with my teeth, slowly dragging it down. His cock nearly slaps me in the face with the force that it pops free, the head swollen and blushed, glossy with precum.

"Fuck, baby," he pants as I run my tongue along his slit, collecting the pearly drops.

"No more wasting this," I chastise, and his eyes widen. "Every drop is mine." I hollow my cheeks and suck him down to the back of my throat in one fluid motion.

A deep growl blooms from his chest as hips involuntarily buck into my mouth, nearly making me gag.

"Gods, fucking, christ—*Ayla*," he babbles, already a sweet little mess for me.

I suck harder, picking up the pace until he's moaning outright, filthy profanities spilling out like a chant. I massage his heavy balls with my hand, loving every second of this. His cock is gorgeous, velvety and long, with thick veins and soft brown pubic hair.

His hand slides into my hair and grips it tight, stalling my movements, and he starts bucking his hips harder, fucking my face, using my throat as his personal toy.

"That's my girl, you look so fucking gorgeous choking on my cock," he praises, a devilish smirk on his face. "Let me see those pretty eyes."

I look up at him while I slide my hand between my legs, my arousal dripping onto the mattress.

"Good girl. Get yourself off while I fuck your face. That's it, kitten." He starts moving my head up and down his shaft, his head falling back against the headboard with a guttural moan.

But after a few moments, I resist, stalling at the head of his cock. His grip loosens, concern skating across his face, but it quickly dissolves when I start swirling my tongue around the swollen tip.

I tease him for awhile, running my tongue up and down the root of his cock, tracing every vein, before swallowing him back down, pushing his cock as deep into my throat as I can manage. I keep going like that, relishing in the whimpering mess he's become, how quickly I'm able to bring him to the precipice of ruin. But every time he teeters too close to the edge, I ease up, starving him of release over and over again.

It's intoxicating, having control over him in this way. Completely at my mercy. Mine to do with what I will, mine to own.

But soon, his patience starts to fray, and his hand in my hair tightens to a fist. He yanks me up off of him and directly towards his mouth, the kiss hot and bruising, tasting himself on my tongue. Before I even realize what's happening, he's flipped us back over, his hips hovering above mine, his cock so close to where I need it.

I'm dizzy with the force of it all, the way he turned the tables so suddenly, wrenched my control away as quickly as I'd taken it. But with Algernon, it's different. Instead of being frightened, I'm overwhelmed with hunger, with *need*.

He wraps a hand around his shaft and drags it through my swollen pussy, making us both moan, breathless.

"Ready?" His eyes meet mine, burning with the intensity of it all.

"Ready," I whisper.

He notches the head at my entrance, and slowly, agonizingly slow, he starts to push in. The stretch is intense, but he whispers praise in my ear, coaching me through every inch.

"Just relax, baby. That's it."

A sharp pinch makes me squeeze my eyes shut, but the pain only last for a second before it's soothed by the heat of his cock.

"Ah, fuck, you feel so fucking good. Better than I could have dreamed," he praises, petting my hair and raining kisses on my cheeks. "Only a little further. You can take it, I know you can."

Finally, his hips nestle against mine, inserted to the hilt.

He pauses, letting me adjust. Quickly, the pain shifts to pleasure, and I need more.

"Please, pup. Fuck me," I pant, digging my nails into his biceps.

Without another word, he pulls out and slams back in, wrenching a cry from my abused throat. He starts fucking me, firm and deliberate, his eyes never leaving my face as I cry out for him, thrashing like a banshee.

After a little while, he starts to lose his composure, his thrusts becoming rougher, and soon the room is filled with the lewd sounds of slapping bodies and load moans of pleasure, both of us lost in the delirious connection between us.

"You're so fucking tight, baby. My Gods, squeezing the life out of me," he pants, dropping his head to my shoulder and kissing the damp skin of my neck. He slides a hand between us and starts strumming my clit, sending me to space.

I cry out as my third orgasm finally arrives, dragging me under a tidal wave of ecstasy. My walls shiver around him, gripping him impossibly tighter.

"Baby, have mercy. I'm not done with you yet," he growls, withdrawing his hand as his hips start to stutter, the muscles of his stomach flexing.

I barely come down from the high, my body already keyed up for another orgasm.

"Algernon!" I cry, bucking my hips up to meet his as stars spark behind my eyes.

"Fuck!" he roars as his cock swells and his orgasm overtakes him, pumping my spasming pussy full of hot release.

I come again, the scalding gush of his seed sending me hurtling over the edge into the most intense orgasm yet. I convulse like a woman possessed, my soul exploding into stardust as my body is lost in the torrent of bliss.

He slowly fucks me through it, stroking my face and holding me close as I come back together, shattered and then reborn.

I gasp for air, clinging tightly to him.

"Fuck, I love you," he murmurs, kissing my sweaty forehead, my eyelids, my nose. "You did so well, Ayla."

"I love you too," I breathe, meeting his eyes, my own blurry with tears.

He smiles, his eyes crinkling and cheeks flushing. "It's you and me, baby." He leans forward and captures my lips in a saccharine sweet kiss.

"You and me," I echo, kissing him back.

We lay together for awhile, skin to skin, just processing, basking, in the liberation we found together. The shattering of our self-imposed chains. I've never felt more free, or more terrified, in my life.

Because now I have a weakness that's undeniable, even to myself. A complication in the path laid out before me. But Algernon's right, I can't live my life mastered by inevitability. I can accept what Fate has in store for me, even go willingly, but until then, I will live on my own terms.

Algernon

I watch her doze in my arms, a snugly, naked bundle of red hair and creamy skin. How quickly we went from tense, pining, semi-friends to full-blown lovers. But I guess that's how towers fall, slowly, then all at once.

I want to tell her what I've found, what I think happened to her, but I'm loathe to ruin this moment, to shatter the pocket of peace we created.

Her stomach growls loudly, and she shifts, furrowing her brows.

"Hungry, love?" I chuckle.

She nods, but doesn't open her eyes.

"C'mon." I nudge her into a slumped, but upright position. "You need to eat, and we have some things to discuss." Her shoulders stiffen a little, and I immediately regret my choice of words.

Brushing her hair out of her face, I tilt her chin up. "I think I know what happened to you, and I think I may have accidentally already fixed it." I smile, sheepish.

She sighs, then smiles softly. "'Course you did." Reaching her arms up, she stretches to the ceiling and lets out a satisfied sigh as her spine pops, pushing her tits up and out.

My cock stirs, and for a second I try to will it away, but with a dizzying wave a delight, I remember I don't have to anymore.

"Keep that up and we'll never leave this bed," I purr, grabbing her by the wrist and dragging her back onto my chest.

"Would that be so terrible?" She reaches down and palms my rapidly hardening cock, stroking it lazily.

"Ah, ah." I remove her hand, much to my bodies chagrin. "Breakfast first."

She rolls her eyes but sits up, throwing the quilt off of her legs and getting to her feet. "You're cooking," she says, pulling one of my favorite argyle sweaters over her head that reaches her mid-thigh.

"Don't I always?" I grin and follow her downstairs to the kitchen.

It's been a chore to bring my mother's kitchen into the 20th century, but at least we have a gas stove and running water.

I start brewing some coffee and chopping fruit, rolling an apple to her so she doesn't get cranky before the oatmeal is done.

"So, what's your theory?" she asks, taking a bite out of the fruit.

"I think it was forced on you, some kind of long-distance dream walking." I add the fruit and oats to a pot, stirring in cream and spices.

"But I wasn't asleep."

"No, but because of your power, there's always a tiny window into your subconscious, an open door to Source." I pour the coffee into an old mug, the white one with blue painted butterflies, and slide it to her.

She reaches up to touch her head, like she could actually feel the open space. "That's a horrible way to think about it."

I shrug, slightly sick with what I have to say next. "Well, that's how Gideon always explained it, how he could get into people's heads."

She freezes. "You think Gideon...?"

"Gideon and Keanu, yes."

Ayla stares down into her coffee cup, shoulders sloping inward.

"Ayla," I murmur, leaning across the counter to take her hands. "I could *kill* him for hurting you like that. Whatever he's become, it isn't my brother."

"I never liked him anyways," she sniffs.

"I know, hellcat." I kiss her knuckles and turn back the pot, letting her have her moment with the hurt, the betrayal that's been eating me from the inside out.

Keanu was always the enemy, the Arcanum. My brother's were just pawns. But now, one of them has possibly taken direct action against Ayla. A part of me had hoped that we could end this without hurting either of them, that my brother's were still in there, but now...I'm not so sure.

"You said you accidentally fixed all this?" she says, pulling me back into the present.

"I did." I set the bowl of oatmeal in front of her, drizzling a generous amount of honey on top.

"Care to elaborate?"

I sit beside her at the counter and reach out to hold the locket, brushing my thumb over the engraved A. "I wanted to give it to you for your birthday, but I had a feeling something about that vision wasn't right, and that maybe it was forced onto you via Psychomancy. I fused some of your hair with the gold." I click open the locket and show her the thin ridges that were once hair. "To protect you. It's just a theory, but it couldn't hurt to try."

She stares at me, eyes soft and round, dare I say misty. "My heads been so quiet, Algernon. It's never been quiet before," she confesses.

I can't help but smile, relief wafting through me like a spring breeze. "Then I suppose it worked."

She throws her arms around my neck and hugs me tightly. "Thank you," she whispers into my ear.

"I just wish I had done it sooner," I murmur. "It always killed me to see you in pain. I'll never forget that first time I watched you have one, that night in the dining hall. I thought my heart was going to fall out of my chest." I smooth her hair and cuddle her closer, still shocked that I can do this, touch her, hold her. That I can tell her all the pathetic, mushy things I've kept to myself.

"A few hours earlier would have been nice," she says, snickering.

"A few hours earlier and you would have thrown it in the river," I growl, biting down on the curve of her shoulder.

She giggles and pushes off of me, blushing fiercely. "Probably."

Gods, I want to make her blush like that every second of the day.

We eat our breakfast and finish the pot of coffee, but neither of us seem particularly keen on what comes next. And after what my brother did to her, on top of what all of them have already put us through, I was ready to slash and burn.

I've never been particularly blood thirsty, but they'd stolen every-thing from me. My home, my brothers, Ayla, my *other* home and friends, a lifetime of work, and now her peace of mind, her autono-my. Not to mention, the countless others whose lives they've ruined, families they've destroyed.

Enough was enough. And maybe I wasn't the perfect hero, more brains then brawn, but I refuse to stand by and let them take anything more from us.

Us. My heart leaps at the thought, and I can't help but reach out and draw her in for a kiss over our empty plates, savoring the cinnamon honey taste of her tongue. She slides off her chair and climbs into my lap, straddling me, her body soft and warm pressed up against me.

I slide my hands up her back and into her hair, tilting her head so I can delve deeper, drinking her down.

A small moan escapes her throat, the sparks between us igniting.

I hook my hands under her thighs and stand up, carrying her into the living room and dropping her on the antique velvet chaise. I kneel at the armless end and grab her ankle, tugging her down and throwing one of her perfect legs over my shoulder to angle her hips up, and her pretty, unclothed pussy, straight at my drooling mouth.

I dive in, lapping at the wetness she's already made for me. She lets out a mewling cry, her hands falling into my hair and tugging at the roots.

"Gods, yes," she groans, grinding back against my mouth and I suck her sensitive rosebud between my teeth.

"You make the prettiest sounds, kitten," I murmur, sliding two fingers over her dripping entrance before easing them inside her while nursing her clit. Her walls are velvet, soft and shivering. With an upwards curl, I force another cry from her throat, like playing an instrument, a song I'll never tire of.

A few more strokes like that and I feel her walls pull my fingers in, tightening around like a vice. I lash at her clit with my tongue, making her lift off the chaise with a shriek.

"That's it, baby. Come for me," I purr, lifting my head to watch as the orgasm slams into her, stealing her breath and making her muscles tremble. Her release coats me to the wrist, sticky sweet, and I lap up every fucking drop.

I sit back on my knees once she settles, sucking her honey off my fingers and trying not to look smug. I'll be damned if it's not satisfying to turn my hellcat into a mewling kitten. The raging erection tenting my trousers is a clear indication of that.

"Ready to prepare for tonight?" I ask as she finally sits up.

She doesn't respond. Instead, she turns over and crawls to the other end of the chaise, draping her upper body over the arm and arching her ass up, rendering me speechless.

"What's the matter, pup? Cat got your tongue?" She asks, glancing at me over her shoulder and swaying her hips in a lazy circle, glistening, puffy cunt and ass on perfect display.

I can only stare, my brain turned to horny soup.

"Bark like you want it," she teases, and my body finally takes the reigns.

I prowl up onto the chaise behind her, delivering a sharp slap to her left cheek. I lean forward, forcing her chest down and ass up even further. "Woof," I growl in her ear, freeing my cock from it's confines and slamming into her, bottoming out in one punishing thrust.

A guttural moan tears out of her, and with it goes her bravado, turning her into a pliant little slut once again. I fuck her mercilessly, finding myself devoid of any of the control I had earlier. I waited my entire life for a bite of her, and now that I've had it, I'm a godsdamn glutton.

I sneak my arm around her waist and start petting her clit, making her back arch even further and my cock reach even deeper. My balls start to tighten, the perfect squeeze of her cunt quickly dragging me to ruin.

"One more, pretty girl. I know you can give me one more," I encourage, grabbing a fistful of her hair and dragging her up and back into my chest. My other hand cups one of her tits, pinching and rolling the hardened nipple between my thumb and forefinger.

"Oh fuck! I'm coming!" She screams just as I feel her walls constrict, sending me hurtling over the edge along with her.

"Gods, yes!" I roar, slamming her back down on the the chaise while I roughly fuck her through it, draining my balls into her greedy cunt, stars sparking behind my eyelids. I collapse on top of her, squashing her into the cushions.

She wriggles and laughs underneath me, trying in vain to throw me off.

"I think we'll just stay here. No need to save the world," I murmur, faking a dramatic yawn.

Ayla manages to get leverage on the back of the chaise and dumps me onto the ground with a solid thud, bruising my tailbone. I can't even be angry, though, because she peers over the edge at me, her eyes crinkled with laughter.

I prop myself up onto my elbows, feigning annoyance. "That was uncalled for."

"Poor pup," she teases, ruffling my hair.

I lunge to grab her, but she skitters out of reach and runs up the stairs, laughing with abandon. The sound makes my chest ache, my heart near bursting with affection.

It's short-lived, though, and soon anxiety creeps in to gnaw away at my joy. What we're doing tonight is unbelievably risky, so much so that I'm tempted to leave her at home, not that she'd stand for it. I know that this is something that we need to do; we can't make any kind of offensive move without more information. I can't keep her safe without more information. I can't free my brother's without more information. All of that and more is inside the Dean's Manor, is inside Folke.

But what if it costs me the life I've only just begun?

Ayla

I dress all in black, hoping it'll grant me some kind of cover. It's really just a formality, though. A vain attempt at comforting myself. I can't control the outcome of this, but I can control what I wear.

I've asked my deck and pendulum a dozen times what to expect. The deck refuses to put out anything but the Magician, which is beyond frustratingly vague. And the pendulum just swings in lazy circles, ignoring me entirely.

At first I blamed it on the locket, but nothing changed after removing it.Was it punishment for wearing it in the first place? For thinking I could control the front gates to my own mind?

Maybe, but a team of wild horses couldn't take the locket from me. I will take it to my grave, clutched in a bloody fist if I must.

I pad down the stairs, finding Algernon waiting in the living room, wringing his hands. I cross the room and sit beside him, taking his hands in mine.

"We probably won't even run into anyone," I assure him, admiring the way his eyes glitter in the setting sunlight.

"I know," he says, gaze fixed on our joined hands.

"Then why do you look so anxious?"

"What if it doesn't matter what we show Oberon? What if we do all of this, put you in danger, for a person that doesn't exist anymore?"

I run my thumb across his knuckles. "I can't promise you what he'll do. But we have to try." My throat constricts, Leda's smiling face flashing through my mind. "She wouldn't give up on him."

Algernon squeezes my hands, understanding who 'she' is, and his eyes harden, determined.

As soon as the sun sets, we venture out, carrying only a sleeping drought and a notebook. We decided copying down the information would be the safer option than stealing anything.

No better crime than one they never know was committed.

We park in the woods circling the Manor and make the brief trek to home itself.

The house is mostly dark, with only a few windows on the main floor illuminated. In them, we can see about a dozen or so people gathered around a dining table, feasting on what appears to be a giant roast boar.

All of their faces are obscured by masks, a practice favored by Keanu during formal dinners. Immediately, I spot Keanu reclined at the head of the table, wearing his haunting deer skull over his head, the antlers nearly four feet across.

Keanu was one of the only witches I've known to have a familiar. It was a tradition that died out around the Witch Trials. Just an overly friendly cat could spell death for a woman, let alone an affectionate raven or sweet snake. But Keanu refused to abide by humanities rules, and when a black stag presented itself to him when he was a child, he accepted.

The stag, gifted the name Arden, was long gone by now, but clearly, what it symbolized continues to resonate.

There's an empty chair beside him, Oberon's place, I realize with a start. *Where is he?*

I search through the other masks, and find some that are familiar, and other's I don't recognize. My grip on Algernon's arm tightens when I finally spot my parents, James in a pig mask, my mother a lamb. I spot Gideon too, his iron hawk mask reflecting the flickering light of the candelabra's, but Oberon's wolf mask is nowhere in sight. *Maybe he's in his room*, I assuage myself. He often retired early when I was still a member.

"This way," Algernon whispers, breaking me from my thoughts.

We creep around the Manor, searching for a servants entrance, which we find nearly completely blocked off by brambles.

Algernon holds up his hands, furrowing his brows together. It's *much* harder to manipulate living matter, but if anyone had the strength, it was Algernon. The brambles shake in protest, but still slump to the side. The door swings open, revealing a dark tunnel.

"I don't see any wards," I mutter, feeling around the edge of the door.

Algernon smirks. "Arrogance has always been his weakness."

I roll my eyes at his bravado, the Raith brothers always had a flair for the dramatics, and step into the tunnel.

Algernon leads the way with a palm full of softly flickering fire, and we eventually reach the doors to the kitchen, where a massive chocolate cherry trifle sits, as if it was waiting for us.

There isn't a soul in sight, so Algernon dashes out, pouring the entire bottle of the drought over the trifle. Thankfully, it disappears into the whipped cream without a trace.

Voices carry from the top of the stairs at the corner of the room and he hurries back into the tunnel, crowding me against the wall.

Two women step into the kitchen, whispering excitedly to themselves. They lift the trifle and with some effort, carry it up the stairs and out of sight.

Algernon relaxes against me.

"Step one, complete," I whisper, running my hands up his chest. Normally, I'd try to will away the butterflies fluttering in my stomach, but I let them fly. To touch him is the greatest luxury, one I simply can no longer deny myself.

He cups my cheek and tilts my head up, fixing his lips tenderly against mine. I kiss him back, the butterflies turning into a raging storm. Gods, he tastes so good.

But, ever the responsible one, he pulls away, running his thumb over my bottom lip. "Lets go watch, shall we?"

We sneak back into the kitchen and up the stairs.

The servant girls linger in the hallway, but they're far to preoccupied with their heaping dish of trifle to notice us in the shadows. The smaller of the two suddenly drops her fork, swaying slightly on her feet.

"How much brandy did they put in this?" she yawns, slumping down into the small bench beside them.

The other girl hardly has time to register what she's said before she collapses next to her, both of them snoring loudly.

Algernon winks at me, then creeps closer to the doors leading to the dining room. Where a moment before there was laughter and conversation, there's now silence, broken by the occasional snore or grunt.

I let my shoulders inch down. That actually fucking *worked*.

Now, the real work begins.

I guide us through the halls of the Manor to the wing where Keanu lives, his office the first door on the right. But, of course, this door *is* warded.

"I have an idea," I whisper, taking the sachet of gold flakes from Algernon's jacket pocket. I shake some into my hand, crush it up, then raise it to my lips. I draw in a big inhale, then blow the glittering dust all around the door, like Sophia taught me to do with cinnamon on the first of the month.

The wards flicker, then fizzle out.

Algernon grins, pulling me in for a crushing hug. "Atta girl." He kisses the top of my head, then releases me.

The office walls are adorned with rich, velvet drapes in deep, regal hues, their fabric seeming to absorb light rather than reflect it. They hang heavily, creating a sense of intimacy and seclusion. Candle sconces line the walls, casting a soft, flickering glow that dances playfully across the room, sending strange shadows up the walls. A small, crackling fireplace sits in one corner, the flame an opalescent blue, although it emits no warmth.

Shelves upon shelves of curious objects fill the space. Crystal orbs, each capturing a swirling galaxy of colors, rest alongside peculiar, enchanted artifacts in varying states of preservation. Dusty, leather-bound books with worn pages line the shelves, along with jars of rare and peculiar specimens, from jarred reptiles to mutated animal bones. An old, ornate mirror hangs nearby, its surface slightly warped, giving off an unsettling, fun house-like reflection.

I head straight for the desk, rifling through the stack of papers on top of it. Mostly letters and ledgers, none of which is in a language I can even begin to decipher.

Algernon trails around the bookshelves, running his hands along the spines and inspecting specimen jars. He picks up an open bottle of wine, and nearly drops it. His fingers come away black and sooty.

"Oberon was here," he says quietly, almost to himself.

"You know they're lovers, right?" I ask, watching him carefully.

He sighs, setting the bottle back where he found it and wiping his hands on his pants. "There's no love there, just obsession."

"What's the difference?"

His eyes hook mine, looking particularly bright in the blue light of the fire. "There's a very important difference." He crosses the room and takes my head in his hands, shaking me slightly. "Obsession leads to ruin, always."

"And love?" I can't look away from him, absolutely enraptured by the intensity of his gaze.

"Love leads to you." He leans in, stealing my breath with a brief kiss.

I can't bare to tell him that those two things are one and the same, so I turn back to my search.

We only find a few letters worth copying in the fifteen minutes we allow ourselves. The deed to dozens of city blocks in the city, several letters from prominent political figures, including the Mayor, and what appears to be a ledger of names, including Gideon, Oberon, and my parents. Then, I find a black book tucked beneath a tilting stack of books, a crude skull with wings embossed on the worn leather cover.

I pull it out and crack the spine, finding another long list of names, all with dark slashes through them, rendering the names themselves illegible. Part of me doesn't want to look for her name, can't bear the thought of it being contained within the pages of this ledger of death, but I look anyways. I make it to the last page of the book, with every scrap of white filled, every name crossed out. No Leda.

I sigh, unsure if it's relief or disappointment coursing through me.

Algernon tucks the book into his jacket pocket without a word, and converts the ink on the other documents to carbon, enabling him to rapidly make copies of everything for us to take back to the farm.

Satisfied, we sneak back out of the house, passing by the dining room to ensure everyone is as we left them. Blessedly, not a soul has moved.

I pause at the door to the dining room, looking at Keanu's slumped figure, the antlers dragging his head down at a painful angle.

I could kill him. The thought rears up without warning, surprising, but not unwelcome.

Algernon's hand slides into mine and tugs me away, as if he's read my mind. *Not yet*, his eyes say.

We hurry down to the kitchens and out the way we came. Algernon repairs the brambles, leaving no trace of our trespassing.

It's only half a mile to the main school building of Folke University, and we make it there without incident. The hard part is over, and the relief makes us light on our feet.

I use the same trick with the gold leaf to break down the wards at the entrance and we sneak in. It's pitch black, entirely too dark to see anything but our own feet. Algernon creates another palm of light, illuminating the strange and ornate hall, complete with marble statues and candelabras.

One of the statues turns towards us.

No, not a statue. *A man*.

I grab at my waist, unsheathing my gun from its holster, and level it at the interloper, who's mostly obscured by shadow.

"Show yourself! What are you doing on campus at this hour?" Algernon demands, half-heartedly hoping its an errant student. His free hand is aimed at the statue nearest to the man, the marble already starting to liquefy.

The man steps forward and into the ring of firelight.

"Skipped dinner," Oberon says, lifting his chin so the dark hair falls away from his face.

We both freeze. I can feel my heart thundering in my chest, making my vision pulse and hands shake. I've seen first hand what Oberon can do, how he can snuff out your soul with the flick of his wrist. To kill comes to him as naturally as breathing.

It would require no effort at all for him to end us both right now.

But instead, he frowns.

"Oberon—" Algernon starts, taking a step towards his little brother, his closest friend.

I try to snag his coat, but he's too far.

"You shouldn't have come here," Oberon says, sizing up his older brother. "I hoped Sane was wrong, that you wouldn't do something so reckless."

My heart quickens. Sane wouldn't sell me out, so why did he tell Oberon we were coming?

"Let us go." I click the hammer, aiming the gun at his head.

"You know I can't do that." His lip quirks up a fraction, a horrible, twisted version of his boyish grin. In a blink, his hand is on Algernon's neck, dragging him to the floor.

Algernon grits his teeth, but doesn't resist. "Run," he growls, not looking at me.

Instead, I squeeze off a warning shot. It ricochets off the marble statue, right beside his head, but he doesn't even flinch, his gaze firmly fixed on Algernon.

"Now, Ayla" Algernon grates, his breath wheezing through his teeth. Shaking, he dips his hand into his pocket and withdraws the black book, showing it to Oberon.

Oberon's hold wavers, confusion softening the edges of his face.

I take a step forward, but an arm snakes around my waist from the shadows and yanks me backwards into the night, forcing me to drop the gun, and slams the door behind me. Locking me out, and Algernon in.

I scream and rail, desperately trying to yank the door open, but the arm is a steel band around me, and drags me backwards into the woods.

"Shhh! Ayla, please!" A familiar voice hisses, and I finally whirl around to face my kidnapper.

He's tall, dressed in an opulent plum colored suit. His skin is as fair as moonlight, the kind of porcelain that glows. Even his hair is snow white, from the top of his head to this thick beard. Golden spectacles rest over warm violet eyes.

Theodore Sane.

"What the fuck, Teddy?" I yell, and he puts his hands up in a placating gesture.

"Hold on, just let me explain—"

"You knew we were coming?" I snap, my heart in my throat. I swallow down the tears that burn behind my eyes. I can't cry yet, not until I save him. I need to be strong.

He looks at his shoes, a bit sheepish. "I did."

"Who did you tell?" Terror turns my blood to ice, freezing over the rest of my emotions.

"Just Oberon. I'd hoped, in vain, that his love for his brother would outweigh his loyalty. Clearly, I was mistaken."

Voices float through the air form the Manor, rageful and loud. The drought wore off. They're headed straight for the school.

I turn to run back to Algernon, to do something, but Teddy catches me again, clamping a hand over my mouth.

"You cannot help him now," he whispers. "Keanu will not kill him. He has plans for him."

"Plans?" I ask, my voice muffled by his hand. I know he's right, anything I do would probably just get me killed. Unlike Algernon, I had no useful skills worth my life, especially with Teddy around, a much more skilled Diviner.

"I will explain everything, but first we must go." He releases me gently, straightening his bow tie and blazer.

"And why should I trust you?" I seethe, the feeling of helplessness and desperation sharp in my chest.

"Because I'm your only friend right now."

I raise an eyebrow, skeptical. I can't detect any lies, something I'm usually quite good at. If anything, his energy screams sincerity. Even with my heightened awareness, the adrenaline honing my senses, nothing about him triggers alarm bells. If anything, I feel a strange comfort, I'm not alone in this.

"He's going to make Algernon create terrible things, things that no one person should possess. I'm a man of logic, of balance. I cannot abide by a scale tipped so extremely in favor of one man."

I sigh. There's no way in hell I can rescue Algernon on my own, and here stands the only person that might be able to help.

"You'll help me save him?" I ask, crossing my arms over my chest.

"I swear it." He places a hand over his heart.

"Then follow me." I turn on my heels and stomp in the direction of the Model A.

Teddy scurries after me, muttering about his loafers.

Algernon

I'm falling through time and space, blackness billowing around me. It's endless emptiness. I've been falling for hours, days, weeks.

My back slams onto frigid concrete, and I'm shocked awake, reality drawing in like a vacuum towards my sluggish brain.

I blink and things slow, the room rolling in lazy circles around me, a brilliant gold light pouring over everything. It doesn't occur to me to sit up. I can only watch the chains on the ceiling sway, chiming softly as they brush together.

The floor doesn't feel cold anymore, the rock melting under my body, cushioning me like the finest goose feather mattress. I'm warm all over, my muscles turned to marshmallows, my blood caramel.

I roll my head to the left, gods it weighs a million pounds, and see a pig crouched beside me, withdrawing a syringe from my bicep with human hands.

That's odd.

"Why are you a pig?" I ask, my tongue thick.

"That's your question? Really?"

I shrug and roll my head the other way, immediately forgetting about the Pig Man. This is *definitely* not my house. I would never put in a concrete toilet, that's barbaric.

"Ah, finally. I was afraid you'd never wake up," a low voice reaches my ears through the fog.

"Who?" I mumble, trying and failing to sit up. Something in my subconscious stirs, brittle with fear.

Someone delivers a swift kick to my temple, snapping my head around. The pain is dull and distant, but it's enough to drag me partially back to reality.

"Algernon," the voice coos, crouching beside me. His black boots are shined to brilliance, his pants starched and ironed to perfection. A long black coat pools on the floor around it.

I crane my head up, looking him in his coal black eyes.

Keanu.

He smiles, teeth white and sharp. A lock of raven hair falls over his brow, a garish contrast to his otherwise precise appearance.

I dig deep, dehydration making my throat dry and raw, and spit in his face. "Fuck you," I snarl.

He wipes his cheek, unfazed. "Your baby brother is *much* better at that."

I try to lunge for him, but he moves out of my way easily, my sluggish muscles barely able to lift me off the ground.

"You made some potent stuff, Al. I'll give you that," he chuckles, nudging at the discarded syringe with his foot.

"You can't keep me here," I growl, already working to accelerate the Synth's half-life. In the span of a few heartbeats, I'm sober and climbing to my feet. Keanu is not a small man, but I tower over him, and grab him by the collar, dragging him up to my nose. "You think my own drug can hurt me? You think those chains, or those bars can hold me?" I seethe.

"Of course not, I wouldn't dream of underestimating you. You won't be going anywhere, but because you'll choose to stay." Those soulless eyes bore into mine, unnerving in their emptiness.

"Why the fuck would I do that?"

A high pitched scream echoes through the hall, and my blood turns to ice.

Ayla.

Keanu leans in closer. "I've got your girl," he whispers, his dragon blood cologne wrapping around me like smoke.

I release my grip, dropping him back onto the ground. I can barely hear what he's saying to me, my heartbeat is roaring in my ears, blotting out everything around me but the sounds of her screams.

"So, cooperate, and your *kitten* will remain unharmed. Deal?"

I level my gaze at him, hearing him use that sacred name making my skin crawl. But I find myself nodding, her safety matters more to me than anything else. I don't care what I have to do.

"Deal," I say, shaking his outstretched hand.

He flashes that same wolfish grin. "Now I've got the whole set. James? With me." Keanu turns his back to me and strides out of the room, the pig man following him out and shutting the door behind him.

Of course it was James. A pig mask was apt. That man was the definition of swine.

Her screams stop and I sag onto the cot on the floor, which is about a foot too short for me. I finally did it. I sold my soul to the devil, without even knowing what the cost would be. But for her, I'd do it again. I'd live in chains for the rest of my immortal life if it meant she would be free.

I only get a few minutes of rest before another masked figure pulls my door open and beckons me forward. I follow him through the winding catacombs under the school, peering into every cell hoping to see Ayla, but no such luck.

The masked figure leads to me a steel door, which he knocks on three times. It swings open, revealing an older man in a white lab coat, his cuffs rolled neatly and glasses straight.

He doesn't smile, just waves me in with hardly a glance.

As I step into the laboratory, a musty, stagnant air greets me, carrying the heavy scent of decaying wood and the acrid sting of experiments gone awry. The feeble light from the thin, grimy windows just below the ceiling struggles to pierce the gloom, casting uneven shadows on the worn workbenches. The instruments, once gleaming with promise, now bear the scars of time and neglect.

To the left, the shelves sag under the weight of dusty glass containers, their labels faded or illegible. The rubber tubing, once vibrant with purpose, now seems brittle and frail. The microscope on the bench stands as a relic, its lenses clouded with the residue. Beside it, the Bunsen burner emits a feeble sigh, its once-bold flame now a mere flicker.

"You may go, Thurman," he says, sounding almost bored.

The masked man nods and closes the door behind him.

"Who are you?" I ask, looking back at the old man. His hair is gray and thin, the purple rings under his eyes heavy.

"I've been your stand-in for 50 years," he glowers, moving toward a filing cabinet in the corner and pulling out a massive stack of papers. He dumps it on the workbench in front of me.

"My stand-in?" I ask, sliding the top paper towards me. *Schema of Atomic Weaponry*, it reads, and my stomach does a nervous flip.

"Keanu doesn't seem to grasp that Transfiguration and Alchemy are not one in the same. I am a Professor of Transfiguration, *not* a scientist."

"What is all of this?" I ask, barely listening to him as I thumb through the pages.

Anatomy of Disease and Biowarfare.

Serum of Superhuman Strength.

The Nucleus, In Pieces.

Submission and Truth Serums.

Noxious Gases and their Usage.

"The recipe to the end of the world, son," he says, sliding his lab coat off of his shoulders. "It's your burden now—" he lays a hand on my shoulder. "—and do what I didn't have the courage to do, and drink that gallon of bleach. Stop him before he can start."

I jump back, slapping his hand away. "You're insane."

He doesn't flinch, just shakes his head sadly. "Coward," he tuts, then pulls open the steel door, lets the masked man slip back inside, then closes it behind him.

The mask stands at the door, watching as I try to wrap my head around this.

"Your job is simple," he says, dragging over a stool to sit on. "Do what he couldn't. Finish the experiments. Or we will finish her." He throws a crushed hunk of metal at my feet.

I scoop it up, realizing it's Ayla's beloved Colt .25. Running my thumb over the flattened barrel, I take a deep breath.

What was I willing to do to keep her safe?

I pull out *Submission and Truth Serums* and start reading.

The days blend together, sleep, eat, work, repeat. The only person I've seen is my masked guard, who hasn't spoken a word to me since that first day. He mostly kicks over half of my single meal onto the floor and grinds it into the concrete with his boot.

Truthfully, the only reason I haven't withered away to nothing is the small meal I find in the supply closet every afternoon, a scrap of meat, a boiled potato, and an apple that must be from the orchard outside.

The first time I found the plate, I assumed it was a trick and left it untouched. But the next day, it had been replaced with fresh food, and I was so hungry that I took the gamble.

At least someone was looking out for me, whoever they were.

I've managed to crack the truth serum, creating a similar blend to Synth mixed with a mild, salt-based anesthetic. Now, I've moved onto the power enhancing serum, although at a decidedly slower pace.

The atomic bomb and nuclear plans are breathing down my neck, inching closer every day.

I write and rewrite my notes, the burner on low as I distill salt water. I've dragged my feet today, testing how closely the masked man is watching me. I hear the stool scrape as he stands. He approaches me casually, unhurried, like he's curious about what I'm doing.

The brutal lash of something sharp knocks the air out of me, sending me to my knees. Something warm and wet pours down my back, the knife having ripped clean through my lab coat and shirt.

I look up, trying to shield my face.

He flips the Bowie knife in his hand, catching the blade in his gloved palm. He pulls his arm back, then arks the knife forward. I lunge away, the pommel missing my temple by a half inch.

His foot kicks out, nailing me in the knee as I scramble to my feet. I don't buckle, instead grabbing the scalding glass double boiler with my bare hand and hurling it at him. Burning hot glass and boiling salt water crash directly over his face, shattering into a million pieces and pouring water down his mask and shirt.

He screams, tearing off his mask and his clothes, mutilating his hands in the process.

I don't recognize the boy underneath the mask. He can't be older than 21, and I've scarred him for life. I try to reach for a semblance of guilt, but nothing reaches back. I just watch as he runs out of the lab and into the dark hall, wailing.

I stagger to the sink, running my scalded hand under cold water. The water licks at my palm like flames, and I grit my teeth to keep from screaming. The wound in my back stings, hot and achy, but it's distant, adrenaline muffling the pain.

Out of the corner of my eye, I see someone step into the room.

I whirl around, prepared to chuck the microscope at their head, but the sight of my younger brother stops me in my tracks.

"Oberon," I breathe, loosening my grip on the neck of the scope.

"Hey, Al," he says gently. He looks much worse than the last time I saw him—*Gods, was it only a week ago?*—his skin sallow, his face gaunt. Darkness stains his fingertips and ears, has discolored his lips a cracked purple color. A walking corpse.

"What happened to you?" I can't help but step towards him, not seeing the monster of death before me, but my mop headed little brother.

He shakes his head, greasy dark hair falling into his eyes. "I only have a second."

I stop, not wanting to spook him out of whatever risk he's taken by coming to see me.

"You have to finish the Serum tomorrow. Do you understand?"

I shake my head.

"He will make *me* kill you, Al. And he'll convince me that it's an honor."

I take another step towards him and he flinches. "Oberon—"

"I know I don't deserve any more of your mercy, but please don't make me kill you. I can't—" A loud bang cuts him off, and I hear Keanu shout from down the hall.

Oberon rushes forward and grabs my hand, his fingers like ice. A warm tingle spreads across my back and hand, the pain quickly dissipating.

He releases my hand and turns, running down the hall and around the corner, just before Keanu rounds the bend at the other end of the hall.

I look down and flex my hand, where there were blisters moments ago is blemish free skin, smooth and pink. I reach around to feel my back, finding nothing but a slightly raised crescent line.

Keanu stops at the door and narrows his eyes at me, and I realize I've never seen rage on his face before, only that cool, composed mask.

Was this what my brother brought out of him?

"Did he speak to you?" He barks.

"Who?"

Keanu bares his teeth, but says nothing more, just turns and storms down the hall that Oberon escaped down.

Another masked figure appears in the doorway and crosses his arms.

"Back to work."

I finish the serum just before midnight the next night, and when the town bell tolls a twelfth time, Keanu appears.

I do nothing but slide him the stack of notes with the crystal syringe on top, a reddish orange liquid inside. Stabilized aqua regia, a mixture of nitric acid and hydrochloric acid, with flax, ashwaganda, poppy, and ginseng. A short lived, but effective power-enhancing serum.

The color reminds me of Ayla's hair, and for the first time, I can't will away the ache of being away from her, the depth of it choking every other emotion from my mind.

The fog of grief is so dense, I barely register him speaking to me, just watch him lift the syringe and inspect it in the light of a yellow bulb.

Keanu approaches me, his dragon blood stink forcing it's way through the din.

"Are you ignoring me?" he growls.

"No—" The pinch in the side of my neck startles me silent, and I watch him depress the plunger out of the corner of my eye.

I don't flinch, even as the aqua regia burns through the veins under my skin.

Keanu rifles through his pockets and withdraws a copper penny. He holds it out to me.

As soon as my fingers brush against the coin to pick it up, it turns to gold.

"Impressive." He smiles, turning over the coin in his palm.

I don't respond, already feeling the burn evaporate as the serum wears off, and the numbness creep back in.

"Now, turn it back." He holds the penny back out to me.

I take it, turning it back to copper quickly, but not quickly enough.

Keanu tuts and shakes his head. "What good is a power-enhancing serum that only lasts seconds, hm?" His hand shoots out and clasps my throat, hot sparks of his strange blue energy singe my skin, the pain sending me to my knees.

He steps out of the way, and James steps forward, tugging off his pig mask.

"I want you to see my face, motherfucker," he sneers, drawing his fist back. The first punch is electric, bright and bursting, but the dozens that come after may as well fall on a dummy, because I'm entirely numb. My mind retreats somewhere quiet, somewhere safe, and I let the beating unfold.

I wake up in my cell, my eyes nearly swollen shut. Someone is tapping on the bars. I lift my left arm to wave them away, pain erupting through the entire left side of my body.

"Algernon," the voice hisses, and I finally turn my head to look at them, my temples throbbing in protest.

"What?" I garble through my broken jaw and teeth.

"I have something for you." He extends his arm through the door, a folded playing card in his hand. No, not a playing card. I'd recognize the card anywhere.

I drag myself over, ignoring the agony ripping apart my insides, and snatch la Luna out of his hand. I unfold it, the sight of her handwriting making my chest constrict.

Teddy saved me. I'll be there soon.

Yours, A

I look up at the odd man standing above me.

"I should introduce myself. My name is Theodore Sane," he says, smiling slightly.

A manic cackle bubbles out of my throat and I slump backward, my laughter echoing loudly against the stone walls.

Ayla

I speed back to the farm, the ringing in my ears drowning out any conversation Teddy attempts. I swing into the driveway and kill the engine before barging out of the car and across the field toward Algernon's greenhouse.

"Where are you going?" Teddy calls out, chasing after me.

I reach the door and yank on the padlock. The metal heats, then pops open easily. I swallow the flicker of warmth the rises up in my chest, he made an exception for me when setting the ward, and run inside. I have no idea what I'm looking for, but there has to be *something* that could help us save him.

I start ripping through books and cabinets, searching desperately.

Teddy watches me quietly without complaint, and after awhile, starts searching with me.

We tear apart his lab, finding nothing of use besides a temporary tincture of invisibility. Not even a bottle of Cure-All.

"Fuck!" I cry out in defeat, throwing his notebook down and sliding to the floor. My stomach churns, sick with terror and guilt. Not only was Algernon in Keanu's hands, he was in my father's as well. James would go to great lengths to get back at me, torturing Algernon was likely at the top of the list.

Teddy sits next to me, folding his long legs into an awkward pretzel, his spine ramrod straight. He fishes a handkerchief out of his pocket and passes it to me.

"Would you like to cry some more? I do not want to interrupt your process," he says after a few moments.

I shake my head, drying my eyes with the back of my hand. "I want to get him back," I snap.

"Then I may have an idea."

"Oh my Gods, just spit it out." I throw the handkerchief at his head, irritated with his odd, formal cadence.

He catches it and folds it neatly, sliding it back into his blazer pocket. "The full moon is next week—"

"We can't wait a week—"

He holds a hand up, violet eyes flashing. "It's rude to interrupt."

My blood boils, but I clamp my mouth shut.

"The full moon is next week, and the School hosts a mandatory ritual in the courtyard on campus. The Manor will be empty."

"How do you know he's in the Manor?" I ask, leaning slightly forward.

"Because that's where lab is," he replies, as if I asked why the sun is hot.

"Why can't we just—"

"Storm in?"

"It's rude to interrupt," I mock, crossing my arms over my chest.

He cocks an eyebrow, but ignores me. "You must think strategically about this, or all three of us will die. You're of no value to Keanu, he will kill you on sight, as he's said many times."

Fear prickles up my spine. Teddy is absolutely right, I'm just an obstacle in his path to conquer Algernon, and by extension, the natural world.

I rub my face, exhaustion and despair weighing heavy.

"So, the Manor's empty...?"

"The night before, I'll verify Algernon's location in the dungeon, then after the ritual begins, I'll get us into the Manor and underground. With the knowledge that you're safe, he'll be able to free himself. The only thing keeping him there is that he thinks they caught you as well."

Fresh tears burn behind my eyes.

"So Algernon frees himself and we, what, run for it?" I ask incredulously.

Teddy nods. "Save your vengeance for another day. Keanu will be weakened significantly by the next moon cycle."

I narrow my eyes at him. "How do you know that?"

For the first time, he smiles. "The numbers, Ayla. It's simple mathematics."

"You know you're very strange, right?" I ask, bumping his shoulder. It's the closest thing to a 'thank you' I can muster.

"If you stopped hating your gifts, you could be strange as well." He rises to his feet and offers me a hand. I accept and he hauls me up. "Let's rest. You're no good to him half-dead from exhaustion."

I roll my eyes, but I'm so tired that they nearly flutter closed.

We pick our way back to the house. I direct him to one of the other bedrooms then barricade myself in mine, making sure to grab my M1911 before I lay down.

I snuggle into Algernon's pillow, clutching the pistol to my chest, and try to breathe, losing myself in his spicy green scent and pretending that he's here beside me.

The full moon bears down on us, white and gleaming.

Teddy and I wait at the edge of the woods, watching the empty air over the courtyard a few meters away. Finally, embers begin to flutter up and into the stars, a column of smoke reaching for the scattered clouds.

We look to the Manor, not a soul stirring inside of it. Not even the staff, who are mandated to attend the Ritual as well.

If Teddy's right, Algernon should be the only person in the entire building.

My skin tingles at the thought of seeing him again, followed immediately by the nauseating fear that we may be too late. I shift my weight back and forth on my feet, growing impatient.

"Just a few more minutes. I'm counting the embers," he murmurs, patting my head so I stand still.

I don't understand half the shit that came out of his mouth, but he's one of the few true friends I've made in my life. *Algernon would love him*, I think distantly.

"Now," he whispers, and steps out form the tree line, hurrying towards the same servants entrance we'd used last time.

I run ahead of him and blow the last of the gold leaf dust to dissolve the ward that had been put in place after our last breach.

Teddy pushes the door open and peers around. He beckons me forward with an quiet "All clear."

I follow closely at his heels as we wind our way through the Manor, not a soul in sight. It's quiet as a morgue, and twice as creepy.

It doesn't take long for us to reach a...bookshelf? I eye Teddy, but he waves me off and mumbles something under his breath, "*Aperi signatum.*"

The bookshelf swings open with a sigh, the warm air of the Manor sucking into the chill damp of the descending staircase before us.

"Do stay close," Teddy says, before starting down the stairs.

I clamor after him, clutching the back of his coat with one hand and my M1911 with the other.

I may not have defensive powers, but that's why man made guns, right?

We reach the landing relatively quickly, only to be met with a six-way crossroads. I've never been in this part of the Manor, but thankfully, Teddy seems to know exactly where to go, and takes us down the farthest tunnel to the left.

The passage is narrow, the walls hewn from rough, weathered stone, their surfaces marked by the passage of countless years. Swaying light bulbs hang from the arched ceiling, casting shadows that play tricks on the periphery of my vision, creating an eerie, ever-shifting tableau.

The sound of our footsteps reverberate around us, making my hair stand on end. Moisture beads on the walls, trickling down in slow rivulets, leaving glistening trails in the dim light.

The passageway twists and turns, revealing occasional alcoves on either side, each housing ancient relics and ossuaries, their surfaces etched with fading inscriptions and symbols.

As we continue, the passage widens slightly, revealing a long row of barred alcoves. The only sounds are the constant, rhythmic dripping of water and the wheeze of ragged breaths.

"Perhaps I should have warned you," Teddy says, reaching out to lay a hand on my shoulder, but I'm already racing toward the sound.

I nearly pass him in my haste, mistaking the lump on the floor of his cell for a pile of blankets.

"Algernon!" I cry out, crouching down and reaching through the bars to shake him, my heart in my throat. Blood mats his sandy hair, brown and crusted to the side of his blackened face. His eyes are puffy and purple, his brow split and angry looking. His normally aquiline nose is crushed, blood nearly crusting his nostrils shut. Those perfect lips and pale and cracked, his beard tangled and filthy with grime. His glasses lay in a broken pile beside him.

He's alive, but barely moves when I shake him. I stretch painfully against the bars, pinching my shoulder against the metal to pet his cheek. He's burning up.

"Algernon!" I pat his cheek more firmly, fear making my hands shake.

He blinks and raises his head a little, taking a fuller breath. "Ayla?" he rasps, reaching up to hold my hand against his cheek.

"I'm here, fox. I'm here," I whimper, brushing my thumb along his cheekbone.

He struggles to turn his head, wincing in pain, but manages to press his lips against my wrist, making my heart ache.

"Get him water!" I bark at Teddy, who scurries off down the corridor.

"There's, ah—" he struggles to prop himself up "—down the hall and to the left, there's a lab. I hid a vial of Cure All under the desk," he says, squeezing my hand before pushing me away.

Teddy returns with some water and passes it to Algernon through the bars. He guzzles it greedily, then promptly vomits half of it onto the floor.

"I'll be right back, I promise." I back away from the cell, everything in me protesting leaving him. But he slumps back onto the floor, panting with agony, and I start running.

It doesn't take long to find the lab, and I blow out the lock with my gun, refusing to waste a second on trying to be quiet. I run over to the table scattered with papers and notes, in the far right hand corner where he could survey the entire room.

My heart twists, he must have been so afraid.

I move to start searching under the tabletop when the stack of papers catches my eye. I flip through them, growing more horrified by the second at the violent and cruel plans laid out before me. Plans Keanu was forcing Algernon to bring to life.

I cover my mouth, holding back a scream, of rage or terror I'm not sure.

I fling the papers away and crawl under the table, spotting the vial of serum against one of the legs, secured with a thin wire. Quickly, I unwind the wire and shove the vial into my pocket.

I crawl out from under the table, looking around the lab, then back down at the scattered papers, and the dozens of notebooks and filing cabinets around the room. It's only a matter of time before Keanu finds someone else to do what Algernon wouldn't.

Without thinking, I run over to the display case and break it open. I sweep my arm along the shelves, knocking row after row of precious vials and jars to the ground, shattering them on the cement floor. I tear the papers apart, rips pages out of books, knock over filing cabinets, turn the gas on high.

I hold my hand up, remembering Algernon's little trick, and snap my fingers, a tiny flame jumping up on my pointer finger. A lab coat hangs to my right, and I hold my finger against the hem, watching the fabric blacken, then catch and start to burn.

I shut the door and run as fast as I can. Just as I turn the corner, a boom rattles the stone and sends me sprawling, but I stagger back to my feet and keep running.

"What in Gods name was that?" Teddy asks as I round the final corner and nearly crash into him.

Algernon just smiles at me, leaning against the wall beside bars. "Hell-cat."

"Shut up. Open." I pull out the vial and uncork it.

He smirks and tilts his head back, opening his mouth for me.

I pour the serum down his throat and he swallows it, immediately sighing with relief.

We watch in awe as his face knits itself back together in moments, color spreading back into his cheeks and lips. He stands and stretches, audible cracks echoing around the cell as his bones mend and click back into place.

Teddy looks a bit green, but I'm beaming.

Algernon lets out a jagged laugh, my mad scientist, and grasps the bars, which immediately start to change in his grip. It takes only a few seconds for the entire wall of steel to turn to crystalline glass.

"Might want to take a step back," he smirks.

We scurry away just before he sends his foot through the glass, shattering it to pieces. He steps into the hall, shards crunching under his boots.

I run back over, throwing my arms around his neck and clinging to him, tears dripping down my cheeks. He's so solid, so real, so Algernon. Safe and whole. I can barely breathe from the swelling of my heart.

"Apologies, Ted," Algernon says, winking at him, before taking a fistful of my hair and tilting my head roughly backwards, claiming my lips in a ravenous kiss.

I melt into him, basking in the burn of his mouth, his tongue gliding alongside mine.

He breaks the kiss and leans his forehead against mine. "I love you so much, Ayla," he whispers, eyes locked on mine.

"I love you too." I tug him in for another kiss, but a burning warmth licks at my side just as Teddy clears his throat.

We break apart and look up, seeing a dancing orange light bathing the hall at the end of this one.

The fire is approaching, and fast.

"Shall we?" Teddy asks.

We all turn to run, but come to a staggering halt.

Gideon and Oberon wait for us at the mouth of the tunnel.

"Well, well," Gideon says, striding forward. "I knew you'd wear her down someday," he sneers.

Oberon follows behind him, a shadow of death, blue eyes never wavering from Algernon, the only other real threat in the room.

"Let us go," Algernon growls, stepping slightly in front of me. "You'd have to kill me now, and you know it."

Gideon raises a brow. "You say that as if it will be a challenge," he chuckles, then his eyes slide to me and flicker gold. "Ayla, come."

The locket warms slightly on my throat, and Gideon's brow furrows a fraction.

I draw my M1911 and aim it at Oberon's chest, who has crept within a few feet of us. "Do not speak to me like I'm your wolfhound, *Geo*." I use the pet name like a whip, watching it sting as his lips flatten into a hard line.

Oberon doesn't flinch, just levels his heavy gaze at me. He takes another step forward, pressing the barrel against his sternum, the same place he'd been killed.

"Do it," he growls. "You'd be doing us all a godsdamn favor."

We can hear the fire now, the roar of it getting closer. The air is thickening with smoke and steam, heat lashing at our backs. The room is illuminated an eerie orange.

"Ayla," Algernon whispers, sliding a hand around my waist to pull me back.

"Do it," Oberon snaps, leaning his weight into gun.

It takes everything in me not to shake.

"Oberon." Gideon places a hand on his shoulder. "Now's not—"

"We can all leave, together—" Algernon starts.

Oberon's gaze flicks to Algernon, quick as lighting, and I see the darkness swallow the cerulean blue.

I don't even think about it, my finger just curls on the trigger, and the gun goes off, directly into Oberon's chest. I made the mistake of hesitating once, I wasn't going to do it again.

"No!" Algernon screams as Oberon flies backward and into the wall, black blood pouring from a crater in his chest. He rushes to him, desperately trying to apply pressure.

Teddy touches my hand gently, and lowers my arms. I stare, numb with shock, as I watch Oberon gasp for air.

The flames are too close, burning at our backs, singing our hair. The smoke is making it difficult to see.

I see Gideon mentally running through his options, but there's only one.

Run.

"Gods, fuck!" He shouts, tugging at his hair before pointing at Teddy. "Get her out of her and into the woods."

Maybe he's not so lost after all.

"What, no!" I scream as Teddy grabs me and throws me over his shoulder, shockingly strong considering his temperament.

"Algernon!" I cry, and he looks up at me, eyes vacant and red.

Gideon grabs him and tries to haul him up, but he doesn't budge, refusing to release Oberon. "Algernon, *please*," Gideon begs, his voice cracking. "I'm sorry, I never wanted any of this to happen. We have to go!"

"Fire!" Voices carry through the tunnels, Keanu's rising above the rest.

"Keanu can save him, we have to go *now* or none of us will survive this," Gideon pleads, pulling at him again, and this time Algernon allows it.

Gideon leads us down a different set of tunnels and eventually we end up at a grate leading to the outside, bathed in moonlight.

There's a horrible boom that shakes the tunnels, and a bone-chilling scream rips through the air, a frigid blue light overpowering the orange heat of the fire for a moment. Keanu must have found Oberon's body.

Gideon grips the rails of the gate and pulls, the muscles of his arms straining through his shirt. With a metallic scrape, the grate comes loose and crashes to the ground.

"*Go,*" Gideon commands, eyes flashing gold in the darkness and Teddy tosses me out onto the damp grass like a sack of potatoes.

Algernon looks back and forth between me, Gideon, and the tunnel.

A part of me hates that he's being made to choose. The other, selfish part prays that he chooses me.

He rolls his shoulders and sighs, that dead-eyed mask sliding into place. "I won't forget this," Algernon says, shaking his bloody hand with Teddy's. He points at Gideon. "Know that he followed *you*. This is on you." And with that, he turns his back on them and climbs out of the mouth of the tunnel, to me.

He pulls me up and drapes an arm over my shoulders, tucking me into his side and pressing a kiss on the top of my head.

"You and me," he murmurs.

Together, we walk away.

Algernon

Silently, Ayla leads us through the woods and to the Model A and I plod along beside her, numb. The night is warm, with a gentle breeze rustling the leaves overhead. The moon glows brightly, Her light making it easy for us to pick through the underbrush.

All I want to do is lay down, let the roots and moss take me home. But Ayla's pull on my hand is steady, her pulse thrumming against my palm. For her, I endure.

The rest of the walk and the ride home is shrouded in fog. She tells me we don't have much time, drags me up the stairs and into the bathroom. My clothes are tugged off of me, stiff and rancid, and she shoves me under a torrent of hot water.

I stare down at my feet, watching murky brown water swirl down the drain as the spray pelts my hair and shoulders. She's talking to me, touching my face and hair, but the words don't reach my ears. Her clothes have come off as well, her skin soft and pale as the moonlight.

Distantly, I want to touch her, hold her, but I can't make myself move, can't make myself speak. It's like a switch has been flipped in my brain, disconnecting my thoughts from my body.

Ayla lathers the bar of soap in her hands and stands on her toes, dragging her fingers along my scalp and scrubbing the soap through my knotted hair.

I focus on her touch, leaning into it as she slowly draws me back into my body. A small sigh escapes my lips, and she smiles softly.

She tilts my head back to rinse, and more disgusting brown water rains down. It takes three washes for the water to run clear, and by the last rinse I've started to thaw, my skin uncomfortable against my bones, my thoughts loud.

"Just a little longer," she murmurs, lathering up her hands again and sliding them along my chest. If she notices the weight I've lost, she doesn't mention it, just washes away the dirt and grime.

I lift my gaze from my feet and look at her face, seeing dark shadows and smudges of soot for the first time. The ends of her hair are singed and her hands shake slightly.

There's a twinge deep inside my chest, my sternum cracked like a tectonic plate, bone shards stabbing into my heart.

Ayla may not have been captive, but she's suffered all the same.

Anger licks up my throat, humming like bees under my skin, their sharp sting setting me ablaze. A horrible sound rises in my chest, something wrathful, and her tired eyes flick up to meet mine.

She must see something dark, because she takes a half-step back.

The beast rears up, called not by desire, but rage, that primal need to protect, to *own*. It's agitated, rabid, like I want to sink my teeth into the meat of her throat and pin her down while I fuck her.

She steps back towards me, fearless.

Foolish girl, the rage growls inside my head.

"I can't tell if you want to kill me or fuck me," she purrs, sliding her soapy hands down my chest and brushing against my rigid cock.

My hand flies up, wrapping around her throat and shoving her back into the shower wall. I lick a streak of soot off her cheek, savoring the gritty, smokey flavor against my tongue.

"I like this scary side of you, pup," she giggles, gliding her nails down my back.

Little minx, she wants to fuck to forget too.

"Up," I order, and she wraps her arms around my neck, jumping as I scoop her up under her thighs.

I drag the head of my cock through her slit, letting out another low growl when I discover that she's already dripping for me.

She shivers slightly at the sound, her hips raising up involuntarily.

I chuckle, the sound dark and strange. "You don't seem scared," I whisper, nibbling at the shell of her ear and down her neck.

"I could never be scared of you. But you'll be scared of me if you don't fuck me *now*."

Hellcat.

I slam into her, sinking my teeth into the curve of her neck at the same time.

The sound that tears out of her is nearly as feral as I feel, her hot cunt like a vice around my cock. I fuck her viciously, the wet slaps of our skin drowning out the voices in my head, her gorgeous cries soothing the beast tearing at my insides.

Gods, she's so fucking tight, soft and slightly ribbed, the thrumming of her heart massaging my cock until I'm drooling, brainlessly rutting into her.

She's not fairing much better, her eyes glassy and rolled back, her jaw slack as she sings for me. Her walls start to shiver, the tell tale sign of an orgasm rapidly approaching.

I need her release more than I need to breathe.

"Come on this fucking cock, hellcat. I want to watch you fall apart," I snarl, grabbing her face and forcing her to look at me. "Give it to me." I slide my hand back around her throat and squeeze, cutting of her cry as her walls constrict.

Her orgasm hits her like a train, her walls wringing my cock mercilessly as they spasm. She thrashes in my arms, her whole body swept up in it's intensity.

I release her throat and she gasps for air, clinging desperately to my shoulders and shivering as she comes down. But I'm not done with her yet.

I drop her legs and spin her around, pressing her chest into the shower wall, my cock still buried inside her.

"Gods, fuck," she whimpers, shaking on unsteady legs.

I don't reply, just drag my hips back and snap them forward, burying to the hilt.

A screech rips from her lungs as she comes up on her toes, her body trying to escape the intensity.

I tighten my grip and drive harder, deeper, her ass glowing red from the force of my thrusts. I'm lost in the chase of my own release, using her little cunt like a greedy monster.

She starts to bounce back against me, chasing her second orgasm, and I love her so much I could explode.

I come instead, spilling into her with a roar that makes my ears ring. She tips over the edge with me, and we fuck each other through it, hungry and selfish, until ever drop of pleasure is wrought.

I ease her to the floor, her legs unable to hold her up any longer and lean my palms against the wall, panting for breath as water pours over my head. *What the fuck did I do?*

She carefully gets to her feet and cups my cheek, hazel eyes searching my face. I can't bring myself to look at her, shame and sorrow eclipsing every good feeling she just coaxed out of me.

"We can't stay here," she whispers, wiping a drop of water from my cheek. "This is the first place they'll look."

I nod. I know this, but my body just wants to lay here and wait for whatever may come. I've always been a runner, but I can't run from this.

My brother is dead. Maybe they both are. If Keanu found out that Gideon let Oberon's murderers escape?

I shudder.

Sane might be dead too, if Keanu finds out that he was helping us.

The loneliness sucks at my chest, hollowing me out. I reach for that numbness I'd carefully curated over my lifetime, and it reaches back like a trusted friend.

We finish showering in silence and dry off before collecting the essentials: clothes, food, water, and my notebooks. I snag a few vials of Cure All as well, just in case, before placing a more permanent ward and fire protection.

I have no idea if it will hold, but it makes it easier to turn my back and walk away.

We pile our meager belongings into the Model A and I slide into the driver's seat.

"Back to Lake Ontario?" Ayla asks, pulling her knees up to her chest.

I shake my head. "We should stay close," I say. I don't say that we should stay close in case my brother's alive and needs me.

"Al—"

"Just for a little while, I can't...I can't go yet." My fingers grip the steering wheel, knuckles white.

She nods, gently placing a hand on top of mine, and a bit of affection leaks through the barricade.

I drive into town, which is completely vacant at this hour, not a soul on the street. There are only a few shops in this part of Alder Bridge, including a general store, a cobbler, a grocer, and the post office. Each have hand painted signs and window boxes with fresh flowers, and verdant green oak trees line the cobbled sidewalk.

Most of the town is coalesced around the college campus, but I head in the opposite direction, searching for something abandoned and unassuming.

An abandoned all-black, craftsman style home catches my eye and I pull over. It has a wrought iron fence around the overgrown yard, which has almost completely taken over the massive wrap around porch. They few other buildings around it are also abandoned, so it's unlikely to see any foot traffic.

Perfect.

I pull into the driveway, which loops oddly around the backside of the house and to a huge set of garage doors.

With a little focus, I get the garage doors open and pull the car in, effectively hiding it from any potential passerby. The only other things in the garage are a shovel, some rope, and an old Model J motorcycle.

Ayla picks the lock into the house and we creep inside. By some miracle, it's sparsely furnished, has power, and running water, so we should be able to camp out here until we get our bearings.

I walk around the property setting wards and come back inside to find Ayla sound asleep on the couch, my sweater bunched under her head as a pillow. I dig a blanket out of the trunk of the car and throw it over her, tucking her in gently.

Guilt gnaws at me, breaking through the wall I've built up so I could get us to relative safety.

I lay down beside her, cuddling her into my chest as exhaustion settles over me. Grief pulls me down, sticky, black, emotional tar slowing my movements and blotting out my vision.

I've encountered dark before, but never quite like this. I've never been helpless, never been without my brothers, not truly. Or maybe I'm just naive, and I've refused to accept that no one is coming to save me. That at some point, I have to take charge, and not just with Ayla, with everything.

I can't hide in my lab. I can't hide behind gold plated walls. I can't run anymore.

At some point, I have to take a stand, not for my brothers, not for Ayla, but for me. For what *I* want.

What do I want?

Ayla squirms beside me, nuzzling closer.

I press a kiss to her temple, shushing her back to sleep. Looking down at her, the delicate wisps of copper hair across her cheek, the easy way her chest rises and falls, the soft flush of her cheeks, it becomes glaringly clear what I want.

I want her, and I want our freedom.

No abusive parents, no evil cults, no debt to society.

Just Ayla and the world at our feet.

The ward at the front gate fracturing jars me awake.

I jump up, rousing Ayla, and creep to the front door. It's still early, maybe 6 in the morning, with the breaking sun just barely bleeding into the night sky. A thick mist covers the lawn and street, obscuring the figure standing on the wrong side of the gate.

Ayla sneaks up to the front window, nudging the curtains out of the way, and aims her gun.

"Haven't you shot me enough?" a voice rings out, familiar as my own.

I wrench open the door and run out to him, crushing him into a bone-breaking bear hug. Oberon hugs me back, solid and strong. hardly the waif he was last night, and a bit of my soul clicks into place.

"I don't understand..." I hold him out at arms length, checking him over.

He reaches into his pocket and withdraws a vial of Cure All, the label yellow and faded from time.

"It was in my hand." He shrugs, his eyes flicking over my shoulder.

I turn, and see Ayla standing on the front stoop. The gun is lowered, but her shoulders are still tight by her ears, her lips a thin frown.

"Ayla, I—" Oberon says, braving a step around me and towards her.

"You betrayed her," Ayla snaps, her jaw quivering slightly.

She may as well have shot him from the look on his face.

"I know I did. Let me try to make it right." He steps closer.

I forget sometimes how close the three of them were, how jealous I would get when she'd hug him and blow past me.

They were the last pieces they had of Leda, the only people that *really* knew and loved her. In being enemies, they were neglecting her legacy of kindness.

I see the moment Ayla wavers, the way her brows soften and her shoulders sink, and she flies down the stairs and into his arms.

"I hate you so much, but I'm so glad I didn't kill you," she sobs, clinging to his neck.

He smiles, just a fraction, and glances back at me, but I'm not faring much better, tears running freely down my face.

Oberon's alive, he's here, and that means we have a chance.

I can turn even the ugliest lump of lead to gold, given a chance.

Act 4

Ayla

Oberon's dark hair tickles my nose and he smells heavily of smoke and rot, but I don't care, I just hug him tighter. A day hasn't passed where I don't miss Leda, but her absence is even more acute now, having Oberon, the real Oberon, back. I'd lost them both that day, my two closest friends in the world.

Nothing could bring Leda back, but we could protect Oberon, and that would be more than enough for her. I haven't forgiven him, but that doesn't change that fact that I love him like a brother, that he's one of my favorite people in the world.

He squeezes me tighter, and I know he must be thinking the same thing.

After another moment, he sets me onto my feet and pulls back, pushing his hair out of his face while trying to discreetly wipe away the tears collecting on his cheeks and nose.

"Come on, let's go inside," Algernon insists lightly, nudging us both toward the front door.

I immediately send Oberon to the shower with fresh clothes and a blanket he can use as a towel, which he gratefully accepts and disappears into the bathroom.

Al leans against the wall beside the door, looking somehow relieved and anxious simultaneously.

I slide my arms around his torso, pressing up against his chest.

"I keep waiting for this to be a trick," he says, absently twirling the ends of my hair.

"What? Me or Oberon?" I ask, resting my chin on his sternum so I look up at his face.

He half-smiles. "Both, I guess." He looks down at me, runs a finger from my forehead, between my eyebrows, over my nose and lips, to my chin. "Fortune favors the brave, and brave I am not."

I scoff and pull back a little. "Are you kidding me? You're the bravest man I know!"

His cheeks pinken. "Hardly, but thank you. I'm not used to you complimenting me," he teases, tugging me in close and turning so I'm pressed between his body and the wall.

I stand on my toes and kiss him, his lips tender and inviting. He kisses me back, tongue grazing my bottom lip, asking for permission. I open up for him, letting his tongue caress mine.

I slide my hands down his chest and under the hem of his shirt, brushing along the architecture of his hips and grabbing the waist band of his pants to bring him closer.

He smiles against my mouth, and withdraws his tongue slowly before sliding it back in, a breathtaking tease that makes my pussy shiver in anticipation. He repeats the motion a few times, rocking his hips against me in time with his tongue, and already I can feel myself unraveling, the need for him overwhelming.

I nip at his tongue, lungs burning for air and he relents, leaning his forehead against mine as we both pant, overheated.

"We should probably get a room set up for him and scrounge up some food, aye?" Algernon says, tracing his thumb over my lip.

I sigh. "Probably."

"Atta girl." He steals one last kiss before heading off towards the kitchen to throw some breakfast together.

The best I can do for a bed is drag an old mattress off it's broken frame, beat the dust off of it, and throw a blanket over top. A sweater pillow will have to do, because I wouldn't subject my worst enemy to that yellow lump.

When I hear the water cut off, I head out into the living room to wait with Algernon.

He's standing over the stove, stirring a big cauldron of something over the open flame. It smells like potatoes and herbs, and my mouth starts to water. Both of us have gone a good week or so without a hearty meal, and all though it wasn't luxurious, it was hot and carb-loaded.

As soon as he notices me, he ladles out a generous bowl and slides it over.

"Eat," he orders, and I don't waste a second diving in.

It's salty and herby, with buttery potatoes, bright carrots, and rich beans. Only Algernon could make a culinary masterpiece out of old canned food and an overgrown garden.

Oberon pokes his head in, his long hair sticking to his face and dripping onto his shoulders. He looks slightly flushed and sleepy from the warm shower, but his eyes are brighter than I've seen them in decades.

Algernon ladles out another bowl and sets it beside mine. "Eat."

Oberon slides into the chair and digs in. We polish off our bowls quickly, and Algernon immediately dishes out a second serving, then makes himself a bowl.

We eat in silence until the pot is empty and our bellies are full to bursting. Algernon moves us into the living room, where Oberon sinks into the overstuffed arm chair and Algernon and I land on the couch.

"So, you're out?" Algernon asks, cutting to the chase.

Oberon nods, looking down at his hands and spinning an onyx signet ring around his finger. "He thinks I'm dead," he says quietly, sounding almost guilty. He glances up at me. "Death was the only escape, so thanks for shooting me. Made the whole thing a lot more believable. The wall caved before he could find me, I was starting to think that maybe I *would* die. I must have passed out, and I woke up outside in the woods, the empty vial in my hand. By the time they got through the rubble, everything would have been ash. No trace of me."

I open my mouth, then close it again.

"What changed your mind?" Algernon rests his elbows on his knees and clasps his hands together under his chin.

Oberon is quiet for a moment. "I saw you, flipped through that book, and I couldn't ignore who I was anymore. When I woke up after the fire, it felt like a second chance. I want to be the man she loved, not his puppet."

My heart twinges, and Algernon rests a hand on my knee.

"Things have gotten out of control. He's established Guilds in almost every continent, witches practicing dark magic and using it to dispose of government leaders. The kids at Folke are being trained like his own personal army. He's completely lost sight of what this all was for, although, I'm starting to think that none of this was *for* anything..." He trails off. "All those deaths for nothing. Just to serve his own greed." His face contorts with anguish, his hands starting to shake.

"Gideon and I were the only voices of fucking reason, everyone else would gladly see the world burn as long as they were the ones that struck the match. Your fucking father—"

"Oberon," Algernon cuts him off.

"I'm sorry," he breathes, shoulders drooping. "Monsters. Every single one of us are monsters."

"You aren't one of them anymore," Algernon soothes.

Oberon's attention suddenly shifts to me. "I have to tell you something."

I stiffen and Algernon narrows his eyes.

"What is it?" I ask.

"Your mother is dead."

The words land hollow in the pit of my stomach, a new reality setting in around me. I try to feel grief, or any kind of sadness, but can find nothing but selfish dread. I knew this was coming, her death was as inevitable as mine. I always knew I would outlive her, at least for a little while, and that means the wheel of my fate is in motion, and turning quickly.

I swallow a bubble of tears, trying to suppress the instant spike in anxiety.

Both men watch me carefully, gauging my reaction. I can't let them know the truth, that my mother's death is one of the last dominoes to fall before my own.

"H-how?" *You're emotional because your mother died, that's all.* No horrible secrets here.

"We found her in the garden, she'd fallen from the roof."

I can't help but snort, the panic rising. "Yeah, she fell," I cackle, the sound ugly and sharp.

"Baby," Algernon tries to pull me into his side, but I rebuff him, getting to my my feet.

"I need some air. Don't follow me." I turn tail and run out of the room before my stilted laughter turns to tears.

I barricade myself in the bathroom, trying to take hiccuping lungfuls of air. Black clouds the edges of my vision, and the room bows and stretches around me. My heartbeat is deafening, the rush of my blood a roar. The locket sears my skin, a white-hot brand against my collar and I rip it off, flinging it into the sink.

A vision hits me square between the eyes and sucks me in.

Paloma rocks an infant in her arms, it's chubby hands reaching up to play with her cocoa colored ringlets. A shadow in the shape of a man falls over us. I turn to see my father, his face twisted and blurry, his nose upturned and bloody like a sucker-punched pig.

The vision flickers and a small girl lays in the grass, pale and still, her green dress spattered with mud, her copper hair tangled with sticks and leaves. She clutches a fox to her chest, it's head hanging at a strange angle, it's tongue lolling out of it mouth. Both of their eyes stare blankly into space.

Someone runs past me, slamming into my shoulder, and then I'm swallowed up by a massive crowd of people. All of them are wearing heavy black cloaks, their faces obscure. They push and pull me, my body lost in the sea of black as they rush towards something I can't see.

The bodies vanish, and I'm plummeting, down, down, down, my red hair and green dress billowing behind me. I crash into the water below.

I open my eyes underwater and try to swim, but my limbs are thick and heavy, useless. I look down and meet Leda's eyes, her corpse bloated and half-eaten by fish.

Something grabs my ankle and drags me backwards into darkness, the only evidence of my scream a trail of bubbles.

I sputter and cough, dirt being flung into my face. I'm at the bottom of a hole, a grave, and my mother shovels piles of dirt on top of me. I blink, and I'm standing on the ground, a shovel in hand. When I peer down into the hole, Leda's dead eyes stare back at me. I blink again, and now it's my mother's corpse, purple rings around her throat.

"Hello, dove," Keanu's voice calls from behind me.

I whirl around and my father is there, like he always is, his hands closing around my throat. I try to fight him, like I always do, but his grip gets tighter and tighter until my vision starts to tunnel, and the strength runs from my limps like water through a sieve.

His face flickers from his own to Keanu's, until I can't tell them apart anymore, my oxygen deprived brain sluggish. I'm tired, so tired, and my eyes finally close.

I jerk awake, very nearly cracking my head on the side of the toilet. Scrambling to my feet, I grab the locket and secure it around my neck once more. It feels cool and heavy, reassuring.

Sorrow settles on my chest, and I sink back to the floor.

My fate hasn't changed, and I was naive to hope that maybe it would. That by saving Oberon, we'd stand a chance. That I'd stand a chance.

But I'm going to die by my father's hand at Keanu's order, and Algernon will break.

I am a pawn for the Arcanum, for Keanu, to use to get his hands on Algernon, just like Leda.

Tears roll down my cheeks, helpless, angry, tears, and I feel like a child again, waiting for my father to come into my room and punish me, where I've always been.

There's a soft knock on the door.

"Ayla?" Algernon calls gently. "Are you alright?"

I wipe my cheeks, take a deep breath, and open the door.

He pulls me into his chest, and I lean into him, tears welling up again. I let the dam fall, and sob into his chest, gripping his sweater in my fists.

I'm not sure how long I cry for, with him rocking me gently and whispering words of reassurance in my ear, but eventually the sobs turn to hiccups, and those turn to whimpers, and I settle, the panic ebbed for now.

He guides me back out into the living room, where Oberon waits, looking a little uncomfortable and very guilty.

"I'm sorry, I just thought you should know..." he says sheepishly.

I hold up a hand to shush him. "I'm glad you did. It's okay," I say, pulling a blanket up over my body and lapsing into silence.

"So, will you?" Oberon asks, turning to Algernon.

"I don't know, Ben. I've never done something like that." He rubs the back of his head. "Are you sure it's necessary?"

I look back and forth between the brothers, completely lost.

Oberon nods. "It's too much. I can't carry it anymore." *Carry what?* Whatever they're talking about, Oberon seems resolute in his decision.

Algernon sighs, then gets up and rummages through the kitchen, returning with a silver butter knife.

Okay, what the hell is happening?

"What are you doing?" I ask, sitting up as Algernon holds the knife between his palms and makes his concentration face.

"Binding my power," Oberon replies, the relief clear as day in his voice.

"What?! Why the hell would you do that?" I jump up and try to wrestle the butter knife away from Algernon, but he just holds his hands above his head and out of my reach.

"I don't have a choice," Oberon says flatly, and I stop.

"He'll retain some of it, it'll just weaken him," Algernon says, lowering his hands and revealing a thin, flat piece of solid gold.

I have a million questions, but I just sit back on the couch and curl back up in the blanket. It's Oberon's power, so it's his choice, even though his full power would be *very* helpful during a possible all out magic battle with the Arcanum. But *whatever.*

Algernon crouches in front of Oberon and lays the gold across his wrist. He bends it into the shape of a band, fusing the ends together on the other side so it can't come off. It looks uncomfortably tight, but Oberon won't be able to cut it off himself.

"I don't feel any different," Oberon says, holding his wrist up and inspecting it.

Algernon smiles, looking a little guilty. "That was the easy part."

Oberon quirks a brow. "Easy part?"

"Now I have to fuse it with your skin," Algernon mumbles. "So the bind is as strong as possible, and not easily reversable."

Oberon's eyes widen, but he doesn't argue, just places his wrist back in Algernon's hand. "Do your worst," he breathes, squeezing his eyes shut.

Algernon grimaces, then holds his hand over the band.

Oberon immediately starts to scream, his muscles bunching with tension, the veins in his neck throbbing. But Algernon doesn't falter, and eventually Oberon settles into agonized whimpers, gritting his teeth against the pain.

Adrenaline carries him most of the way through, but after 45 minutes, he loses consciousness. It's pain-stacking work, and Algernon is pouring sweat and just as tense as his brother. Cell by cell, he binds Oberon's skin with the gold band, creating a connection only he can break.

As it's been since the day Oberon was born, Algernon is his keeper.

When he finishes, they both slump over with exhaustion, but the relief is palpable. Algernon because he's finished hurting his brother, and Oberon because he has control for the first time in half a century.

I haul them both up, tossing Oberon into his room and dragging Algernon into ours. He collapses onto bed and immediately falls asleep, shoes and all.

Carefully, I unlace his boots and remove his sweaty clothes before tossing the blanket over him. I crawl into the remaining space under his right arm and tuck into his side.

His arm wraps around me, even in sleep, and cuddles me closer. It's the middle of the afternoon, but exhaustion takes hold and drags me under.

I keep my hand clasped tightly around the locket.

Algernon

Late afternoon sun streams in through the windows and across my eyes, dragging me out of a deep sleep. I prop up onto my elbows and look around, taking in the unfamiliar room. *Where the hell am I?*

Ayla's gentle breaths catch my attention, and the events of this morning come flooding back.

Oberon is home, relatively safe and sound. He left the Arcanum, and Keanu, behind.

I slide out from under the blanket and walk out into the hall. I peak my head in Oberon's room, and sure enough, there he is. Curled into a tight ball with his back pressed against the wall, he sleeps fitfully. The binder I placed on him glows orange in the retreating sunlight.

I sigh. He's safe, and whether he likes it or not, he's stuck with me.

I go back to our room, and the sight before me stills my heart.

Splashes of golden sunlight have set her hair ablaze, drawing out the natural highlights of her copper strands. Her cheeks are flushed a delicate rose color, the freckles across her nose a winding constellation, placed perfectly by the Gods themselves.

I step forward, careful not to make a sound, and drop onto my knees at the foot of the bed. I crawl forward, inching the blanket up, revealing the soft curves of her calves, the sumptuous flesh of her thighs, and let it pool around her hips.

Even as I part her legs, raining kisses across her inner thighs, she doesn't stir.

I brush my knuckles over the silk gusset of her panties, earning a tiny shiver. Moisture blooms through the fabric as I caress her.

Slowly, I pull the fabric to the side, unwrapping her perfect pussy like a birthday gift.

My mouth waters at the sight of her, shining with honey, unfurling for me already. I can't resist and drag my flat tongue through her slit, catching every drop she's made for me.

Fucking scrumptious.

My cock throbs painfully underneath me, but a team of wild horses couldn't tear my mouth off of her cunt. I devour her, greedy, no longer caring if I wake her up. I take her clit between my lips and suck hard, lashing the bud with the tip of my tongue, and she wakes up with a cry.

Quickly, I slap a hand over her mouth so she doesn't wake Oberon and suck harder. Her hips buck up against me, smearing my beard with her slick.

Fuck, I could live the rest of my immortal life down here and want for nothing.

I move back down to tease her entrance, spearing her with my tongue and thrusting in and out. I feel her tongue caress my fingers, and I slide two into her mouth, letting her suck on them to keep herself quiet.

A fresh gush of honey fills my mouth, and I pick up the pace, holding her down with an arm slung across her hips. She comes with a stifled cry and bites down on my fingers, the delicious bolt of pain rocketing straight to my cock.

I lap up every drop of her release, but don't relent, even though my cock is absolutely begging to be buried inside of her.

She squirms and tries to jerk away, but I hold her tightly.

"I'm not finished eating, kitten," I growl, withdrawing my hand from her mouth and slapping the outside of her thigh lightly. A warning.

She whimpers, but stays put, burying her face in her pillow to keep quiet.

I slide my fingers soaked with her drool inside of her. Her muscles are coiled so tight, it takes a concerted effort to sink to my knuckles. Gods, she'd squeeze my dick off all wound up like this.

"Gotta relax, baby. I don't want to hurt you," I say, and drop some soft kisses onto her thighs. "Let me make you feel good."

She takes a deep breath and her muscles start to loosen enough for me to move without fear of tearing her.

"That's my girl, just relax and take what I have to give you, okay?" I dip my head back between her legs and lap at her clit, her walls fluttering around my fingers.

She nods, clutching the pillow tighter, and starts to rock back against my fingers, moaning softly.

"Pretty, pretty girl," I coo, blowing on her puffy bud, just enough to tickle her.

"Gods, wanna come," she mewls, grinding harder against my fingers.

I smirk and curl my fingers up, petting the spot that makes her sing and suck her clit between my teeth.

Her second orgasm tears through her, and I have to practically smother her with the pillow to keep her quiet while I guide her through it.

Once her shivering abates, I take the pillow off her face and am met with a dazzling smile.

"Is that a 'please fuck me' smile?" I ask, bending down to kiss her.

She nods and takes hold of my cock, lining us up.

I tilt my hips forward and sink into her, both of us moaning into each others mouths. She's so fucking tight, I have to fight to push all the way in.

"Fuck, Ayla. Like a damn python," I mumble, gritting my teeth.

She shakes her head. "That's you, my love," she chuckles, voice tight from the painful stretch.

I smile and kiss her again, driving my tongue into her mouth to taste her. She kisses me back, sloppy with need.

I drag my hips back and snap them forward, forcing a gasp from us both, the pleasure making my legs shake.

"Need more," she pants, arching into me and digging her nails into my shoulder.

I pull out even slower, and slide back in inch by inch, torturing us both.

"So bossy," I reprimand, dipping my hand between us to graze her clit. "Greedy girls have to pay a price," I purr in her ear, relishing in the shiver that passes through her body.

Lucky for her, I demand payment in orgasms.

She bites down on my shoulder, frustrated, and I laugh, snapping my hips forward again as I apply pressure to her clit.

"For that, I'll take two more orgasms," I say, nipping at the shell of her ear before moving back to properly fuck her brains out.

And fuck her brains out, I do.

Her third orgasm comes quickly, hard and fast, and she very nearly drags me down with her as her muscles bare down on me, but I manage to hang on.

I don't relent, knowing I won't last much longer, and blessedly, her fourth orgasm rides in on the coattails of the third, and I watch her ascend, her eyes rolling into the back of her head as her whole body quakes with pleasure.

Being quiet was out the window. All I care about is making her come as many times as she possibly could. And then some.

My own release refuses to be kept at bay any longer, and I pull out to paint her stomach and tits with my seed, biting down on my fist to silence a stream of profanities.

"Fuck, that's a gorgeous view," I pant, admiring the ropes of cum criss-crossing her soft stomach and tits, glittering in the golden sunlight.

She smiles lazily at me, eyes fluttering closed as she floats down from her high.

I throw on a pair of pants and check Oberon's room, still fast asleep, thank Gods, and search around for a towel. I wipe her off, then drag her into a hot shower with me.

I wash her up, down, and sideways, massaging out the kinks in her neck and shoulders, savoring the feel of her skin against mine. This might be my favorite thing in the world. Wet, soapy, orgasm-drunk Ayla.

We dry off and get dressed, then head down to make some food. More potatoes and carrots, with some rice I found in the pantry.

It's another hour before Oberon emerges, looking weary, but relatively okay. He sits on a stool and drops his head in his hands, rubbing the sleep out of his eyes.

"Can I ask you something?" He says, picking his head up and looking at me.

I pause my stirring. "Of course."

"What happened to mom and dad? Did you give them—"

I drop the spoon with a clatter and Ayla's head snaps up.

"You don't know?" I ask, my heart sinking. *How could he not know?*

Oberon sighs. "I had a feeling. Just wasn't sure what you chose to do."

Ayla puffs up. "Algernon didn't *choose* anything—"

I pat her head and she quiets, though her eyes stay angry. "I didn't give any to them, and they never asked for it. They left not long after Gideon did. I don't think they cared much to live forever, after everything."

Oberon nods, but doesn't speak.

I plate dinner and pass it around, but Oberon ignores it, staring down at his hands.

"Do you want to go see them?" I ask.

"They're here?" He lifts his head, and he looks so much like his little melancholy, desperate for affection self that I forget what we're talking about for a second.

"At the farm, yeah. Gideon and I arranged it all."

He lets out a dry laugh and shakes his head. "Motherfucker. Can we go now?"

I glance at Ayla, who is pointedly staring down at her plate. She feels my eyes and looks up.

"I can sit in the car, if you want." She shrugs.

I can't help but smile and pull her into my side, pressing a kiss to the top of her head. "Eat, then we'll go," I say, nudging his plate towards him.

He groans, but shoves a forkful into his mouth.

The sun is mostly set, casting a navy blue shadow over the farm. Oberon and I climb out of the car, leaving it idling to keep Ayla warm as she waits with a book. I tap on the window and point at the small door locks, only turning away when she rolls her eyes and the lock *shicks* into the door.

Oberon tries to keep his eyes on the path, but I see his gaze lift towards his old home, the cottage he and Leda had shared. The look on his face is impossible to read, somewhere between agony, rage, and longing. His lips are a grim line, his eyes narrow.

I place a hand on his shoulder to steer him, making sure he doesn't trip. We come around the bend beside the house that leads to the cemetery and his head snaps up.

"Gideon's here," he hisses, nodding toward the direction of the grave site.

I can just barely make out a tall silhouette of a man in the darkness with a large dog by his side, but part of Oberon's gift is that he can sense other peoples life force, their energy. Like a bloodhound, but for souls.

"It's alright," I soothe, feigning confidence. I backtrack a bit, checking on the car. Ayla is curled up in the backseat with a blanket, lost in her book. I hope to the Gods she has her gun.

I join Oberon again and nudge him forward.

"He's not the man you think he is," Oberon says cryptically, but resumes walking.

I shrug. "None of us are."

Gideon doesn't move as we approach him, despite certainly knowing we're there. He just stares down at our parents headstone, holding a bundle of blue hydrangea and smoking a cigarette. But the very large wolfhound, who is thankfully friendly, bounds over to greet us.

I scratch behind the dogs ears and hang back while Oberon approaches him.

"Why didn't you tell me?" Oberon mutters, stopping beside him.

"You've suffered enough loss for one man, kid," Gideon answers, glancing up at me. He snaps his fingers and the dog returns to his side. Even sitting, the dog's head reaches his waist.

"How long?" Oberon asks, crouching down in front of the headstone. It only depict their initials, SJR and ABR.

Gideon takes a drag, thinking, then looks over at me. "Do you remember?"

I rack my brain, and am met with the uncomfortable realization that I don't remember when they died. Time was irrelevant until Ayla came back into my life. And then every moment after was either a moment with her, or a moment forgotten.

"Around the Great War?" I guess.

Gideon nods. "Almost twenty years ago, I wager."

"Do you visit often?" I ask, despite knowing that he doesn't. In the months Ayla and I lived here, the wards weren't tripped once.

"No, not often," he replies, absently scratching the dogs head.

None of us speak for a few moments. I wonder if he came tonight hoping I'd bring Oberon. He always was a few steps ahead of us.

"I didn't know you liked dogs," I say dumbly, trying to fill the awkward silence.

"I don't," he clips, and stops petting the dog, who thumps his tail merrily.

Oberon snorts. "That's Dorian, his giant, drooling son."

I try to hide my smile. Everyone's got a soft spot, even a frigid ass like Gideon.

"Speaking of co-dependent beasts." Gideon ashes his cigarette on Absolon's side of the headstone. "Keanu's out of his fucking mind."

Oberon stiffens and stands up. "He doesn't give a shit about me. It's an act," he says, voice flat. But his eyes stay trained on the ground. *Does he feel guilty for leaving?*

"It's damn annoying. He was already a drama queen, but now he's insufferable." Gideon turns and looks me dead in the eye. "You've managed to kneecap him, now is your chance to cut off his head, clear?"

I keep my face even, despite the spike of fear in my chest. "And what about you?"

"I'm staying the fuck out of your way." He makes a clicking sound so Dorian heels, then turns and strides down a path that leads into the woods, disappearing into the dark.

"So dramatic." I roll my eyes, feeling a deep itch to get back to Ayla, distantly wondering if this was all some kind of elaborate trap.

"He's not wrong, though. Bastard," Oberon grumbles, stalking back down the path we came from.

I catch up to him, breathing a sigh of relief when Ayla's exactly where we left her, nose practically pressed against the page.

"We'll figure something out." I rap my knuckles against the window, making her jump, and she unlocks the car.

I slide into the driver seat, and Oberon climbs into the passenger side. He rolls down the window and turns up the radio, letting the night air blow the hair out of his face.

Ayla

The drive back to the abandoned house is full of chatter and planning between the brothers. Something's got them fired up and ready to storm the campus.

I, on the other hand, feel like I've swallowed a ball of lead, the sinking feeling dragging me down and rendering me silent.

Algernon really sees an end to all of this. He thinks we'll find a way to live happily ever after. He has no idea that sooner or later, probably sooner, I'll be gone.

My eyes burn as tears rise, anxiety coiling in my chest. I can't lie to him anymore. He has to know the truth so he can start to let me go.

We park in the garage and the boys practically bound into the house. I trail behind them, making a beeline for our bedroom. I close the door behind me and slump on to the mattress, dropping my head in my hands as the tears finally come.

I don't want to die, don't want to leave him. I especially don't want to die at the hands of that pig, give him the satisfaction of finally ridding the world of me.

The tears turn to hiccuping sobs, and I'm grasping the pillow to my chest, gasping for air.

I'd do anything to stay. Anything.

I'm not ready.

"Ayla?" Algernon's voice washes over me, heavy with concern. His hands are on my face, brushing away wet clumps of hair from my cheeks. "Baby, what's wrong?" He picks me up and cuddles me into his lap, rocking side to side.

"Is she okay? Did she have a vision?" I hear Oberon ask from the door.

I shake my head and cling tighter to Algernon's shirt.

"No, I'm not sure. Can you give us a second, Ben?"

The door shuts and Oberon's footsteps recede down the hall.

"Kitten, what's wrong?" he murmurs, tilting my chin up so I can't avoid his gaze.

"I don't want to break your heart," I say, sounding embarrassingly pitiful with my blocked nose.

"Break my heart? What are you talking about?"

"Algernon, I...I've been keeping something from you," I begin, taking a deep breath. *Here we go.*

He pulls back a little, brows furrowed.

Gods, I want to smooth his handsome features back into easy contentment. But I have to do this. I have to, even it's the worst thing I ever do.

"I'm going to die," I say finally.

"We all—"

"No, I need you to hear me. I'm *going* to die. Not in twenty, fifty, or even a hundred years. I'm going to die soon, Algernon—" My voice cracks. "Very soon."

"I don't understand, no one is going to hurt you Ayla. I-I'm right here," he stutters, cupping my face. But I see the fear in his eyes, the wild terror I've walked alongside every day of my life.

"I've always known. It was the first vision I ever had. It's never changed." I place my hand against his, leaning into his touch. My chest feels lighter, like I've shed a concrete coat, even while my heart is breaking. There's freedom in telling my deepest secret, even if it's also the darkest.

He's quiet for a long time, just staring at my face. Then he whispers, "What do you see?"

"My mother dies first. She's dancing in the grass, wearing a white dress." I sniffle, the image of my mother clear as day in my minds eyes. She was cruel, but so beautiful. "Then something pushes her, invisible hands, and she falls back. I think she's going to fall into the grass, but she keeps falling, through the ground and out of sight. I rush over, but she's already dead, a broken heap at the bottom of her grave."

Algernon brushes my tears away, looking so sweet and sincere that I almost lose my nerve.

"I start running through the woods, I hear your voice. I scream your name."

He throat bobs, tears starting to run down his cheeks.

"But I get caught in the brambles, it's like they reach out and grab me, the thorns cutting into my skin and dress. Then—" I shudder, the image sending a chill up my spine. "My father steps out of the woods, and grabs my neck."

Algernon's thumb brushes against the column of my throat, almost possessive, as anger starts to bleed into the anguish in his eyes.

"He tilts me backwards, and suddenly I'm underwater." Claustrophobia crawls under my skin. I can almost feel the frigid bite of the water, taste the metallic, salty zing as it rushes into my mouth.

Algernon squeezes his eyes shut, shaking his head like he can't stand the image, can't bear to hear anymore.

"I will die at the hands of my father, Algernon. It's set in stone. He will kill me." I finish, exhaling.

"No!" His eyes snap open, jumpy and feral. "I wont let it happen. I'll fucking *gut* him. You can't—"

"You aren't listening to me!" I place my hands on his shoulders and shake him. "Its going to happen. The vision has never changed. It has been confirmed hundreds of times over. I'm going to die, and there's nothing you or I can do about it."

"Ayla, I can't lose you." He grabs my hands, places them over his thundering heart. "I refuse to let you be taken from me."

"You were always going to lose me," I say bitterly. "This is my Fate."

"You think I give a single fuck about Fate?" He growls, eyes narrowing. "We are not slaves to Fate, Ayla. We can stop this. I'll go burn that fucking Manor down *right now*. I'll rip out his heart and give it to you, for Gods sake. We have the advantage, we know what's going to happen—"

"Don't give me false hope, Algernon," I snap, angry now. "You'll only break both of our hearts. There's nothing we can do."

"You aren't powerless! You've always doubted yourself," his voice softens, his grip on my hands loosening. "Look at the power you have over me," he murmurs, leaning his forehead against mine.

"Al, I don't—"

"You have control, you have power. Nothing can take that from you." He moves our hands to press against my sternum. "What would happen if you embraced your power, instead of running from it?"

I blink at him. "I don't know what you mean..."

"Ayla. Your visions have always just happened to you. What is you *looked*, instead of just seeing?"

"I look with cards," I bite out, irritated and confused.

"Not with cards." He taps my forehead.

I recoil, anger flaring. "You think I wouldn't? I *can't*, Algernon." It's too vast, out there. Too unknown. I hate to admit it, shame like a thorn in my side, but I'm terrified. Terrified of trying, of resisting, of *wanting*. For so long, passivity has been the only thing that's saved me.

"Try, love. I'm right here." He pulls me back into his lap, trying to smooth my ruffled feathers. "Just try. What are we having for breakfast tomorrow?"

I huff, trying to ignore the churning fear in my stomach. It's just breakfast. Just a few hours away. And I said I'd do anything to stay.

I reach up and unclasp the locket from around my neck, placing it in his open palm, and close my eyes.

"I'm right here to pull you back, Ayla. I promise," he whispers.

I take a few deep breaths, sinking into the deep blue of my third eye, tapping into the energy I call on when I divine with tools. My hands itch for something to channel it through, something to contain the energy, but I bare down.

I am the conduit.

The smell of strawberries reaches me before the image does. Algernon has powdered sugar all over his shirt, some has even collected in his beard and on the tip of his nose. He flips a pancake in the pan and grins at me, waggling his eyebrows. A pile of pancakes sits in front of me, topped with a mountain of fresh strawberries, thick syrup, and an avalanche of powdered sugar.

I jolt back into the present, my eyes snapping open.

"Pancakes with strawberries," I blurt out, looking up at Algernon's face.

A breathtaking smile splits his worried expression. "You did it!"

A rush of adrenaline steals my breath, a surge of power like I've never felt before. *I fucking did it.* For so long, my gift has been something that's just happened to me, beyond my control or understanding. I could use tools, sure, but they always muddied the message and required twice the amount of energy.

But now, now I can point and shoot. I have *control,* the thing I've longed for all my life.

A manic giggle bubbles up and out, and I throw my head back and laugh.

"I'm so fucking proud of you," Algernon laughs, hugging me close.

Heat flushes through me, heady and thick. Without thinking, I grab him by the hair and yank his head back, earning a surprised gasp. I adjust myself in his lap so I'm straddling him up on my knees, looking down at his pretty face.

"Thank you," I purr, before capturing his lips in a scalding kiss. I drive my tongue in his mouth, licking along his teeth, feeling the sharpness of his canines. He growls low in his throat and opens up for me, hands kneading my ass.

I feel drunk with power, delirious with it, consumed by the need to dominate him, mark him as mine. I pull my head back and grab his face, forcing his jaw open, and spit on his tongue.

His cock lurches beneath me as he swallows thickly, squirming under my touch.

"Good boy," I whisper, dragging my tongue up his cheek and nipping at his ear.

He whimpers, grinding up against my core. *So needy*.

I push him backwards on to the bed and pull my shirt over my head, baring myself to his hungry gaze. He looks me up and down, jaw slack, the race of his heartbeat making his cock bounce.

I start climbing up his body. I'm going to sit on that beautiful, sweet face.

Algernon reads my mind and yanks me up the rest of the way, ripping my panties off of me and diving straight into my pussy with an eager tongue.

"Fuck!" I cry out, grinding down on his face as he devours me, seemingly perfectly content to drown. He sucks on my clit mercilessly, grazing it with his teeth and lashing it with his sharp tongue.

His hands are all over me, gripping my tits and rolling my pebbled nipples, massaging my thighs and dragging his nails down my back.

It's fucking bliss.

I dig my fingers into his fluffy hair and grind harder, an orgasm fast approaching. He moans against me, the vibrations sending a delicious arc of pleasure up my spine.

He spears his tongue into my entrance and throws me over the edge, lightning striking every nerve in my body. I come with a scream, riding his tongue into oblivion.

He grabs me by the hips and lifts me off of him as he sits up, throwing me down on the bed in front of him. His beard is soaked with honey, and his eyes sparkle like a madman.

My legs immediately fall open as he unbuttons his trousers, wasting no time burying himself to the hilt. His pace is blistering, pummeling my bones and muscles to mush with the power of his cock.

His mouth finds mine in the frenzy, sloppy and intense. The taste of my pussy mixed with him is too much, intoxicating and filthy, and my walls clench as a fresh wave of arousal sends me into space.

"That's it, kitten. Take what's yours," he growls in my ear, his hips starting to stutter as his release approaches.

"All mine." I bite down hard on his shoulder, eliciting a guttural moan from him. Both of us hurtle towards the finish line, fucking wildly, not allowing an inch of space to come between us.

I slide my hands up his chest and wrap them around his neck, squeezing hard enough to pinch off his air. His hips falter, eyes rolling back.

"Don't move," I coo, taking his lower lip between my teeth and nipping at the soft flesh.

With great effort, he still his hips, eyes searching my face, confused but hopelessly turned on, swimming with desperation.

I lower my hips, sliding his cock half-way out of me, then roll them back up until he's buried to the hilt.

Understanding blooms across his face and I feel his hands fist the comforter beneath us.

I repeat the motion, earning a pained whimper, and keep going until we're both panting, dancing along the knife's edge of oblivion.

Every time his cock starts to swell, his balls tighten, I freeze, edging him over and over and over again until he's practically in tears, his whole body shaking above me as he clings to his resolve.

So obedient.

"Are you ready to come?" I ask, stroking his cheek with my fingers.

He nods, gritting his teeth. "Please."

I snap my hips up, knocking a grunt from his throat, and this time I don't stop. His hips surge back into motion, fucking me down into the mattress.

"Fuck, Ayla!" he bellows as his release hits him. My walls clench around him as my own orgasm crashes over me. I must black out for a second, my soul lifting out of my body as I watch us come together, clinging together like we might float away. Refusing to be separated, even in bliss.

We lay together for awhile, my head tucked into his neck and our arms wound tightly around on another.

"I won't let you go," he murmurs into my hair. "I don't care what I have to do."

I press a kiss to his pulse point, taking in the scent of his skin, the warmth of his thrumming blood.

"I'll do everything I can to stay."

We wake up in the late morning, sticky and stiff, but more hopeful than I've been in a long time. Maybe ever.

After a quick shower, Algernon starts whipping up pancakes while I chop the strawberries we found in the overgrown garden.

Oberon is already up, reading quietly in the living room with a cup of coffee. He scowled at us when we first appeared, but said nothing.

I try to feel guilty, but, I don't. It was way too good. He can be grouchy all he likes.

I stare at him, narrowing my eyes. *Can I look into his future?*

"Quit staring at me," he snarls, clapping his book shut.

"Sh." I silence him, letting the indigo wave wash over me.

I see Oberon, looking much more built and covered in black tattoos standing in a steel room I don't recognize, wearing a white coat with the sleeves pushed up to his elbows. Leda dances up to him, handing him something sharp with a peck on the cheek before dancing away, her own lab coat fluttering behind her.

I gasp, sending me crashing back into the present.

Oberon's waving a hand in my face, looking very annoyed. "What is your problem?" He snaps his fingers in my face.

A pancake flies at his head, narrowly missing him.

"Watch it, little brother," Algernon warns, coming up beside me and throwing an arm over my shoulder.

Oberon sulks and goes back to his chair.

I blink and a tear rolls down, and I can't help but smile.

"What did you see?" Algernon asks, wiping my cheek with his thumb.

I giggle and shake my head, returning to the strawberries. "It's his life, I won't spoil it."

He huffs, but kisses my forehead and returns to the stove, smiling to himself.

I practice the entire morning, searching for random little things, trying not to venture too far into the future. I know when the first frost will be, who's going to be elected President, when Al Carone will go to prison, stupid, inconsequential little things.

But I can tell that the men are growing impatient for me to ask the questions we really need answers too, even though Algernon insists that he doesn't want to rush me, nor does he want me to exhaust myself.

"Hold my hand?" I ask Algernon, who's sitting in an armchair a few feet from me.

He gets up immediately, setting his tinkering aside and joining me on the couch. He clasps both my hands in his, brushing his lips against my knuckles.

"What are you searching for?"

"The rest of my father's week," I say, anxiety already pinching my chest.

"Why James?" Oberon asks, setting his book aside.

"Gideon and Keanu probably have wards up." Both men nod in agreement. "My father's too arrogant for that."

"Be careful. I'm right here," Algernon says, squeezing my hands three times.

I close my eyes, letting the blue wash over me as I think of my father.

A pig mask flashes in my minds eye, and I recoil, but cling to the image, refusing to be spooked out of my own head.

I hear jazz music, and the familiar buzz of a big party. I look around and realize everyone's in disguise. It's a masquerade, and a jumping one at that. There must be hundreds of people crammed into the main lobby of Folke, I recognize it because of the statues and chandelier. Keanu stands in the balcony, donning his deer mask and clutching a whiskey in his hand. His cold blue aura lashes at the air around him.

Fuck, he's mad.

I need to figure out when this is, I think distantly, and turn to the windows. Not a moon in sight.

It's the Spring Equinox, I realize. The new moon falls on the 21st this month.

I squeeze Algernon's hand, and he starts tapping my hand in time with my heartbeat, guiding me back to my body.

I come out of it with a gasp, drawing in a sharp intake of breath. "The Spring Equinox, there's a masquerade."

Oberon slaps his forehead. "I *knew* that! That's perfect!"

"Why is it perfect?" Algernon asks, fussing over me as I come back.

"All of his people will be there. It's the perfect time to undermine him. Show them that he's weak," Oberon says, voice rising with energy.

I nod, and catch Algernon's gaze. "James will be there."

Algernon nods, understanding immediately what I'm insinuating.

"Many birds, one stone." Oberon grins.

Algernon

M y knife glides through the wood, shaving off fragile curls that fall to the floor and leave sawdust all over my pants. The point of the foxes ear slowly sharpens, until finally, the mask is done. I slather a deep red stain across it and set it in the sun to dry, and hopefully it'll be ready for tonight.

Ayla is perched by the kitchen counter, painting the final details on her orange tabby mask. She seems remarkably at ease, considering what we're doing tonight, but she's stared death in it's jagged maw her entire life. I suppose one must grow used to it.

I, on the other hand, am a nervous wreck. I can't sleep, can't eat, can't do anything but putter around and watch her every move.

She's told me more than once that my hovering is pissing her off, but I'd rather her be mad than...something else.

Until she's safe, I'm more than happy to annoy the shit out of her.

The plan for tonight is simple. Sane is sending us a car that will take us to Folke, where Ayla and I will blend with the crowd while Oberon causes a scene with his grand return to the living. Keanu will lose his mind, inadvertently showing his hand to his followers. In the mean time, Ayla and

I will track down her father, I'm looking forward to this part the most, and dispose of him.

Best case scenario, James is the only one that gets hurt and Keanu takes a major blow to his empire.

Worst case scenario, we're walking into a death trap.

We could run, an option I've suggested many times, but Ayla and Oberon won't have it. Fighters, both of them. I'm not sure what I am. Maybe a prudent scientist, but probably just a coward.

If it was just me, I'd follow Oberon into battle wherever he aimed. But with Ayla, I can't help but feel like I'm handing her over to the wolves.

She refuses to go quietly. I don't want her to go at all, but if she must, I'll be right by her side. We'll jump off the cliff together.

Gods, can't we just not jump off the cliff at all?

I fasten the trail of buttons along her spine, ghosting my fingers across the curve of her lower back. The emerald silk spills over her body like liquid jewels, too exquisite to touch, but I can't resist.

She turns in my arms, hazel eyes burning with determination. A soldier prepared for battle; her armor a floor length gown, her shield a wooden cat mask. Tonight, she faces her greatest fear, her constant shadow, and with that look in her eye, Gods help anyone that gets in her way.

"You look radiant, darling," I murmur, twirling a strand of copper hair around my finger.

"As do you," she smiles, straightening my bow tie.

I draw her closer, our lips connecting in a languid kiss. Her tongue drags across my lower lip, always a tease.

"I love you," she says, so close I can feel her lips move with the words.

"I love you too." I slide my hand into her hair and pull her closer, deepening the kiss into something darker, hungrier. Something promising.

"*Ahem*," Oberon clears his throat.

She turns her head, but I don't stop, kissing down her throat and basking in her fresh perfume, the scent of her skin.

"The car is here."

I lick a long strip back up her neck, delighting in the shiver that runs through her, and place a final kiss to her lips before straightening. "Shall we?" I grin at him.

He rolls his eyes and heads back down the hall, black wolf mask in hand.

I secure Ayla's cat mask, then she helps me with my fox, and we meet Oberon on the front steps. He takes a deep breath and slides the wolf mask over his head. The effect it has is immediate, transforming my little brother into something menacing. His spine straightens and his chest broadens, his eyes freeze over.

He opens the back door for Ayla and I, then slides into the front, signaling to the driver to proceed.

The drive is long and silent, Ayla's hand gripped tightly in mine, and when the driver opens my door, I nearly drag her out and make a dash to the woods. But I don't. Instead, I offer her my arm and we follow Oberon up the front steps.

He steps off to the side, letting us enter first.

The room is bathed in candlelight, the chandelier shimmering like diamonds. Lush jazz wraps around us, decadent and dark, and beckons us in. Guests glide gracefully across the mosaic-tiled floor, their costumes a symphony of rich velvet, lace, and brocade. Dresses cascade in dark, dramatic hues, adorned with lace and satin, while gentlemen are clad in tails and waistcoats. Each figure bears a mask, a work of art in its own right, concealing identities behind an intricate dance of feathers, porcelain, and silver filigree.

The atmosphere pulses with magic, the energy electric and intense. It was rare to have so many witches in one place, and it'd been many, many decades since I've interacted with more than a few at a time. My own Source rears up, excited by the thrum of power. It's almost intoxicating, the rush of it all.

I can tell Ayla feels it too, her eyes sparkling behind her mask.

The echoes of laughter and hushed conversations intermingle with the music, creating an energy that seemed to resonate through the very stones of the building. It was a dance of whispers and murmurs, secrets exchanged beneath the veneer of masks and the shroud of night.

I wrap an arm around Ayla's waist and escort her to the bar, making way for Oberon's dramatic entrance.

As soon as he steps through the doors, the festivities come to a crashing halt, everyone gasping and shrieking at the sight of him.

His name drifts over the crowd like smoke. *Oberon. The Necromancer.*

I glance up and see Keanu on the balcony, his bone mask casting an eerie shadow over the room, the antlers stretching like branches. The only indication of his reaction is the tendrils of blue whipping around his arms and legs, his aura a vivid sapphire. His knuckles are white on the banister.

Oberon lifts his mask and winks at him.

The banister cracks.

"As you were," Keanu orders, his deep voice echoing against the walls.

Everyone jumps into motion, dancing and drinking, although a bit stilted. The crowd parts like the sea as Oberon walks through the center of the room. He brushes past us and the bartender slides him a glass of blood red wine with a curt nod.

Murmurs follow him like a shadow, eyes flicking between him and where Keanu stood moments before.

He ascends the stairs and disappears into a shadowed hall.

Worry prickles up my spine, but he insisted on doing this alone. Insisted that Keanu wouldn't hurt him.

"Well, look what the cat dragged in," a familiar voice pipes up from behind us.

"Gideon," I sigh, turning towards him and tucking Ayla closer to my side. He's wearing a fierce iron hawk mask, his gray eyes cold and calculating.

"This was bold." He says with a smirk, taking a sip of his whiskey. "But clever. The rats are craving a display of power, and Oberon delivered. Well done."

"Fuck off," Ayla snaps. "You're a fucking coward."

Gideon tilts his head slightly, assessing her. "When will you learn not to run your mouth, Abbott?"

I lunge forward to grab him by the collar, but Teddy steps between us, his white owl mask doing nothing to obscure his identity.

"Gentleman, please. We're on the same side," he hisses, shoving us both backwards. "Do you hear them?" he whispers, and we quiet down, really listening to the chatter of the crowd.

They sing of dissension, swift and cruel. That without Oberon, Keanu is weak, too weak.

"The cards are set," Sane continues. "Stay the course." He leans down and whispers something to Ayla before turning and being reabsorbed by the crowd.

Gideon bends in a dramatic, mock bow before ducking into the crowd himself.

"What did he say to you?" I place my hands on her hips, turning her to face me.

"James isn't here yet," she whispers, picking invisible lint off my lapel.

A small burst of hope lights up my chest. Maybe he won't come at all. *Smash!*

A thundering crash echoes around the building and the party freezes. Oberon comes flying out of the shadows, slamming into the banister of the balcony with a sickening crunch. A high-pitch whistle slices through the air.

"Do not move from this bar. I will be right back." I press a quick kiss to her temple and bolt for the stairs, nearly colliding with Gideon as he does the same.

We dash up the stairs and to Oberon, who's already getting to his feet. The veins in his face are a sickly blue, the skin of his throat blistered and black. His eyes are that horrible onyx, his hands blackened by dark magic.

He rushes back down the hall, Gideon and I on his heels, and tackles Keanu to the ground, delivering blow after blow to the other man's face.

I do the first thing I can think of and raise the floor boards, creating wooden cuffs around Keanu's arms and legs to hold him place. Gideon pulls Oberon off of him, wrangling him like a feral dog.

"Enough!" Gideon bellows, throwing Oberon aside. "You'll *kill* each other."

"Good," Oberon snarls, before lunging at Keanu again.

Keanu opens his mouth to scream, creating a cannon of blue electricity. At the last second, I throw a wall of friction around Oberon, the effort of it nearly taking me to my knees, but when the kinetic energy makes contact with the barrier, it dissolves to nothing. Keanu stares in disbelief.

Gideon steps between them, his eyes flickering gold. "I said *enough*." His voice has a distorted echo, like it's coming from inside my head, and we all halt in place.

"I will kill all three of you, I swear to the Gods," Keanu snarls, breaking through one of his wrist restraints.

"And then what?" Gideon snaps, turning towards him. "You know what they're saying out there. Without Oberon, you're nothing."

Keanu narrows his eyes, breaking the other restraints with a blast of blue light from his palm. "You have no idea what I am, Raith." He takes aim at me, but Oberon throws himself between us, taking the cerulean bullet into his shoulder.

But he doesn't falter, just stands tall between us and Keanu.

"It's over, Key." Oberon's voice looses a bit of it's edge, sounding almost remorseful. "You know it's over."

A wolfish grin stretches across his face, and his eyes flick to me. "Not yet, it isn't."

My stomach drops.

"James was so excited when I told him that his daughter was here."

"You motherfucker!" I roar, lunging at him, but Gideon grabs me around the middle. "Where is she?" I scream, trashing against my brother's hold.

"Better be quick, fox." He checks his watch and *tsks*, shaking his head. "You've wasted so much time already."

Gideon practically throws me out the door and all three of us break into a sprint, barreling down the stairs and directly into a crowd of party goers.

"Move!" Gideon bellows, his eyes lighting up that same incandescent gold, and the crowd parts like the red sea. The glass surrounding the courtyard is obscured by black clouds, rain pelting against it.

I send my shoulder through the doors, shattering them on impact, too panicked to consider using magic.

"*Ayla!*" I scream as the rain slows to a gentle patter, the clouds lifting away, revealing Ayla sprawled on the ground, soaking wet and still.

Ayla

I run after Algernon to the stairs, but someone snags me around the waist and drags me back.

I open my mouth to scream, but a hand claps over my mouth.

"Ayla, stop. You'll only get in their way," Teddy hisses in my ear, carrying me out into the courtyard. He deposits me on a concrete bench. "They're stronger than him. Together, they'll be fine."

"Fuck!" I shout, dropping my head in my hands. This wasn't how it was supposed to go. Oberon was supposed to be safe with him. No one was supposed to get hurt. Well, almost no one.

"It's going to be alright, Ayla. I promise." Teddy offers a reassuring smile, easing some of the tension in my shoulders.

A rumble of thunder makes the ground shake, dark clouds rolling in over the school. Static crackles through the air.

"Was it supposed to storm?" I ask, a sick feeling crawling up my spine.

"I don't think—" A wooden beam comes swinging out of the shadows beside us, connecting squarely with the back of Teddy's head. He crumbles to a heap on the ground, eyes vacant, crimson blooming through his white hair.

My legs move before my brain and I'm running, but something tangles in my hair and drags me backwards, the pain bright and sharp.

"Let me go!" I scream, slapping and kicking, but they keep dragging me, unperturbed by my thrashing. I realize with a dull pang that no one can see us. The glass room is completely hidden by a thick haze of black clouds, the deluge of rain and heavy thunder obscuring any sounds, and ensuring that no one will dare venture out.

Oh, fuck.

James throws me onto the ground in front of him, a gruesome pig mask with rotten tusks and a bloody snout hides his face.

"Hello, babygirl," he sneers, kicking me in the stomach as soon as I lift my head. "I've missed you." He stomps his boot down on my ankle, shattering the bones to smithereens.

I let out a keening cry, black spots swimming in my vision. I can't move, can barely see through the heavy torrent of rain.

"Where's your little boyfriend?" He picks up his boot and stomps down on my knee. Everything goes white, my ears deafened by a teeth chattering ring. I wonder if he's killed me, if one could die from pain, but then reality comes flooding back, and I'm choking on my own screams.

James rips the cat mask off my face and smashes it on the ground, leaving it splintered like my bones.

I try to drag myself away, but the pain is too much, the rain is too much, and I collapse into a heap.

"Nowhere to run now, bitch." James grabs me by the hair and throws me into the fountain, the water so cold I can't breathe. He rips his own mask off and then his hands are around my neck, shaking me hard.

I gasp and claw at his hands, flaying the skin to ribbons, but he doesn't relent, just squeezes tighter, gets angrier. My vision starts to tunnel, red spots floating in and out of focus. Everything burns, from my lungs to my toes, like my whole body is on fire.

He shoves his arms forward, dunking my head underwater. The blood from his hands swirls around me, mixing with my tendrils of hair. I watch them dance, almost the same color.

My arms are so heavy, *when did they get so heavy*? I let them fall to my sides, let the water hold them up. Yes, that's easier. That feels better.

His face is distorted by the rippling water, by the bubbles escaping my mouth. Is he my father? I don't recognize him. Just a man, any man. Men aren't so scary. Men are all the same.

Men are monsters.

Pathetic, controlling monsters.

My fingers brush against something solid, something rough and cold.

I've been at the mercy of others my entire life. At the mercy of their needs, their moods, their fleeting fantasies. Waiting for them to tell me what to do, where to go, what to believe in, what I'm capable of.

A man killed my mother, killed my best friend, stole my childhood, is trying to steal my life.

It was *mine*. It was all mine. Mine to live and lose, mine to love and cherish.

It was *my* choice.

My fingers wrap around the stone.

I'm so fucking tired of other people making choices for me.

It's *my* life. *My* future.

No one will take anything from me again.

I heave the rock off the bottom of the fountain and up, pouring every ounce of rage behind it. The rock breaks the surface of the water, suddenly moving twice as fast, and slams home on something hard.

My father's hands immediately release my throat and I rush up for air, using the momentum to carry the swing all the way through.

The rock bursts through his skull and slams into the ground with a deafening crack.

I scream, water rushing up with the sound, and vomit slimy fountain muck all over the ground. I gasp for air, hacking up blood and bile.

The storm is starting to dissipate, the rain softening to a spring shower.

My father is unrecognizable, his skull completely demolished between the rock and the ground. Blood runs through the gaps in the cobblestones, spreading around us like a spiderweb.

I look to my left and see Sane starting to stir. That's good.

Exhaustion starts to pull at my muscles, dragging my eyelids down.

"Ayla?" I hear someone say, Teddy maybe, but the moss covered cobblestone is far too welcoming to resist, and I let it embrace me.

"She's breathing," someone says. I can feel hands on my throat, on my chest.

Gods, it *hurts.*

I try to slap them away. "Hurts," I mumble.

"Yeah, she's alive." Oberon?

"Ayla, baby, wake up. C'mon, hellcat. Please," Algernon whispers, and I feel his hands grasp mine.

I focus on his touch, the warmth of his palm, and try to squeeze.

"That's it! Hey, baby. I'm right here." He kisses all over my hands, so warm and soft.

"C-cold," I mutter, feeling starting to return as the fog dissipates.

Something warm and heavy is laid over my body, it smells spicy and green, like home.

"Can you sit up, love?" Algernon asks, gently sliding a hand under my head.

I blink the water from my eyes and finally see him, his thick lashes and tawny beard. His flushed cheeks and bloodshot eyes. Tears run salty tracks down his face, but his smile is breathtaking.

He eases me up slowly and cuddles me into his chest, his lips finding every part of me within reach. "Gods, I love you so much. I'm so sorry," he whispers, burying his face in my hair. "I'm so sorry."

"I love you too," I whisper back, nuzzling closer.

I'm alive. I'm *alive!*

"You did it." He cups my cheek and turns my face up towards his, his smile like the sun. "You're free."

I press my lips to his, needing to taste him, to know that this is real.

"She turned him to mincemeat is what she did. Gods above," Gideon snickers, nudging the gore covered brick with his foot.

"That's my girl," Algernon purrs, kissing me again.

"Yes, yes, well done to our favorite little *brat*," Keanu spits out the last word, surprising us all from the doorway.

Algernon holds me tighter and glares daggers at him. Oberon, Gideon, and Teddy step in front of us. The rest of the party presses in against the glass, watching with wide eyes.

Keanu waves lazily at them and leans against a tree. "You heroes are such a bore. You want me to leave Alder Bridge? Fine, but know this." He opens his palm and blue tendrils of smoke snake upwards, taking the shape of a stag. "Ideas never die." He closes his fist and vanishes, blue light popping like a flash bulb.

A murmur passes through the crowd, followed by a few clapping hands.

"We're all free," Sane laughs, breathless, and beams at me.

"For now," Oberon says under his breath, so only the five of us can hear.

"For now is good enough, I think," Algernon says, standing up with me cradled in his arms. "I'm taking her home, coming?" He looks between his brothers, then pushes through them and over a broken pile of glass.

Oberon and Gideon glance at each other, shrug, and trail after us.

The crowd parts, whispering about Algernon and I, probably wondering who the hell we are. But I don't care about them.

I press my lips to Algernon's neck, still in disbelief that I'm here. That I'm alive and James isn't. That Keanu surrendered.

I had no doubts that he'd be back, but like Algernon said, safe for now is enough. Alive today is enough.

Algernon

Gideon pulls his car around and I tuck Ayla into the backseat, sliding in beside her.

I expect to head back to the abandoned house, but instead Gideon drives us to the Farm, knowing the way by heart even on a moonless night.

Ayla shivers against my side, still soaking wet and in shock, but every time I glance down at her, she's smiling.

I hold her tighter, allowing myself a second to breathe, to just be happy that she's alive instead of pummeling myself with guilt. When I saw her passed out on the ground, a dark circlet of bruises around her neck, her body so still, I felt the edges of my soul start to unravel.

I should have never left her alone, should have never followed Oberon, should have never gone to that fucking party in the first place. I don't care that Keanu surrendered, I don't care that James is dead. None of that would have meant a godsdamn thing if I'd lost Ayla.

I'm not a hero. My only purpose in this world is to keep her safe, to love her. And instead I left her alone in the wolf's den. It's because of her own grit, her own strength, and a small miracle, that she survived.

It's the last time she'll have to fight for her life. The last time she'll know suffering.

I press a kiss onto the top of her head, lifting the soaked strands of hair off of her neck and tucking my suit jacket tighter around her body. Her color looks much better, but I'm afraid she'll catch another fever.

Mental note, give her a dose of Cure All the second she's out of these wet clothes.

We pull into the drive and I immediately climb out with her cradled in my arms, wasting no time. Oberon opens the doors for us and I push inside, heading straight for our bedroom.

If I don't get these clothes off of her, she'll catch her death.

I set her on her feet and push the jacket off her shoulders and get to work on the twenty million fucking buttons down the back of her dress.

"Algernon," she says, voice still hoarse.

"Hmm?" I ask, swallowing the urge to just tear the damned thing off.

"Are you alright?"

I pause, biting back a laugh. I spin her around, placing my hands on the slope of her rib cage. "Did you just ask if *I'm* alright?"

She chews her lip, nodding.

I can't help the exasperated exhale that forces its way out. "Baby, I'm fine. You're the one that was throttled and nearly drowned."

"And you're the one undoing buttons like they personally victimized you," she counters.

"I'm sorry," I sigh, relaxing my grips on her sides. "I just...I'm so sorry, Ayla."

She reaches up and brushes a tear off my cheek. I hadn't realized I was crying.

"You have nothing to apologize for, love," she murmurs, wrapping her arms around my neck and hugging me to her, her frame molding itself snugly against my chest.

"I could have lost you," I whisper, burying my face in her hair.

"But you didn't," her voice sounds muffled against my shirt.

"Because you kicked some serious ass, you wild thing." I smirk, reaching down to finish undoing the last of the buttons. The dress slides off her body and into a wet heap, revealing the extent of her injuries. Bruises stain her back and arms, her hands and legs covered in scrapes. She's standing on one foot, the other hovering slightly off the ground. The ankle is three times it's usual size and a horrible magenta color, with spots of deep purple spreading down her foot and up her shin. Her knee isn't any better, angled wrong and bulbous.

"Ayla, what the fuck?" I scoop her up and set her on the bed, wrapping a quilt around her and dropping to my knees to access the damage. "Did he fucking stomp on your leg?" I ask as I gently prod her ankle.

"Yes," she hisses, teeth gritted against the pain. "That's exactly what he did."

I wrestle down my rage. He's dead, and me losing my shit isn't going to help her right now.

"Oberon!" I call, moving up to check her knee.

My brother appears in the doorway, looking exhausted. "Yes?" His eyes fall to her leg and he grimaces.

"I don't want to let the Cure All set the bones, it'll hurt too much." I'll never forget the pain of my ribs snapping back into place when I was still in that cell. "Is there anything you can do?"

He looks down at his binding and back at her leg. "I can try." He comes closer, glancing at Ayla for permission before laying his hand lightly on her ankle.

Gideon hovers in the hall, whispering with who I assume is Teddy.

"Fuck, it's like bone mulch," Oberon grunts. "I can set some of it, but it's not going to feel great," he says, looking back up at Ayla.

I slide up the bed and wrap my arms around her, partly for comfort, partly to hold her still.

"Go ahead," she says, pressing her face into my shoulder.

Oberon concentrates on her ankle, and she gasps.

"That's not so bad—*fuck*!" she cries out, trying to jerk away from him as I hear a horrible grind and crunch.

"Now, the knee," Oberon says, setting his hand just below the swollen knot that used to be her knee.

"Get it over with," she snaps, biting down on my shoulder.

Pain licks through my arm, but I ignore it. If I could take every bump and bruise, every broken bone, I would.

Oberon doesn't flinch when he bears down with his magic, and Ayla screams. There's an audible pop that makes my stomach flip, along with some loud cracks, and then he releases her.

She sags back into me, panting.

I reach for the drawer and grab a vial of Cure All, popping the cork and holding it up for her.

She just tilts her head back and opens her mouth. I pour the serum down her throat and seal it with a kiss. She hums as the medicine flows through her, all the bruises fading and scrapes closing. Her knee and ankle return to their normal proportions, and the flush returns to her cheeks.

"Better?" I mumble against her lips, smiling.

"Much." She gives me a quick peck, then glances over at Oberon.

"You okay?" he asks, raising a brow.

"Yes. You have ten seconds to get out before you get an eyeful."

He snorts and holds up his hands, backing towards the door and shutting it behind him.

I lay her back onto the bed, kissing the corner of her mouth, along her jaw, and down the column of her throat, savoring the silken feel of her skin under my tongue. She arches up into my touch, small breaths panting from her parted lips.

"Need you," she breathes, lifting her hips up.

My hand finds its way between her legs, parting those velvet lips, and finding her wanting, practically weeping for me. I slip in one finger, then another, encouraged by the satisfied sigh she makes. I drag my fingers in and out, stretching her, melting away her residual stress until she's a pliable little puddle.

"My precious kitten," I purr, sucking a rosy nipple into my mouth and grazing the sensitive flesh with my teeth.

She mewls in response, walls clamping rhythmically around my fingers. So ready to get fucked.

"Please, fox. I need you," she pants, grabbing at my shoulders to drag me up.

Who am I kidding, how can I resist that? Every part of me was screaming to claim her, to feel her heartbeat from the inside, to know that she's alive and well. That she's mine.

I shift on top of her, spreading her legs wide with my hips, and line up my cock with her entrance. I slide my arms underneath her shoulders, cradling her head in my hands, and kiss her deeply, slowly pushing inside of her. She stretches around me beautifully, slick and hot, *made for me*.

She moans into my mouth, dragging her nails along my back, and there's no where else in the world I'd rather be. This is heaven, wrapped in every part of her, feeling her soul as keenly as her kiss.

"Gods, I love you," I moan, angling her hips up to drive deeper.

"I love you too." She licks along the seam of my lips, pressing her tits against my chest as she fights to get closer.

"Touch yourself, hellcat. Show me how fierce you can be," I growl, notching up to a blistering pace.

She slides her hands between us and starts stroking her clit, her moans turning to cries of ecstasy. Her walls start to flutter around me, her orgasm so close I can taste it.

"That's it, baby. Scream for me. Show Fate just how alive you are."

She comes with a cry that makes my ears ring, her whole body seizing like she'd been struck by lightning.

I fuck her through it, relishing in the vicious squeeze of her spasming cunt, licking the sweat and tears from her face.

She grabs me by the shoulders and flips me over, straddling me like a hunter over their freshly caught prey. My cock jumps with excitement, throbbing deep inside of her.

She starts bouncing up and down on my cock, those perfect thighs flexing with the effort, her tits bouncing gloriously. I can't do anything but stare up at her, absolutely enraptured by the goddess above me wringing out every drop of pleasure that she can.

Fuck, I'd let her bleed me dry just to see that smile on her face, that mischievous light in her eyes. She's a marvel to behold, a gift from the Gods.

Her hands drop to my chest, nails digging deep as she chases her second orgasm. I grab her hips hard, lifting her up a bit, and start pistoning in and out of her, knocking the breath out of us both.

It's a fucking rapture, and we fly over the peak together, clinging to each other as we plummet.

She collapses onto my chest with a *umph*, and we both start laughing uncontrollably, giddy with bliss and relief. We fucking made it. We survived.

Now, we can start over.

Epilogue

Ayla, Spring, 1940

After ten years in Alder Bridge, tending the farm and helping Oberon establish his mortuary practice, Algernon was craving a change of pace. I could tell he longed to go back to the city, to the energy and electricity he craved, and I'd be lying if I said I didn't want to experience what his life as a rich inventor had been like before it all fell apart.

He'd been reluctant all the same to leave Oberon and Gideon behind after everything, especially with their relationship still strained on a good day. But Gideon had Folke and Teddy, and Oberon had his burgeoning business, and it was long overdue that Algernon did something for himself, even if I was tagging along for the ride.

We left in the early morning, taking a train from the rural mountains to the concrete jungle, then hailing a cab out of Grand Central Station.

My mind can barely grasp how different the city looks but, I suppose a lot can change in a decade. It rolls by like a film reel as we drive, almost dreamlike in the blush of the early morning.

The driver turns down an alleyway, and anxiety spikes through me, but Algernon gives my hand a reassuring squeeze.

"Just wait, darling," he murmurs against the shell of my ear.

A few moments later, we pass through the two buildings and into an even stranger dream. Algernon's mansion soars before us, surrounded by lush green and color. It's exactly as I remember it, gilded and mighty, breathtaking in it's detailed architecture.

"I had built it for you," he continues, kissing down the exposed slope of my neck while I crane my neck to take it all in. "But you never got the chance to enjoy it."

I whip my head around, nearly knocking into his. "For me?"

He grins. "For you, kitten. Everything I've ever done was for you."

The driver comes to a stop in front of the marble steps, and the entry doors are flung open. An older woman, wearing a stunning crimson blouse and black pencil skirt teeters down the steps on impressive heels, some how staying upright despite her haste.

Algernon jumps out of the car and scoops her up into a warm hug, smiling from ear to ear. "Gods, Mags, I missed you," he says, setting her gently back onto her feet. "How have you been?"

"Just ducky, Mr. Raith, thanks to you," she replies, reaching up to pat his cheek.

I climb out of the car, smoothing my forest green dress, nerves prickling along my skin. I knew Algernon was obscenely wealthy, but being confronted with it in the glaring light of day is jarring, especially after living humbly for my entire life.

Those few times I'd visited his house before had been more like a dream than reality, and it never fully hit home that it was *Algernon's* house. Bought with the millions of dollars he's earned through his patents.

Algernon was generous with his money, and rarely ever spoke about it. He gave Oberon every cent to start the funeral home, and donated a large sum to help Folke rebuild, so long as they named the new lab after him. But beyond that, he lived modestly and deliberately, a trait that often left me in awe of him, like right now.

I reach to grab my bag when I'm pulled backwards, spun around, and yanked into Magda's arms for a spine-severing hug.

"Don't be so shy, dear!" She says, pulling back to give me a once over, her cheeks ruddy with joy. "He's been treating you well?"

I smile, clutching my bag to my chest. "Would you expect anything less?"

"Not at all." She pinches my cheek and turns back to Al, who flashes me a wink. "I've taken care of everything to your specifications, and it's ready for you to move in!" Magda claps her hands together, then turns towards the driver, hustling him along with our bags.

"Move in?" I ask, raising an eyebrow.

"What, you don't want to bunk with me?" he teases, grabbing my hips and pulling me close.

"I'm not sure," I taunt, turning my head to look over the estate. "I was hoping for something bigger."

"Brat," he growls, tickling his fingers up my sides and diving in for a kiss. His lips are soft and teasing, nipping at my lower lip in a light warning. "I have something for you," he murmurs, pulling away.

I tilt my head in confusion, thinking he's about to pull out another egregiously expensive surprise, but then he pulls a black velvet ring box from his coat pocket and everything freezes.

"I can make a fuss if you want, but figured you might prefer something quieter," he says, cracking open the box to reveal a gorgeous golden ring, with a crystal-clear rose cut diamond and carved filigree along the delicate band. Simple but exquisite.

My heart ricochets in my chest, elation fizzing through my blood and bringing tears to my eyes.

"Ayla, will you mar—"

"Yes!" I fling my arms around his neck, dragging him down to press my lips to his, but the grin's on our faces make it nearly impossible. "Took you long enough," I grumble through my tears, kissing all over her cheeks and forehead.

He nips at my ear and pulls away. "Let me put it on you then, hellcat."

I hold my hand out, and he carefully takes the ring from the box and slides it over my finger, the diamond glittering in the rising sun. I hold it up to admire it, turning it this way and that, emotion stealing any words that come to mind.

"It was my mother's," he says, taking my hand and bringing the ring to his lips, kissing it gently. "I hope you love it as much as she did."

A question burns through my joy, grief sapping the air from my lungs. "Why didn't she give to Oberon for Leda?" I ask, closing my other hand over it and pressing it against my sternum.

Algernon smiles, sheepish, a blush crawling up his neck.

"What?" I snap, his reaction taking me aback. "Leda deserved—"

His hands come up to cup my cheeks, quieting my protest. "It was years before then, kitten."

My racing heart trips over itself. "What?" I ask again, softer.

"She gave it to me after your 21st birthday," he says, brushing away a tear with his thumb. "With specific orders to give it to *you*, when you were ready."

"My 21st..." I try to tally up the years, but it makes my head spin. "You held onto it all this time?"

"Well, for awhile, and then Magda did. It was in the safe I gave to her after the fire. I had forgotten about it in the chaos. She was kind enough not to hock it. She's our house manager now, by the way." He smiles and all I can do is stare at him in disbelief.

"Did I fall and hit my head when I got out of the cab?" I ask, and he throws his head back with a peal of laughter.

"Not on my watch." He presses a kiss to my forehead and reaches for my hand. I twine my fingers with his and he leads me up the stairs and into his—our home.

Memento Sentire

M *row!*

Grendel yowls from outside my door, impatient to receive her morning offering. I pull the white duvet over my head, but it does little to stifle her incessant protest. My snoozed alarm blares to life for the fifth time, Mitski coaxing me out of bed.

I silence the alarm and check the time, 7:25. *Shit*. My first class is at 8. Whoever picked an 8 am for my first class on the first day was a monster. And it definitely was not because I choose my classes whilst wine drunk during a girl's night. Definitely not.

It was my final semester, just a few months from completing my Master's in Creative Writing, and an 8 am was *not* going to kill my vibe.

I throw on an oversized Bat Boys tee and open the bedroom door, releasing the beast. She rises up on her 3 legs and puffs, like I don't come out of this door every single morning, and takes off down the hall into the kitchen. All of six feet. My one bedroom apartment is hardly something to write home about, hardly 700 square feet, but it has exposed brick and huge windows, so small victories.

I dump some wet food in Grendel's ceramic bowl, which I hand-made to look like a flat cap mushroom so she doesn't have to crane her neck *or* overstimulate her whiskers, while she screams at my feet.

"Here, you wretch." I set the food down in front of her and sneak in a head scratch while she's distracted before dashing back to my room.

I pull on some fresh underwear and a white pleated skirt, then open my closet and start riffling through cardigans, settling on a lightweight, cropped navy and baby blue argyle one. Warm enough that I won't freeze in the Humanities air conditioning, but not so thick I'll melt outside. I pull on black thigh high socks and scamper into the take-out box sized bathroom.

I pull my hair back with a white headband, brush my teeth, and splash some cold water on my face before applying a light layer of Ponds and a drop of rosehip oil, my grandmother's sworn combination.

With light brown gel, I fluff up my eyebrows and glue them in place, then sweep some plum colored mascara over my lashes. I dab my rose-pink lipstick on my cheeks and blend it out, giving me a little color, then apply it to my lips.

I pull off the headband and shake out my hair. It barely scrapes my jawbone, all choppy layers and texture so it doesn't fall flat. I spray my bangs with water and blow them out with a round brush, a habit so practiced it takes moments. They lay across my forehead and frame my eyes, hiding my terribly large forehead.

With a flourish, I mist it all with texturizing spray and give it a final fluff before I slip on my Mary Janes and dash out the door, snagging my already packed back and tossing a goodbye to Grendel over my shoulder.

When I slide into the drivers seat of my blue Prius, my phone buzzes to life.

"*Mère du matin,*" I say, a smile lifting my cheeks.

"*Cherie*, you sound so tired," My mother, Lillian, says, sounding none too excited herself. I can hear men chatting in the background, along with the unmistakable crash of waves and creaking of a ship.

"It's not even 8 a.m. here. The first day of my final semester, *maman*. What are you up to?"

"Your father and I just boarded a sailboat in Spain, *le Bonaparte*, and it made me think of your failed manuscript."

Of course it did.

"And I was wondering if you'd made any progress with it? I'd love to share with the Captain, he's absolutely enamored with the Empress, and thinks we're so clever for naming you after her."

I sigh. "No, *maman*. I haven't. But I'll sit down with it if I have time today."

"*Merci*, Eugenie. Kisses!"

I open my mouth to say goodbye, but the line goes dead. Typical. I toss my phone into the passenger seat and pull out, heading towards campus.

By the time I find a parking spot on campus, I'm ten minutes late. Fifteen by the time I hoof it to the classroom. But, by some miracle, the Professor is late too.

I slide out my laptop and pull up my schedule to check whose teaching. Professor Hallor, rings a bell. I type the name into my school inbox, and several emails pop up from my advisor, Dr. Lahara.

No wonder it sounds familiar, I'm his Teaching Assistant this year for his advanced Creative Writing Workshop. Another detail that fell through the steel trap that is my brain.

I hover over an email from my advisor that came in this morning and open it.

Gin,

Just received some unexpected news that Professor Hallor will not be returning to Folke this year. Every other English Professor has an assigned TA, but I'll figure something out. At least you can scrap that 8 am!

Best,

Dr. La

Well, shit. There go my plans for this semester, and the very necessary check I need to pay my bills. I close my laptop with an audible *clack.*

"Hallor's not coming, class is canceled," I say to the other students, most of whom I've shared classes with for the last six years, packing up my stuff.

They all groan.

"See you assholes later!" I call over my shoulder as I skip out the door, heading straight to Folkepour.

When I step into the cafe and wave to Farrah, the manager, she comes running out from behind the counter and throws her arms around me. I melt a little, letting the inconvenience of this morning roll off as I squeeze her back.

"I missed you, darling!" she says, pulling back to inspect my outfit.

"I missed you more." I grin, tucking some hair behind my ear.

She urges me towards the counter as she prattles off questions. "What were you working on this summer? Did you get to visit your parents? Are you and Pietro still together?"

"I'm still working on that biography of Empress Eugénie, but I started drafting some absolutely heinous monster smut that you'll *love.* I couldn't afford to fly to fucking Munich, so no parents. And Pietro can choke on his own cock." I think that about sums it up.

Farrah blinks at me, then bursts out laughing. "I never liked Pietro anyway." She tamps my preferred blonde espresso and clicks the portafilter into the machine. "Now tell me, does your monster have horns?"

Farrah and I chat for awhile in one of the window booths, splitting a breakfast flatbread and sipping iced lattes, but eventually she has to return to the counter and I have to get some work done.

Opening my laptop, I pull up my draft about Empress Eugénie, although, calling it a draft might be too generous. It's more like a jumbled outline with random bursts of nonsensical prose. I just can't pin her, can't quite get the plot arc right. She was a mess of contradictions, and tempest in her own right, with an immeasurable impact on the world and the feminist movement. But she was also materialistic, and pious, and cold, all traits that I struggle to wrap my head around, to emulate. You'd think I'd have more of a connection with my namesake, but she feels as foreign to me as Mars.

I waste the next few hours combing through my outline, adding here, tweaking there, but altogether making very little progress. I sit back in my seat with a huff, throwing back the last dregs of my third latte.

The back of my neck prickles, my ears heating, and I glance up.

Slate gray eyes catch mine across the cafe, pinning me to the spot. He looks familiar, a professor, I think. But I can't place him. And he had a face I would *definitely* remember. His jaw could cut glass, his cheekbones high and regal. His hair is dark, with a dusting of silver at his temples and in his perfectly groomed facial hair. The linen shirt he wears does little to hide the muscles underneath, dark curls of chest hair peaking out from the low v-neck.

Holy hell, that guys gorgeous. Like movie star gorgeous. And he's looking at *me*.

"Raith!" the barista calls out, passing him a very large, very black iced coffee.

Immediately, my warming core freezes over. Of course, the infamous Professor Gideon Raith, as gorgeous as he is viciously unkind. I turn back to my draft, willing his gaze to move elsewhere. That guy can sit and spin, based on the shit his students have told me.

Pretentiousness doesn't sit well with me, and it doesn't get more pretentious than the Religious Studies Department, of which he is the Head. The only thing worse than a philosopher is a philosopher with a Bible.

Gag.

"Hey, Gin!"

I turn my head and spot Carsin, a fellow Creative Writing major, and one of my few friends, making a beeline towards my booth.

"Ah!" I jump up and give them a huge hug, my height barely reaching their shoulder. Carsin and I have gotten close over the years, forming writing groups and being each other's primary beta-readers and critique partners. They spent the summer with their family in Boston, so I haven't seen them in months.

I shove them into the booth across from me and plop down across from them, immediately shutting my laptop and resting my chin on my palm. "Spill."

Carsin dives right into the summertime family drama, including a pregnant cousin going to jail and an aunt having an affair with her personal trainer.

I listen as best I can, but Raith's lingering gaze is like a gnat in my ear. I have half a mind to call him out just to get him to fucking leave. Just ignore him, just ignore him. He's nobody.

After what feels like an eternity, his glare, because it must be a glare, moves away. When I risk a look up, he's gone.

Good riddance. I've made it six years without crossing his path, another four months is nothing. Easy peasy.

Coming late 2024!

Acknowledgments

I know everyone says that writing a book is a labor of love but for me, writing *Memento te Aurum* was a celebration of love. This book was daunting, even more so than my debut, but I had an absolute blast through every stage. There's a lot of pressure on a second book, i.e. 'can lightning strike twice?'. And, in many ways, this book exceeded my wildest dreams.

Algernon and Ayla taught me more about love, loss, and life than any other experience (save my own marriage, of course). Both of them challenged my perceptions of love, of partnership, and what it truly means to *live*. Writing has a funny way of showing us parts of ourselves we've never seen, and providing the very reassurance we've needed all along.

Like Algernon and Ayla, sometimes all you have to do is dig deep and be brave.

Thank you to my beta-readers and writing friends for sharing your beautiful minds and innumerable talents. This book would not be the same without you.

Thank you to my friends and family for never letting me doubt myself, not for a single second, and for gifting me their bravery when my own ran low. Your faith in me and my pen is the greatest gift I've ever been given.

Thank you to my husband, Hunter, for your endless support, encouragement, patience, and inspiration. There's a piece of you in everything I write. I love you, endlessly.

Thank you, my beloved reader, for allowing my story to occupy a little space in your life and your heart. I will forever be grateful.

And lastly, I must extend a thank you to myself, for showing up and doing the damn thing.

If you haven't already, please consider leaving a review of *Memento te Aurum* wherever you purchased the book, as well as Goodreads. For indie author's like myself, one review can be the difference between our careers sinking or swimming.

Thank you for taking the time.

About the Author

Alice Greene is a former gifted kid from Upstate New York with a love of all things spooky, magical, and literary.

With a degree in English Literature and a passion for storytelling, Alice's writing style is a toothsome blend of angst, dark humor, and whimsy that explores the shadowy recesses of the human heart.

Today, she lives in South Carolina with her husband and pets.